BILLIONAIRE DEVIL

JULIE CAPULET

Hot playboy billionaires? Definitely not my type. Until one offers me a ride to California—with some dangerously irresistible "lessons" thrown in … and he somehow starts to change my mind about what dreams are actually made of.

Making it as a fashion designer in New York City feels a lot like trying to fly to the moon with homemade wings. My Instagram is slowly gaining traction, but the grind is exhausting. So when my best friend asks me to be the maid of honor at her shotgun wedding in Malibu, I'm tempted to head back to L.A. for good. Especially since my unrequited crush is also on the guest list.

The night before my road trip, my friend Sloane drags me along to a swanky Hamptons party where I happen to meet her drop-dead gorgeous billionaire boss, Colton Maddox—also known as the King of Heartbreak. Definitely one to steer well and truly clear of.

But the next morning, I open the door to find Colton standing there with coffee in one hand and the keys to a luxury tour bus in the other. In my tequila haze, I must have told him about my road trip—*and* my unrequited crush. Now he's insisting we had a deal.

Did I really agree to travel across the country with a hot,

cocky devil? Even worse, did I also agree to let him give me "lessons" on how to seduce a man, after I admitted I have zero experience? How mortifying.

Turns out, Colton Maddox is maddeningly persuasive. He's also an *exceptionally* good teacher. He showers me with luxurious gifts and takes me to all the hot spots on my wish list. Including Vegas.

As we get closer to L.A., the insufferably sexy billionaire is starting to convince me that maybe, all along, I've been holding out for the wrong man…especially since the cocky devil is now my husband.

Sometimes what happens in Vegas doesn't end up staying in Vegas after all…

Billionaire Devil is a steamy billionaire romance in the New York Billionaires series, starring the four Maddox brothers. Each book in the series is a complete standalone with a sexy fairy tale HEA.

New York Billionaires

Julie Capulet LLC

BILLIONAIRE DEVIL
New York Billionaires
Copyright © 2025 by Julie Capulet

BILLIONAIRE DEVIL

1

Wednesday
Southampton, New York

"I WISH I could help you, Miss Bailey, I really do," says the woman on the phone. "But I can't forward your information to my boss for the simple reason that she doesn't take unsolicited phone calls. At all. You'll have to go through the usual application process just like everyone else."

"I have," I tell her. "I never heard back."

"That means you weren't selected. They only get in touch with people they're interested in meeting with."

"But if she could take a quick look at my Insta—"

"There's nothing else I can do," the woman interrupts sharply. "You'll just have to wait until another position is advertised and try again. Have a nice afternoon." She hangs up on me.

Damn it.

I sigh, putting my phone face down on the tiny kitchen table in my postage-stamp-sized studio apartment, gazing out the window at my neighbor's rusty air conditioning unit in the back alley of what most people would consider a very beautiful town. Southampton *is* beautiful, of course. Once you get out of the back alleys and away from the air conditioning units that happen to whir very loudly at all hours of the day and night.

Not that I'm complaining. I chose to be here and I'm doing my best to make the most of it. I moved to the east coast from L.A. almost a year ago, leaving the only home I've ever known, because I desperately needed a change. The place never felt the same after my mom passed away suddenly, two and a half years ago. Once I graduated from UCLA with a degree in fashion, I figured the best thing to do was to dream big and try my luck in the fashion mecca of New York City.

I also wanted to get away from the love of my life, who—and yes, I'm aware of how pathetic this sounds— I've only actually spoken to a handful of times. Usually when he was being drooled over by other women. Even so, I hold onto those rare moments of charged eye contact—which are etched into my memories like they've been lasered there with a sadistically red-hot blowtorch— like little gems.

Troy Beckett. Star hockey player. Center for the Bruins and record-holder for the most goals scored in one season. Playboy of the highest order. Gorgeous, in a tousled, just-rolled-out-of-bed kind of way that was basically the equivalent of crack to every woman with a heartbeat during all four years of my college experience.

I never really even got close to him.

Of course I regret that the only man I've ever loved— from afar—might not even know my last name. It was another reason I needed to leave L.A.

You'd think in a city of almost four million people, a girl could have figured out how to avoid one ego-inflated jock.

But luck was never on my side in that regard. I ran into him everywhere. On campus, at the beach, during my part-time job at a trendy café. The one right around the corner from the Bruins' practice rink, as it turned out.

He was always being fawned over by beautiful, scant-ily-clad puck bunnies. He'd catch me staring. He'd smile. He'd say things like, *Hey, Lila,* which caused my heart to erupt with joy because he actually *did* know my name. Or, with a grin, *You're not stalking me, are you, babe?*

As I said: etched into my brain on a repeating loop that I had to move clear across the country to try to escape from.

It's worked, mostly.

I've been too busy holding down two jobs while also trying to make inroads for myself as a designer to think much about my unrequited love. I'm grateful for that, as exhausted as I might be. At least I don't run into him during my waitressing shifts or through the long hours at my job as a stylist in the boutique on Main Street. Both of which are slowly but surely destroying my soul.

The job in the boutique, Threads on Main, was offered to me before I left L.A. The owner was a contact of one of my design collaborators on the last of my senior projects. A girl named Solange whose mom had a couple of rich friends in Southampton.

The boutique looked amazing on paper. I accepted the job offer, rented out my old apartment in Venice, packed my bags, thanked my lucky stars I was finally getting a change of scene, and drove my mostly-trusty Toyota Corolla three thousand miles to start work the following week. It's an exclusive store in the Hamptons with direct links to several of the major fashion houses and it sounded like a dream come true.

I fantasized it might be a launchpad to New York Fashion Week. *Bryant Park, here I come*, I'd thought. I pictured myself sipping coffee in one of the park's little cafes, then rushing off—in some impossibly cute outfit of my own design—to get my very first solo show ready for the catwalk, where the front row would be full of Kardashians and Beckhams.

For a whole year now, after my other jobs' shifts are over, I work late into the night, painstakingly sketching and sewing pieces that might catch the eye of my boss and, with her contacts, maybe even the design houses themselves.

Things haven't worked out quite like my fantasies, to say the least. My boss, Veronica Wade, fits every stereotype of the steely, ball-breaking fashion dragon a la Miranda Priestley. She thinks of herself as the go-to know-all of Southampton. She attends parties with the likes of Christian Siriano and—once—Ralph Lauren and his wife Ricky, who, for reasons known only to herself, she considers not only equals but close friends.

Veronica won't even look at my designs. Which means that asking her to show them to people in the industry is out of the question. She also pays me so little, I had to get a second job as a waitress four nights a week just to make ends meet. The tips from the old school billionaires—who are misogynistic dinosaurs but throw money around like it grows on trees—help pay the bills, but they're not getting me any closer to my dream of making it as a designer.

I scour the internet looking for opportunities. I work on my Instagram profile, which is slowly gaining some traction. I spend my nights sewing my garments. But none it seems to get me any closer to making my goals a reality.

The non-stop grind is starting to make dents in my stamina. Maybe because I haven't had a solid night's sleep in months.

My phone vibrates. Hoping it might be one of the jobs I've applied for calling me back, I pick it up.

Jess's name pops up on the screen. My bestie from home, who grew up a few houses down from mine. We also went to UCLA together. I majored in fashion and she majored in film.

"Hey, Jess."

"Hi, honey. How's life? You haven't called me in over a week, just saying."

"Sorry. I've been so busy." Just hearing her voice makes me pine for familiarity. I'm surprised to feel the slightest sting behind my eyes. God, I really must be strung out.

Jessie is like a sister to me. We were both only children, both raised by single moms. The difference is, hers is alive and well and thriving as a Hollywood casting director. Mine got sprinkled into the ocean, which she made me promise I would do, months before she had any idea she would drop dead of a sudden brain aneurism in the middle of a regular Tuesday afternoon.

Reading my voice like only Jess can, she comments, "You sound tired."

"I am, a little," I admit.

"Well, the good news is, you're about to get a vacation."

"Yeah, right." I exhale a light laugh. "I can't take a vacation."

"You have to. I'm getting married."

"What?" I splutter. "To who?"

"Remember the guy I was telling you about a few months ago?"

"The hot tech guy you met at that beach party?"

"Yes. His name is Jacob."

"But…you're *marrying* him?"

"We've seen a lot of each other over the past three months and, well, the thing is…"

Her pause goes on just a little too long. "The thing is what, Jess?"

"I'm pregnant."

I'm speechless for a couple of seconds. "Holy shit, Jess." Jessie has always wanted kids. It's been a dream of hers for as long as I've known her.

"I know. It's a lot. But I'm happy. It feels like it's meant to be."

"It's a little *sudden*." I'm about to say, *you barely even know the guy*, but it's hardly going to be helpful right now to point that out.

"Yeah. It is sudden. It just kind of happened. It was a shock. We used condoms and everything, but one of them must have broken. I like him so much and he's been so incredibly *nice* about the whole thing. He's sweet and caring—and hot and also loaded—and we both know those attributes don't converge in one human being very often. He's basically perfect. And then the look on his face when I told him my period was late…he was *excited*, Lila. Not scared or spooked or trying to worm his way out of anything. His reaction really made me want to…I don't know, just go with it. His parents are still married and they still live in their family home in Mendocino. We went up there last month and he introduced me to his whole family. He's got two older brothers and his parents were so welcoming and they're all so *normal*, Lila. He's stable and…*real*. Not like every loser I've ever dated—and God knows there have been plenty of them. He has a house in Malibu. An *amazing* house. With a view of the ocean. And then two nights ago he got down on one knee out of the blue and he asked me to marry him. With a big-ass diamond ring. So I said yes. We want to do it soon. We want to do it before I start to show and we can't see any reason to wait."

Maybe so you can get to know each other? I want to say. But the truth is, I've barely talked to Jessie for months. I've been too busy to make the time to chat for hours, which is what we always end up doing.

I mean, maybe it *is* possible to make decisions like this on the fly if it feels right. How would *I* know? The only man I've ever connected with was too busy connecting with every other female within a three-mile radius to even notice me. I'm hardly the best judge of these things. "Wow, Jess. I'm so happy for you. If you're really sure."

"I'm sure I want to have this baby. And so is he. We just…clicked. Before this even happened. I don't know if I've ever felt this excited in my entire life, Lila. For all of it. So I figure that's a good sign."

"Yeah. It must be a good sign. This is amazing."

I can tell she's crying. "I know, right? Who would have thought I'd be married and knocked up before I even turn twenty-four? Will you come? Will you be my maid of honor, Lila? I can't do this without you."

"Next Saturday? Way to give a girl some advanced warning, honey."

"I know. It's quick. Please please please come, Lila. I need you there."

"Of course I'll come." I actually do have some time off accumulated at the boutique since I haven't taken a single day off for the whole year. I'm owed two weeks, in fact. My boss at my waitressing job is laid back enough to also give me time off, at least I hope he is. Even if he isn't, it hardly matters. I can't exactly say things have worked out for me here in New York. I haven't even come close to achieving a single one of my goals. I'm still stuck in this overpriced limbo that involves styling billionaires' wives whose faces are pumped so full of Botox they look like they're made of plastic, and whose only fashion consideration is flaunting price tags to their equally-obscenely-loaded friends.

"I can send you a plane ticket if you want," Jess offers. "If that's helpful."

"You know me." I laugh off my fear of flying. "I prefer to remain on solid ground, rather than suspend myself thirty thousand feet in the air inside a flimsy metal tube."

"I thought you were going to go to therapy about your phobia," she chides me.

"I haven't had time. It's on the list."

"It's a long drive, Lila."

In some ways I feel like this might be a sign. Maybe it's time for me to cut my losses and accept defeat. I *tried* to make it in New York, I really did. I gave it a year. I've worked my ass off with nothing to show for it. I've made progress, but I still have such a long way to go. Plenty of designers base themselves in L.A., after all. It's not like I can't build up a following from the West Coast. "I was actually thinking of coming home." I hate that, as I say it, a piece of me feels like I'm a failure who's giving up too soon.

"For good?" She can't disguise her hopefulness.

"I don't know. I've made one friend and I can't get an interview for a job I actually *want* to save my life."

"Would you move back into your apartment?"

"The tenant just signed another six-month lease, so no, not right away." I inherited the one-bedroom apartment I grew up in (and its mortgage) when my mom died. My mom was a working actor and single mother and she did the best she could. I admire her for so many reasons, but most of all because no matter how hard things got, she always stayed true to her art. It was her passion. The one lucrative role she ever got allowed us to buy a tiny apartment only one block from one of the more scenic canals, in a quaint but run-down house that was converted in the seventies into two apartments. Ours is on the top floor, with its own rickety exterior staircase and a closed-in balcony with a peek-a-boo view of the water.

My apartment is cozy and cute and still my favorite place on earth, with all its memories and its quirky little Californian personality. It needs a lot of work and there's still a substantial mortgage to pay off, as well as the forever-ongoing expenses of taxes and insurance. The rent barely covers its costs, and even though property values have skyrocketed over the past few years, I could never sell it. That would feel like selling off a big chunk of my soul.

"Move in with *us!*" Jess gushes. "Jacob's house in Malibu has five bedrooms."

"Wow, Jess. That's incredible. But I'm not moving in with you and your new husband—and baby, soon enough. Thanks for the offer though."

"You could stay with us until you find somewhere else. Just think about it, at least. You'll have plenty of time to mull it over on the 40-hour drive."

"True."

"So you'll come?"

"Yes. I'll be there by noon on Saturday. Does that work?"

"You can't get here by Friday night?"

"I'm going to say Saturday just to be on the safe side. It's going to take me all week to get there."

"Okay. The ceremony starts at three. If you could get

here by noon so we could get ready together, that would be perfect."

"It's a date."

"Lila, I'm *so* excited to see you. L.A. isn't the same without you in it."

"I've missed you too, bestie."

"Listen, my mom's here to take me to try on wedding dresses. I would've asked you to make me one, if it wasn't so rushed. Call me tomorrow though. We need to talk through details."

"Okay. I'm working two shifts but I'll call you in between."

"You work way too much. There's seriously a free room for you to call your own here if you want it. You could sew all day and put your own show together."

As tempting as that might be, it would never work. I'm far too independent to rely on other people. Just like my mother was. The mere thought of mooching off Jess's new fiancé makes me feel uneasy. I guess it's one of my quirks. I always need to feel like I'm fully in control of my own destiny. "I'm really happy for you, Jess. I'll call you tomorrow."

"Thanks, honey. It means the world to me that you're coming. Oh, and Lila?"

"Yeah?"

"Remember Brittany Wells?"

"Yeah." She lived down the street from us when we

were teenagers. We used to go to the Santa Monica pier together sometimes.

"You know how she was always baking cupcakes and started that cupcake business a while ago?"

"I think I remember you mentioning it."

"Well, she's offered to make our wedding cake."

"Great."

"And since she offered to make the cake, I invited her to the wedding. She asked if she could bring…a plus one."

"Is that a problem?"

"She said…" Jessie pauses. "I'm just going to blurt this out because I don't know how else to say it, but her plus one is Troy Beckett. She's been dating him off and on and…he's coming to the wedding. They're not exclusive. She said they're 'friends with benefits'. That's how she put it."

I feel myself pale. "Oh."

"I just wanted to tell you, so you weren't caught off-guard or anything. But you're over him now, right? That was a long time ago."

"Of course," I laugh breezily. "Are you kidding? As if I'd still be pining for that loser."

"Thank God." She sounds relieved. "I knew that. I just wanted to make sure."

"Don't give it another thought."

"Okay. Good. I better go. I'll talk to you tomorrow."

"Bye, Jess."

We end the call.

Fuck.

I *am* over that loser. Totally. It's ridiculous that I ever loved him in the first place. He hardly even gave me the time of day and I hate that I wasted so much of my life on him. I *saved* myself for him, all through college. Hoping maybe he'd notice me. Fantasizing that maybe once he got to know me, he'd fall in love with me and leave all the others behind.

Which means I'm a huge sucker and a complete idiot.

And I'm basically *still* saving myself for him—not intentionally, but it's not like I'm out on the town every weekend picking up men. I'm too busy working.

I also hate that my heart is beating faster at the thought of seeing him again. *They're not exclusive? Does that mean…maybe, just maybe, there's a chance that he might finally…*

Stop it.

I force myself to snap out of it. I've given way too much of my energy to that black hole of a not-even-close relationship. I can't allow myself to spend another second of angst or longing on a guy who's never treated me like anything more than a piece of furniture.

Snap out of it, girl! You're better than that.

Of course I am. I've moved on. I'm a strong, independent woman, taking the world by storm.

Who's also thinking of giving up on her dream of making it in

New York because it's lonely and nearly impossible to get ahead. And who still hasn't met anyone else because she spends all her time striving like a madwoman but basically getting nowhere.

Anyway, I'm *trying* to take the world by storm, that's got to count for something.

2

Lila

My phone rings again and this time it's Sloane. The one and only true friend I've made since I've been here.

"Hey, Sloane." She came into the restaurant one night with friends, soon after I started working at the restaurant. I just happened to be finishing my shift. We ended up having a drink together because she complimented the skirt I'd made and we talked for hours. It felt good to find a friendship that was so easy and spontaneous. She's bubbly and outgoing and fun. She lives in Chelsea and sometimes, if my schedule allows—which has only happened twice—I'll take the Jitney into the city and meet her for a drink somewhere.

When Sloane found out I design clothes she looked me up and bought a few of my pieces online. She told her friends about me and it's been Sloane's orbit of Instagram fashionistas that have given me the most exposure so far.

"Honey, what are you doing Saturday night?" she asks. "Will you come with me to a party? Technically, I'm working, but I need reinforcements. I can't bear to talk shop all night with the finance nerd brigade."

"Whose party is it?"

"My boss's brother, Noah. It's at his to-die-for house in Southampton." Sloane has a job as the assistant for Colton Maddox, one of the four very successful Maddox brothers, famous for their good looks and their money. And for supposedly being Manhattan's most eligible bachelors. Colton is the playboy brother, according to Sloane. She tells me wild stories about how he charms all the most beautiful women in Manhattan into bed but refuses to commit to any one of them beyond one night. "Usually I'd go alone but I need a buffer since it'll be mainly work people. They're celebrating the best quarter they've ever had at Invested Enterprises."

"Sounds fun. But I'm heading back to California for a friend's wedding this weekend."

"Oh," she says, disappointed. "When are you leaving?"

"Sunday morning."

She perks up. "Then you *can* come."

"I was going to have an early night on Saturday and try to leave early on Sunday. I'm driving all the way to L.A., if you can believe that."

"You're *driving*?"

"I know, it's a long way. But I'm scared of flying." I

don't mention to Sloane that I'm thinking of moving back to L.A. for good. "And I thought I could see a few places along the way that I've always wanted to see." I don't love the idea of going alone, but then again maybe it'll be a good opportunity to get some headspace and reassess my life. I haven't had a chance to do that in a while.

"Please come?" Sloane pleads. "I need you, girlfriend. Plus I haven't seen you in weeks and we need to catch up. You can still get an early night. Wear one of those sexy-ass designs you're so good at. It'll be a good opportunity to get noticed by some seriously loaded Hamptonites and it could be good for business."

Maybe she's right. Besides, I can admit I've been lonely lately, mired in my grueling work schedule. It might be nice to have some fun for a change. "Okay. I'll come. But just for a few hours."

"Fantastic! Thank you, sweetie. I'll die of boredom if I have to spend the evening discussing spreadsheets and cost benefit analyses. You're way more interesting."

I laugh. "Sure I am."

"Who knows, you might meet some hot billionaire who will sweep you off your feet and fall madly in love with you."

"Yeah, right," I scoff.

"I'll see you on Saturday, honey. I'll pick you up at six."

3

COLTON

Saturday
Southampton, New York

I LOOK out over the water, taking a minute to appreciate the killer view from the palatial deck of Noah's Hamptons house. The whole sky is lit with fiery shades of red and orange. Tonight we're celebrating the best quarter we've had yet. And the backdrop fits. I get the eerie feeling that something monumental has opened up or shifted somewhere out there in the universe—which is fucked up. The sky is absolutely on fire with cosmic power tonight.

Would you listen to yourself, asshole?

I don't usually stop to consider shit like "cosmic power" or sunsets in general. In fact I can't remember the last time I took the time to notice the color of the sky.

I'm not sure why I'm feeling philosophical tonight. Maybe because we've worked our asses off and are finally beginning to reap some serious rewards for all our colossal efforts.

Invested Enterprises was my brother Cash's creation, but Noah and I have put just as much blood, sweat and tears into the company's success as Cash has.

Cash had something to prove. At first I came along for the ride, because it was a challenge and it was also an escape hatch from the family business. Maddox Enterprises was founded by my great grandfather. It's well known to be one of the most profitable investment companies in New York State history. Not a bad legacy, sure. But trying to work there with my father, before he dropped dead of a whiskey, cigar and meanness-induced heart attack—as well as my three older brothers and the long list of ancient executives—was a little like trying to conduct business in an overcrowded pond full of blood-thirsty sharks.

The layers of stifling expectations were so entrenched, it was like pulling teeth just to present any inkling of a new idea. The decrepit old board members, some of them relics from our grandfather's era, saw every modern concept as a threat to their traditions and, even worse, to their gigantic investment portfolios. We tried to tell them we could have taken those portfolios to the next level, but it was no use.

Alexander was always going to be CEO of Maddox Enterprises because he's the oldest son. Noah is the second son and the most accepting of all of us. If nothing better had come along, Noah probably would have stayed and made a good career out of being second-in-command while also keeping the peace because that's what he does.

Cash was the one with the most strained relationship with our father. The thing he craved most of all was to be out from under the thumb of A.J. Benjamin Maddox III. And because our father was so convinced Cash would fail, it lit a bonfire under Cash like nothing else could have. Cash was hell-bent on making IE succeed no matter what it cost him.

Noah and I understood that. We wanted the company to thrive as much as he did, because it meant we were no longer indebted to Maddox Enterprises, not only for our jobs but for our entire fucking identities.

For me, as the youngest of four sons, I was always an afterthought. I was never going to have any kind of role that was about *me* and not just my last name. So as soon as Cash offered another option, I was eager to jump the family ship.

But building a company from the ground up has been fucking hard work. We've had every imaginable curveball thrown at us and we've caught most of them, but not all. The company floundered a few months ago when we were investigated for an insider trading accusation, which turned out to be Cash's jealous bitch of an ex trying to get revenge. When that story broke and we could assure our investors that the problem was nothing more than a petty argument that was now over, our company went into overdrive. As painful as the fiasco was at the time, the spike of publicity turned out to be the best thing that could have happened to us.

Business is most definitely booming.

The live band starts up from the corner of the patio, the humid summer air carrying the sound. I grab a glass of champagne from the lined-up flutes being poured by the bartenders and make my way toward the hub of the party, which is revving up.

For most of the year, this place is wasted on Noah. He's the most chilled person I know, the kind of guy who prefers a low-key bottle of red by the fire to an all-night rager. But this house is showy as fuck and built for parties.

Maybe with the newfound success of the company, Noah will finally start to let loose a little.

He's surrounded by a group of women who are draping themselves over him for a photo and it makes me laugh. I kind of like this side of him. Since Noah is a romantic and now that Cash and Alexander are both head over heels for the women of their dreams, my brothers like to joke about how I'm the only ladies' man in the family now. Which isn't entirely accurate.

But I'm definitely not feeling it tonight.

In fact I haven't been feeling it for a while.

It's not that I *can't* get women's attention—at least ten are ogling me right now. It's just that some internal switch seems to have flicked recently and I've suddenly become incredibly fucking…picky.

The sunset tonight is only making it worse. It's a beautiful night. It would be nice to *feel* something other than just a surface-level tendency to go with the flow because you can.

I've been called the "smoke show" and the "pretty boy" Maddox brother—irritating, but I often get featured on magazine covers and I have more followers on social media than all three of my brothers combined, possibly because none of them could care less about being seen. I don't mind it.

I don't post often. Maybe a few times a month, and my posts usually make headlines. I've always been athletic and I'm ripped as fuck from years of hockey training during college and, ever since, a punishing sixty-lap swim every morning followed by weight training. I have blue eyes and dark brown hair. I'm 6'2" and built. And I tend to get noticed.

The media talks me up as a person who knows how to have a good time. I guess it's not a terrible reputation to have.

And then there's my money. I was born with more than I could ever spend in several lifetimes and I've managed to quadruple it since I turned eighteen.

It's easy for us. We learned how to read investment spreadsheets before we learned how to read comic books. Our father made damn sure his sons knew their way around a portfolio. He considered anyone who couldn't double their money every three years a dim-witted idiot. It was a crime worthy of being disinherited, so we paid attention.

So I've lived my entire life with the knowledge that I can have any woman I want, whenever I want, wherever I want. It's obviously a win-win.

Which is why I can't figure out why I've been so badly off my game lately.

I've wondered if it's because two of my brothers are sickeningly in love, so much that it's changed their entire personalities. The two most stoic, uptight people I know are whipped so hard they spend all their time following their new fiancées around like lovestruck puppies, buying them mind-bogglingly expensive jewelry, luxury apartments and month-long trips to the tropics. And these are workaholics on steroids who have never taken a vacation in their lives.

The thing that gets me the most is that they're so fucking *happy*.

It's got me thinking.

What would that *feel* like? To fall in love like that? To be so besotted with *one* person that you want to spend not just all your time with them but the rest of your goddamn *life*.

It's hard to imagine.

"Hi, Colton." A girl I hadn't noticed sidles up to me, twirling a long strand of bleach-blond hair.

"Hey."

"We met a few weeks ago. At my friend's party in Soho. Do you remember me?"

"Sure." Nope.

"My name's Mandy."

"Right. I remember." Not even close.

Charm usually comes naturally to me. I'm the cruisey, easy-going member of my family, the one who's first to laugh and who has, until now, been perfectly content to bask in my reputation as a fun-loving playboy having the time of his life.

I don't remember meeting this girl.

And I don't particularly want to.

Her fake lashes blink at me, her brown eyes full of hopefulness and visions of a life of ease, with two point five kids raised in some eight-bedroom saltbox mansion in this neighborhood, their trust funds fully in place before they've even been conceived.

I'm not feeling it at all. "I've got to go talk to my brother, but maybe we'll run into each other later on."

"Oh. Okay." I brush past her disappointment before she feels compelled to give me her number.

Making my way toward the bar at the far end of the porch, I have the sudden urge to get inebriated.

What the hell's wrong with you? That was a slam dunk.

As I said, I've been off my game lately. Which is starting to piss me off.

I don't want another meaningless fling tonight.

Why the fuck not?

Because I want to know what it feels like to experience some-thing real.

4

COLTON

I LOOK out over the crowd.

I know most of the people here, of course, and there are the inevitable hangers-on, who have crashed the party to get close to Noah, Cash or me. There's a buzz in the air, the kind that only comes when you're coasting on the high tide of victory.

We don't intentionally hire *only* outrageously good-looking people, but you wouldn't guess it from standing here on Noah's patio. With the sunset as our backdrop, we could all be movie stars.

And yet I can't find even one person who appeals to me in the way I need them to appeal to me tonight.

What the fuck's going on?

I see Cash at one of the tables, his fingers entwined with Dusty's. Those two would annoy the hell out of me if they weren't so perfect for each other. Cash is totally besotted and I can see why. Dusty is gorgeous, with a cute Texan flair and a softness that's rubbed off on my brother. He's calmer when she's around.

Dusty whispers something in Cash's ear and he bends down to kiss her with a tenderness I've never seen in him before.

Alexander is equally annoying with his new fiancée, Ivy. Never in a million years would I have expected either of them to fall this hard.

I know it'll never happen to me. And I wouldn't want it to. I can't think of anything worse. Being tied to one person like that for the rest of eternity would be a nightmare.

Still, it would be interesting to feel it. Just once.

A crazy, head-over-heels love that blinds you to everyone else.

I've never felt anything remotely like that. Not even close.

Cash sees me watching him and raises his flute at me in a silent toast. I'm in his good books for the work I've put in this quarter—which, believe me, isn't always the case. Cash didn't sky-rocket this company to where it is by going easy on anyone, especially his little brother.

Cash stands, getting the attention of the crowd almost immediately.

"Thank you for coming tonight, everyone," he says, his deep voice making it clear he's the boss even when mildly intoxicated by both lust and Moët. "You deserve to celebrate tonight. And you have my deepest gratitude. We owe our success to each and every one of you. You've put your trust in me and my brothers over the past two years and we've achieved things even *I* wasn't sure were possible. So here's to Invested Enterprises. And by the way, you're all getting a huge bonus in your next paycheck. Cheers."

Gasps of celebration erupt from around the patio and I can't help but feel proud of them—of *us*.

And now I can get on with the rest of my night and find the most beautiful woman at this party to take home with me. I need to get over whatever dry spell seems to be taking over my love life.

I spot Sloane, which is easy to do since she's five ten, taller than most women, even without the sky-scraper heels.

My assistant is, objectively speaking, a good-looking woman. And not my type at all.

She's also the one woman who has access to my entire life at her fingertips.

Sloane smiles and waves to me. We're all in a good mood tonight.

A woman is talking to Sloane, with her back to me.

She has dark, glossy hair that spills down her back. She's slim, wearing a dress that hugs her curves and leaves her tanned, toned arms bare.

Chances are I've met her before.

But no. I'd remember that hair, which is long and silky, cut in layers. The shorter layers have a jaunty little wave to them. It's an unusual haircut and it's sexy as fuck.

I make my way over to them.

As I get closer, I check out the girl's outfit, which isn't something I would usually take a lot of notice of. I've lived my life in New York, surrounded by rich, beautiful women. They're *all* fashionable. But this friend of Sloane's has a sophisticated flourish to her look.

As I make my way through the crowd, I'm forced by all the people I know to do my duty as a Maddox. Mingling, saying hi, sharing a joke. But I'm in laser-focus mode. Some invisible force is tugging me toward the girl.

I want a better look.

Sloane and the mystery girl are obviously friends, judging by the way they're leaning in, like they're telling secrets.

I'll choose to ignore the fact that Sloane notoriously refuses to introduce me to her female friends.

I guess I can't entirely blame her for that. I'm very up-front about the fact that I don't do commitment. At all. Never have. I make sure women know that from the word go. I'm up for a good time, but when the night ends—which it always inevitably does—the night ends. I make sure they know I won't call before I offer them a second drink. They're fine with that, every single time.

That doesn't, however, stop each and every one of them from thinking she'll be the one to change me. To convince me she's the one worth reforming for. And when that doesn't happen, they start acting like I'm the worst guy alive when I follow through on every single one of the promises I made when I first met them.

That alone seems to be enough to ensure that Sloane doesn't think I'm a good match for any of her friends.

To be fair, I probably wouldn't want a woman *I* cared about platonically sleeping with me, either, unless all she's interested in is the best night of her life.

I realize how arrogant that sounds, but I'm just talking from experience. Before you run for the hills and write me off as an asshole or a man-whore, let me explain one thing. I'm honest, I'm fun, I make people laugh like they haven't laughed in a long time, they often tell me. They can be themselves with me.

But when we get to the bedroom, I'm no gentleman. I'm careful and very thorough in all the ways I need to be. I'm also hung like a fucking Spartan. And I know how to use my gifts.

That's just the way it is. I happen to be very, very good in bed. This isn't me singing my own praises. This is the talk of the town. Which Sloane loves to point out to me every chance she gets. I swear she keeps a digital scrapbook of the quotes.

Colton Maddox is the best lay on the planet, according to one Victoria's Secret supermodel, a headline Sloane insisted on reading to me. *He was gone by morning but, girl-*

friend, I have been SHATTERED in the best kind of way, enlightened beyond recognition, and I'm still high on my three-orgasm endorphin rush. Baby, come back to me.

Or something like that.

Or, according to a starlet I met at a movie premiere a few months ago, *Colton Maddox, CALL ME, you sexy beast! Holy Amazeballs, Batman, I need another night with you. Pretty please with whipped cream on top* 😈 *! Once was never going to be enough, you bad, bad boy. You just can't DO those things to me and then disappear like a hot, ten-inch, dirty-talking ghost, it's not fair!!!*

And so on.

Sloane warns her friends to steer clear of me, but there's an intrigue she can't control. Women fall for me at the drop of a hat and there's nothing Sloane or anyone else can do to curb their enthusiasm. I'm a piece of A-list billionaire prime beef and half of them are madly in love with me before they've even met me.

It is what it is.

I can overhear the girls' conversation now, and I grab a bottle of champagne from an ice bucket.

"So how's stuff going with work?" I hear Sloane ask the girl.

"Today is actually the start of my first vacation in a year," the girl replies. She still has her back to me, but the soft husk to her voice is strangely magnetic. It's the kind of voice that could calm your worst fears or talk you off a ledge. "I've got two weeks off." Mystery girl takes a sip of her champagne and I see her shoulders visibly relax. So wherever she works is stressful, then. Some instinct that feels new to me doesn't like this.

It's then that I get my first look at her face.

5

___

COLTON

I DON'T WANT to sound dramatic here, but with the backdrop of the red sky and the setting sun dipping into the sea, leaking its liquid fire all over the surface of the water, painting the girl's skin, her hair and her face with its golden effect, she looks like some kind of otherworldly fire-lit angel.

Her face is *insanely* beautiful.

Her eyes are silver, catching the reflected glow of the sun like bottled lightning, rimmed by sweeping lashes. She's petite and fine-boned and, in contrast, her lips are almost ridiculously full and lush. Something about the bee-stung plushness and the perfect pink of them reaches into me and grips both my heart and my cock like tight fists.

Fuck.

She notices me and she blinks up at me, her silver eyes widening a fraction.

I can honestly say I have never been so mesmerized in my life. Her dark, gold-lit hair frames her face, with those curls of the shorter layers adding a playful softness and the longer strands hanging to frame her breasts, which are high and full with the faint outline of her nipples barely showing through the fabric of her dress.

Fuck me.

I notice again the style of her outfit. I happen to personally know many of New York's top fashion designers and I get a lot of invitations to their shows, to liven up the front row. I don't pay attention enough to know who this designer might be, but it doesn't look familiar. It looks new and cutting edge, with details of pale suede and off-white fur. Even I can tell that it's well-made in that way that well-designed clothes should be: they make the person wearing them look fucking amazing.

This girl would look gorgeous in a paper bag, but the dress takes her beauty to a whole different level. She's hot and sexy and naturally glamorous, like she wakes up looking like this.

"Don't you dare look at my bestie that way, Colton Maddox," I hear Sloane scold me through my dazed infatuation. "You can't have her."

We'll see about that.

I feel strangely starstruck and drunk on the vision of her.

How can anyone be this fucking beautiful?

"Lila, meet my devastatingly handsome but completely insufferable boss, Colton Maddox."

So her name is Lila.

"Don't believe a word she says. I'm not insufferable at all."

"Really," Lila says softly, like she doesn't believe me.

"Colton, meet Lila Bailey, my gorgeous, talented and exceptionally off-limits best friend."

"Lila, the pleasure's mine." I take her hand carefully, leaning to kiss her cheek because I can't resist. Her skin is cool and silky-smooth. The scent of her hair, all floral spice and lemony freshness, is so mind-numbingly appealing it makes me dizzy. I have a savage urge to wind the long strands around my fist and tilt her head back so she's fully under my power before tasting her insanely inviting mouth.

"Nice to meet you, Colton." Lila smiles, pulling her hand from mine.

For a second I'm speechless—and this might be a first —by the sweetness of her smile and her neat white teeth, but there's something reserved and knowing behind her eyes. Sloane, no doubt, has warned her about me. If she's Sloane's "bestie," Sloane probably gushes every chance she gets about how terrible I am, how I leave a trail of broken-hearted women in my wake wherever I go.

Even if Lila is as intrigued as I am, her eyes lingering on my face, my chest, and lower—as she's biologically hard-wired to do—she's already made up her mind about me. "Sloane's told me a lot about you." There's a pause before she says it. "All good, of course."

"Of course." I slide a look at Sloane, who gives me an overly sweet smile. I can't stop my assistant from gossiping about my night life, and it never bothered me before, but right now I find myself regretting that she knows every damn thing about me.

Damn it, Sloane.

I immediately get the impression that Lila is inexperienced. And a little bit world-weary, like she's been burning the candle at both ends for too long. Not unusual in New York, of course, but I don't like that she has the faintest bruise-like shadows under her silver eyes.

Is she okay? Is she working too hard? Does she have anyone to take care of her?

It's an unfamiliar feeling. To not just care about these details, but to feel the concern leeching deep into psychic fresh dirt, taking on a manic edge.

"Beautiful night for it," Sloane comments.

"Yes," I agree. "The perfect night to celebrate our success." I top up both their glasses and my own, clinking my flute against Sloane's, then Lila's, grinning at the stunning little minx, because I can't *not* grin at her. She's so fucking gorgeous, her beauty is somehow making me feel like I just won one of life's holy jackpots.

"Okay, one more drink, but that's it," Lila says. "I've got a long drive tomorrow."

"Where to?"

"My friend's getting married in L.A. next weekend. It's going to take me all week to get there."

"You're driving to *L.A.*?" My brain is working in the background behind this slightly shocking piece of information. Who drives to fucking L.A.? And the spin of my thoughts is taking me into brand new territory. *This could be your opportunity to spend time with the most beautiful woman you've ever met. To convince her you're not a serial-dating villain. To show her that instead, you're the man of her wildest dreams.* "By yourself?" I'm not even going to acknowledge that last thought. I don't know where the fuck it flew in from.

"Yeah, well, I have this phobia about flying." She laughs lightly, and the sound does weird things to me. Those invisible fists gripping my heart and my cock squeeze tighter. "It's lame, I know, but it's a hang-up I have. So I figured it could be a chance for me to check out a few places I've always wanted to go, along the way."

Her voice is angel-soft but with a light smoky husk to it.

I wonder what it would sound like moaning my name. I have a sudden, feral need to find out.

"Like where?"

"Nashville. I've always wanted to go there. Aspen, maybe for a night or two, but I hear it's super expensive. The Grand Canyon's on my bucket list and it's sort of on the way. So maybe I'll try to fit that in too. And Vegas, believe it or not. I don't even gamble but I feel like I should at least see it once in my lifetime."

Against my will, my brain is continuing to concoct a plan.

A bus. One of those super-sized tour buses with lounges and upstairs bedrooms. I could show her these places in total style. I could blow her mind with how much fun she could have, and how much luxury I could lay on. For a whole week, she could be all mine.

"Are you sure you don't just want to fly, honey?" Sloane asks. "I used to hate flying too, but I just take a sleeping pill now and it knocks me right out."

Lila admits something she's clearly been holding back from Sloane. "I'm actually thinking of going back to L.A. for good."

"No." Sloane takes Lila's hand. "You can't."

"I'm not a hundred percent sure yet, but things aren't really working out for me here like I'd hoped."

Which means you'll never see her again if you don't act on it. She'll slip right through your goddamn fingers and you'll always wonder.

Sloane is upset by the news. "But it's so sudden, Lila. You can't leave for *good*."

"I'm sorry I didn't tell you before, Sloane. I've actually been thinking about it for a while. L.A. is home and I'm…" She glances at me briefly but then overrides whatever hesitation is holding her back. It might be the combination of the champagne and the fact that Sloane's warnings have made her decision to steer clear of me resolute. She tells us more than I might have expected. "Well, the guy I've had a crush on forever is going to be at the wedding. And my best friend from college—the one getting married—has offered me a room in her soon-to-be new husband's house in Malibu, not that I'll probably take her up on it, but it's nice to have the option short-term. So it feels like the timing might be right."

"What guy?" Sloane asks. "You never told me about a guy you've had a crush on."

"Honestly, he's no one. Just a guy I used to basically be in love with even though nothing ever happened between us. I'm kind of dreading seeing him."

There are a few things I can use here. She's single. She's pining for a man who must be the biggest fucking idiot on the planet. And if nothing happened between them and she's been pining for him all this time, that could mean…any number of things which I try not to fixate on or over-analyze.

"I'm hardly fantasizing about a romantic reunion with my old unrequited crush," Lila laughs again, but there's regret in it. "It's probably going to be totally awkward."

"*Or*," Sloane gushes, "he'll realize what he's been missing out on all this time and he'll fall madly in love with you."

The idea of it makes my blood turn hot and it's an

unfamiliar sensation. What the hell? Is this…*jealousy?* Whatever it is, it's intense. I want to kill the fucker.

Lila shrugs lightly. "Highly doubtful."

"All you have to do," Sloane insists, "is to turn up all super-hot and outrageously sexy, like in this insane dress you're wearing right now or one of your other designs—like that catsuit on your Instagram, oh my god. The guy won't stand a chance."

Of course he won't. And neither do I. *Note to self: look up Lila Bailey's Instagram.*

"It's extremely unlikely," Lila says. "Compared to Mr. Hotshot Lawyer in Pasadena, with my two minimum wage jobs and tumbleweeds rolling through my love life, I'm definitely not looking like the best option on paper."

"Girl, those details are irrelevant," Sloane insists. "Don't you dare sell yourself short. Have you looked in the mirror lately? You could have any man you wanted. You just haven't met the right one yet."

The more I watch her the more mesmerized I become. The girl is absolutely stunning.

"That's the thing," Lila says. "Maybe I *have* met the right one but he just didn't want me. I know it's ridiculous. I really should have moved on a long time ago. And I thought I had, but then as soon as I heard he was going to be there…oh, god, why am I even talking about this? The whole thing is ridiculous."

So she's never dated because she was waiting for some asshole from her past to notice her.

Sloane looks around, whispering conspiratorially to Lila. "You know, if you wanted to let off some steam before you see this guy again, to take the edge off those nerves, you could…you know, have a little fun tonight. We're surrounded by hot, rich assholes. Any one of them could be yours for the taking."

I'm gripping my champagne flute so hard I have to make a point of not breaking it.

"What a way to sell your colleagues." Lila bites back a smile.

"I mean, they're not *all* assholes." I know Sloane's not including me in that half-compliment.

Lila laughs. "As if I'm going to have my first one night stand with some random guy just so I don't completely embarrass myself in case I happen to connect with Troy, who's actually with someone else but apparently they're 'not exclusive', according to Jessie. It's so pathetic. Someone please save me from myself."

I grip the back of a bar stool to stop myself from yelling *I volunteer as tribute* at the top of my lungs. I can't suppress the raging urge to save this stunning little stranger from the douchebag named Troy. What kind of Class A moron would overlook this drop-dead gorgeous girl when she was crazy about him?

"Wait," says Sloane. "What do you mean, 'your first'…?"

"It's nothing. Forget I said that."

But Sloane is nothing if not persistent. "Lila, do you mean you've never…at all…even once…?"

Lila's face turns bright red and she glances at me before shielding her eyes from me, as though that'll stop me from overhearing. To Sloane in a hushed plea: "Would you stop? That's the very last thing I would want your billionaire devil of a boss to know about me."

I can't even get offended by that. I *am* a devil. And she's an angel.

"Seriously?" Sloane squawks under her breath. My assistant is good at her job, but tact is not one of her strong points.

Sloane takes Lila's mortified silence as a yes.

"Holy shit," Sloane exclaims in her hushed whisper. "You've been *saving* yourself for this guy?"

"No. Well, not exactly. I just…haven't found someone better yet."

"Girl, you could cash it in now. Here. Tonight. Do you want me to introduce you to some of the lesser-assholes?"

"Of course I don't." Lila's expression is layered. Sadness, almost. Exhaustion. "I decided only a couple of days ago that I'm going to drive back to California on what might end up being a one-way trip. I need to focus on that and not get distracted."

"Lila, it's such a long way. Are you sure you want to do this? God, I'd offer to come with you if I didn't have work."

I'm tempted to offer Sloane the time off. But another idea is gaining momentum and it doesn't want Sloane anywhere near it.

Lila twirls a strand of her hair. "I thought things would fall into place for me here in New York, but the reality is, they haven't. I think the open road and some head space is exactly what I need, to figure out my next move."

Sloane contemplates Lila and I can tell Lila's about to be lectured by my well-meaning but very bossy assistant. I'm on the receiving end of it every damned day, so I know the warning signs and when to run. Lila, it seems, does not.

"It all sounds very Thelma and Louise, Lila—without Thelma—but the reality is you'll be spending your nights in shitty motels, eating dinner alone, spending huge stretches on the road with all those big trucks and endless traffic. All day every day of driving is extremely tiring. It's not even *safe*, Lila. Plus there are predators out there. Lots of them. Is your car even reliable? Maybe you should at least consider taking a bus. I don't think you've thought this all the way through."

Lila sighs. "I have thought it all the way through and unfortunately it's my best option. I've given it a year, Sloane. You're basically my only real friend. I'm still not even close to breaking into the industry. And my car only makes that clunking sound when I turn the air conditioner on. It'll be fine. The weather's cooler now. I *want* to take the time to drive, anyway. I think it's what I need."

Sloane begins to relent. "If you're really sure, honey."

"I am."

None of this is remotely acceptable.

Anything could happen to her out there on the open road by herself. Even if she does make it to L.A. without breaking down or worse, the thought of her showing up to that wedding dressed in some sexy little number to try to win back a dim-witted asshole who most definitely doesn't deserve her makes me feel like bending a crowbar in half before impaling him with it.

A waiter shows up with a tray of tequila shots he's passing around. Sloane picks up two of them, handing one to Lila. "Well, if it's our last night together for a while, we need to at least drink to your journey. And your conquest. You too, boss." I grab one and Sloane clinks her shot against mine, then Lila's. "To the fall of Troy."

Lila giggles and shakes her head. "I'm *really* going to regret this, but what the hell."

They both drink their shots, Lila struggling with it. I tip mine back. They're generously-sized shot glasses. Doubles, if I'm not mistaken.

As I watch Lila's hair lift gently in a passing breeze and I catch the floral scent of her, I suddenly get the unfamiliar feeling that I'm in serious trouble. My brain is on auto-pilot and its plan is fully in place. I have no idea why

I suddenly feel compelled to be this little stranger's white knight but I'm feeling it *hard*.

Someone calls to Sloane from across the patio. One of the girls from Noah's office.

"Oh god, I forgot I was supposed to send Laney those documents. I can do it from my phone. I'll be right back, Lila." Sloane eyeballs me and I expect her to give me her well-practiced speech about my many character flaws but for some reason she doesn't. "Behave," is all she says before slipping away. "And talk her out of driving to California by herself."

I have no idea if Sloane could feel it. But *I* can. This fizz of electricity that's hanging in the air between me and the gorgeous girl whose lips are so lusciously flawless I'm having a hard time not kissing her lustily right here and now.

I take heart from the fact that her cheeks have those soft flags of pink and her silver eyes are locked on mine.

"Do *not* let me have any more shots," Lila says. "I still haven't finished packing and a hangover will definitely not help me. Besides, tequila makes me crazy."

"I'll have one of my drivers make sure you and Sloane get home safe," I tell her. "The bride must be a good friend for you to trek all the way across the country to go to her wedding."

"We've been best friends since we were ten." She blinks up at me. Her eyelashes are naturally long and lightly curved, framing those stunning, light-filled, soulful eyes. "She just found out she's pregnant. To some guy she really likes but hardly knows. Even though I've never met him, I get the feeling things are going to work out for them. He's got plenty of money and he's nice to her. He has a stable family and a nice house. I just hope she gets everything she's ever dreamed of. She deserves it." Her eyes are filled with emotion. She's definitely feeling the alcohol now and I have the urge to protect her in ways I've never thought about before but that are burning me with their ferocity.

"And what about you?" I ask her. "What do you dream of? Besides the loser who let you go."

Her mouth quirks with regret. "I'm sorry I told you all that. It's stupid. Just a guy from my past who I honestly never thought I'd see again. And I was *relieved* about that. But now it turns out he's going to be at this wedding and I can't really not go just for that reason. I'm the maid of honor."

"He must be the stupidest man on the planet, to not notice you when he had the chance. There's clearly something wrong with him."

"Oh, there's nothing wrong with him. He's like the poster child for good decisions."

"If you weren't one of his decisions, honey, I'd have to strongly disagree."

Her expression is hard to read but I can almost hear what she's thinking. That she's half dreading seeing him and half hoping it might be different this time. She's still mired in some mindfuck with a guy who never gave her the time of day.

It's not right. She's too beautiful to be ignored.

"Are you still in love with him?" I brace myself, but I've already decided—and I have no idea where the fuck this is coming from, because it's a complete U-turn to the way I've lived my life until this exact moment—that I'm going to be the one to change her mind.

What the fuck, Maddox.

"No. I'm not in love with him. It was a long time ago. I just want to see him again so I can lay all of it to rest and get on with my life. I thought I'd already done that but I haven't met anyone else and maybe I'm still holding onto something. This is my chance to finally let it go."

I'm not convinced. And I suddenly can't handle the thought of her *not* letting it fucking go.

"The thing is, I'm terrible at reading signals or signs," Lila confesses, the tequila now having its way with her. "That's part of my problem. I think it might be the reason Troy friend-zoned me in college. And why I've had such bad luck with men. If I don't up my game, I'm doomed to be single forever." Her gorgeous face twists into a sulky pout and it's the cutest thing I've ever seen in my goddamn jaded life. "Anyway, I'm sure you don't want to hear another word about my pathetic sob story."

"It's not pathetic. It's romantic. You just wasted your efforts on the wrong guy."

She blinks up at me again, twirling a finger through a

curl of her silky hair. *I want to grab handfuls of it as I fuck that sweet little pink mouth.*

The worst part about this whole clusterfuck is that there's a very real possibility she *would* be better off with Troy. She said it herself: I'm a devil. I'm the guy who breaks every woman's heart. It's my whole identity and there's no reason to think I wouldn't break Lila's too.

I don't know if it's the color of her lips or the fire in her eyes that has me slayed, but for the first time in my life, I crave something I've never had a reason to crave before. I want to be a better man than fucking Troy.

I know that if I confess my sudden knight-in-shining-armor tendencies to this perfect little stranger, she'll probably laugh in my face. So I take a slightly different tact. "Do you have a plan?"

"What do you mean?"

"How are you going to play it? You can't go in there all subservient and self-conscious. You have to stride in there like you own the place. Like you expect every man there to get on his knees for you." Which they all will anyway, even if Lila doesn't realize it. There's no way in hell any straight man in their right mind wouldn't want to devour Lila Bailey.

But she can't see this.

"That's the problem," she admits. "I don't even know where to start. I have zero experience seducing men." She blushes again and I try not to think about how badly I want to make her whimper and writhe with pleasure.

My cock is hard and hot but I ignore it. "So the wedding is next weekend?"

"Next Saturday."

"Well, then, it's obvious, isn't it?"

"What's obvious?" Blinking at me innocently.

"You need a driver. Someone to keep you company." *What the fuck are you offering right now?* "And if that person can give you lessons along the way? Then it's a win all round."

"Lessons?"

"Here's my offer." *Tequila, do your job. Make her say yes.* "I'll drive you to California and, along the way, I teach you how to seduce a man. How to flirt like a pro. How to read signals. I'll teach you how to get any man you want. I'll even teach you what to do with him once you've got him—so well, he'll fall completely, totally head over heels in love with you."

Like this one. And only this one.

6

COLTON

I DON'T EVEN TRY to interpret the shit going on in my brain right now. It must be the tequila having its evil way with me.

And I barely know what I'm offering. All I know is I've got this inexplicable need to be close to her. The thought of letting her walk away, possibly for good, and straight into the arms of some clueless asshat who doesn't appreciate her is unbearable.

"Wow," she breathes. "That's a big promise, Mr. Maddox."

I'm going to be her travel companion. Somehow, between now and L.A., I'm going to change her mind about Dipshit Troy.

The waiter returns with another tray of drinks. This time it's flutes of champagne. I take two, handing one to Lila.

"Not for me," she says.

"You have a driver now. You can be hungover in the passenger seat. Have one more with me. Then I'll have my driver take you girls home if you want."

She relents, taking the flute, but she doesn't drink it. "You really are a devil, you know that?" She looks so damn lovely I basically feel like I'm in the process of being zapped by a slow-moving lightning bolt that's infusing me with a super-powered, full-blown obsession.

"So, we're doing this?" I'm trying to act like my world won't implode if she says no.

"You really think you're that good of a driver—and teacher?" She clearly thinks I'm joking about the offer.

"I know I'm that good, sweetheart."

Her bell-toned laughter kills me. "So what exactly are you going to teach me?"

"Everything you need to know."

"How?" Coquettishly, without even meaning to be, with a sweep of those long lashes.

She might not think she knows how to flirt, but the way she touches her tongue to her plump bottom lip when she's unsure…it's pure torture. I'm fucking hooked.

I feel her eyes on me, studying me. "What do you get out of this, then?"

I lean in close. So close that I can smell the sweet smell of roses and ripe peaches on her skin. I take a sip of my champagne before answering, enjoying that I can see

I've riled her with just one look. My mind might be scrambled, but she's not immune to my charms.

"I get the opportunity to take some time away from work and see some of this great country of ours, of course."

"Of course." Clearly amused, Lila takes a sip of her drink, like she's waiting for the part two of my answer. So I take my cue, leaning in even closer, catching the spark in her eyes as they lock with mine.

"And I get to spend time with the most beautiful woman I've ever seen." I reach out to trace the outline of her delicate jaw with one finger, keeping my voice low. "If I get to kiss you just once along the way, I'll consider it to be the best road trip of my life. And when I demand more—and I will—I'll expect you to do anything I ask."

"Oh yeah?" comes the sassy but breathless reply. She still thinks I'm teasing her.

The problem is, I'm dead serious about all of it. "Oh yeah. Because the demands I'll make will give you the kind of pleasure you never even knew existed."

Her silver eyes get wide. My urge to kiss her is so strong it physically hurts. But I don't want to scare her away.

She laughs. "Wow. You're good, I'll give you that. Those lines are expert level. I'd say you're definitely the right man for the job."

"And you're already better at this than you think."

I take her hand in mine, squeezing it lightly, as though to seal the deal.

Sloane is making her way back toward us and I murmur to Lila, "Let's keep our deal under wraps for now." Sloane will have my head on a platter if she finds out, but I'm facing bigger issues than the wrath of my assistant.

I'm relieved when the band cranks up several gears and a few more people join our circle.

It's probably the alcohol—I'm half hoping it *is* the goddamn alcohol and I'll come to my senses any minute. I can't take a week off. Especially for a girl I've known for exactly twenty minutes. Then again, Cash just took two weeks off. And that was before we'd even fully resolved the issues we were having, which I ended up solving for him.

I haven't taken any time off for over a year.

Whatever excuses I might be making or not making evaporate when Lila smiles at me. And I know for sure that I'm in deep, deep trouble. It's the kind of trouble that somehow feels so fucking good I simply don't care.

7

Sunday
Southampton, New York

I BLINK at the harsh morning sun beaming through my window, which burns into my brain like the hot flames of blowtorches.

Ow.

Why didn't I close the blinds last night? I always close the blinds.

It all comes flooding back to me.

Oh my god.

I went to that party with Sloane last night.

Oh no.

And proceeded to drink *way* too much alcohol and confess *way* too much about my pathetic backstory not only to Sloane but also to her extremely hot boss.

You idiot.

How did I even get back to my apartment?

I vaguely remember some luxury limo-type car dropping me off. Sloane and I were crying and hugging because who knows when we'll see each other again.

"Ugh," I groan, patting my bedside table as I squint in its general direction, hoping that last-night-Lila might have had the foresight to put a glass of water there. She did not.

I can't move. That's it. I'm deceased. My head throbs with a vengeance that could only be matched by a rabid woodpecker, and my mouth is as dry as the mighty Sahara.

Note to self: the next time someone offers me tequila, run in the opposite direction as fast as my legs will carry me.

I should never have accepted Sloane's invitation to her company's swanky Hamptons party. The thing about Sloane is that she can be very persuasive when she puts her mind to it.

When else are you going to get a chance to hang with a bunch of billionaires, she insisted. *Get your ass into a skimpy little dress that shows off that banging body and be ready for me to pick you up at six.*

Or something along those lines.

And so here I am.

My stomach rolls as I suddenly panic that I've missed

my alarm and I'm late for work. *That's what you get for pretending you belonged with those people last night, Lila.*

I'm about to jump up—jump being a relative term when your head and stomach are both spiraling like you've just hit the summit of a rollercoaster and are now headed directly vertical—when I remember I have two weeks off. Which would feel like a relief if I wasn't currently so concerned with hurling all over my clean white sheets.

Then I remember the *reason* I have two weeks off.

I'm driving to L.A. today. Or at least starting my journey westward.

Shit.

Veronica did end up giving me the time off but she was such a passive-aggressive bitch about my request, I'm not sure if I'll be welcome back after my two weeks anyway.

I can handle that. I've already decided I'm moving back to L.A. for good.

Haven't I?

I still haven't completely quit either of my jobs or given notice on my apartment, but I'd planned to do some of that this morning. Or on the way.

I was supposed to wake up early and get organized.

Damn it, Lila, why are you such a mess? No wonder you can't get ahead in life. You can't even make a few simple decisions.

That's what this trip was supposed to be about. Thinking things through.

Except that having a thought right now feels a lot like wading through knee-deep tequila-heavy mud.

Ow. My head.

Lord, I need some water. And Tylenol. And caffeine.

I reach again to my bedside table and feel around for my phone—thank God it's here. And completely dead.

A vivid memory slices into my brain.

Sloane's ridiculously sexy boss.

God, that man was gorgeous.

I vaguely remember a conversation during which I overshared on an *epic* level. Then, when Sloane was talking to a colleague about work stuff, Sloane's boss came up with some absurd plan that involved the two of us driving to California together. *What the hell?*

I groan again, my hand covering my eyes. Did he have a name? Oh shit, of course he did.

Colton Maddox.

The Colton Maddox. On the Forbes list, multi-billion-aire, along with his brothers, who happen to be four of the most successful investors and entrepreneurs in the city.

Colton, I learned somewhere along the line from Sloane, is the youngest brother. The playboy. The most eligible bachelor in Manhattan who, as hard as they try, none of the socialites or influencers can get to commit.

Risking the entire contents of my stomach upending themselves onto my splurge-buy comforter, I sit up a little, trying to make light of the situation.

So I had a little too much to drink. It happens. Not to *me* before last night, but I guess there's a first for everything. I'm sure Colton Maddox is laughing it off as a joke this morning too, just like I am. He probably makes teasing promises like driving across the country on a whim to lots of women. He's notorious for breaking hearts, I remember Sloane telling me.

I cringe at the hazy memories.

I did shots with him. We drank more champagne and flirted. He pretended I was good at it. Then his playful banter was all about coming along on my trip while meanwhile…oh god. Did I…there's another swirl of nausea to complement my morning regret…yes, I told both Sloane *and* Colton my whole sob story about my old college crush. Like, the *whole* sob story. And then I admitted to Sloane I'm still a freaking *virgin*. In front of Colton Maddox.

How completely mortifying.

Then Colton joked about offering to enlighten me in the art of seduction during our road trip across the country.

Help.

I need to call Sloane and tell her to apologize to her boss on my behalf for getting inebriated at the company party and spilling my guts. He probably thinks I'm a total nutcase. Hopefully he's already forgotten about me and has moved on to some jet-setting tycoon's daughter who doesn't have any old college crushes and who definitely isn't a virgin.

Clearly, it wouldn't be safe for the good people on the interstate if I was to attempt to drive this morning. Maybe if I spend the day recovering and finishing up my packing —and getting Sloane to relay my fervent apology to her boss—I could get up super early tomorrow and make up for some of the lost time on the road.

I couldn't have known I'd be nursing a monumental hangover and would need to spend the day over a toilet bowl rather than driving my ancient but hopefully-trusty Toyota Corolla across Pennsylvania.

But, hey, shit happens. At least I did have a tiny bit of *fun* for the first time in a long time.

Maybe a little too much.

Okay, way too much.

I decide to surrender to feeling like death warmed up and just sleep for a few hours. But first I really need to brush my teeth and drink several enormous glasses of water.

Carefully lugging myself out of bed, it takes a few seconds for my equilibrium to settle into place. *Tequila, I'm swearing you off for good. Never, ever again.*

I plug in my phone, limp to the bathroom, take two Tylenol and drink four glasses of water. Then I brush my teeth for five solid minutes and wipe the make-up from around my eyes. I leave my bird's nest hair as is. That can wait.

Just as I get settled back into bed where I can feel sorry for myself and nurse my regrets, there's a knock at my door. It's got to be Sloane coming to beg for forgiveness for the obscene amount of tequila and champagne she allowed me to consume last night. No one else even knows where I live.

But Sloane went back to the city last night.

Maybe she decided to come and check on me to see if I'm still alive.

"We're no longer friends after those shots," I groan.

The knock comes again, more persistently this time. My girl is really pounding.

"Damn it, Sloane," I mutter. "Okay, fine."

I climb out of bed. Wearing nothing but a skimpy pink bralette and matching boy shorts, I shuffle to the door. I pull the door open, ready to give Sloane my most pathetically hungover and in-pain face, when I freeze.

It's not Sloane.

Holy shit.

It's Colton Maddox.

8

Lila

COLTON IS STANDING THERE on the other side of the door, looking like…well, like a ludicrously handsome and slightly windswept ultra-hot billionaire. And not even remotely hungover. How is that possible?

Not only does he *not* look like he's about to die, he's even more beautiful than I remember him being last night. Admittedly, my memory is hazy, but I distinctly recall the butterflies in my stomach that worked their way down to…well, a little lower than my stomach…when he stood next to me at the bar as I marveled at his to-die-for rugged good looks. Which don't even compare to the way the blindingly bright sun is lovingly showcasing him right now.

Wow.

Was his hair this…sexily tousled last night? It's dark

and wavy, like he's overdue for a haircut. It gives him this rakish, panty-melting, gorgeous look.

Really, Lila?

Yes, really. Absolutely panty-melting.

He had this effect on me last night too. And I'm not typically the kind of girl whose panties…well, *melt*. I'm usually too distracted by work and money or lack thereof and trying to establish myself and whatnot to notice a guy's five o'clock shadow and wonder what it would feel like to touch my fingers to the roughed-up surface of his square jaw.

Or to feel a sort of tingling up my spine just from the sound of his deep, rasped voice.

Now, he's wearing jeans and a white polo shirt that's snug around the sculpted muscles of his shoulders and which shows off his tan, accentuating the dark hair and the white teeth. The whole thing is way too colorful and just…roguishly ideal, like he just stepped off a Ralph Lauren photo shoot after a perfect day of living the high life out on his private island.

As for the eyes? I'm sure he had them last night, but I do *not* remember them being this startlingly blue in a way that makes you think of the glittering ocean and hot summer and the best days of your life. They're sparkling with mischief, and his lopsided grin is…ridiculously gorgeous. And darkly intrigued, as though the sight of my hungover state is amusing to him.

"Hey," he drawls, as his eyes rove over my thin and

practically non-existent clothing, if it could even be called that.

My pulse riots. The universe sure does have a sick sense of humor, bringing this demi-god into my morning, when here I am looking like I just escaped from the nearest asylum.

I take a deep breath, trying to not freak out, when I get a whiff of his scent. Of course he smells like crisp mountain air mixed with just a hint of spicy cologne. My senses feel personally attacked.

Without waiting for an invitation, he strides in, broad-shouldered and tall, his athletic body filling my tiny apartment with zinging, stormy man-energy.

"I took the liberty of bringing you a supersized one-sugar black Americano. I figured milk wouldn't go down too well but the sugar might help restore your electrolyte balance." He holds out an extra-large cup of coffee with *The Bear and the Bean*'s logo wrapped around the heat-protective cardboard band. How did he know that place has my favorite coffee? *And* that I like black coffee with one sugar?

It's thoughtful, that he's considered how I might feel. Possibly the most thoughtful thing anyone has done for me in…a while.

He holds out the coffee and I take it from his hands—Jesus, they're big—and try to ignore the sparks that shoot up my entire arm then funnel directly to my *very* intimate regions when our fingers touch. *Yikes. My panties are getting…oh god.* But he's crazy if he thinks me looking like this is a sign I'm ready for anything other than a 90s romcom marathon in bed.

"What are you doing here?" I can't help asking. "And how do you know where I live?"

I watch as he makes himself at home in the midst of my organized chaos, stepping over one of my open suitcases with his long legs, leaning casually against the kitchen counter. "I might have asked a few subtle but well-aimed questions to my somewhat-tipsy assistant last night."

Tipsy. That's a very kind way of putting it. I grab an oversized t-shirt and put it on, since I'm basically standing here in my underwear. "She gave you my address?"

"Affirmative. I really need to check her data protection and confidentiality training is up to date." He smirks briefly, then looks deadly serious as he says, "Are you ready to go?"

I try to fold my arms across my chest while holding hot coffee, to attempt to hide my nipples, which are reacting *a lot* to someone who is essentially a stranger. An extremely hot stranger, but a stranger, nonetheless. "Do I look ready to go anywhere other than my own funeral?" I attempt to deadpan—because making a joke of this is all I've got.

"You did seem to enjoy the tequila last night." His eyes actually twinkle. "And the champagne."

"I blame you entirely for that."

"Sloane's the one who got you started. And she's your 'bestie', so…" he shrugs.

"Yeah, that's a life choice I am starting to reconsider," I mutter. "Look, I'm not sure why you're here, but I'm not exactly up for visitors right now."

A frown darkens his absurdly handsome face. "You don't remember our trip?" For a fraction of a second, he looks at me like a wounded puppy.

"I mean, vaguely, but that was a joke, right? You can't really be serious about wanting to come with me." A light laugh escapes me at the ridiculousness of the situation. "I mean, aren't you some kind of in-demand investment wunderkind—"

"Wunderkind?" he grins.

"Isn't that what they call people who succeed in a very competitive profession at a young age?" Ow, that one hurt my brain.

Colton presses his tongue against his bottom lip like he's attempting to hold back a laugh. "I'm not that young. I'm twenty-six. Plus there was some nepotism involved— not that I'm *not* a successful investor. I am. My private portfolio outperforms all three of my brothers' most quarters. I was trained well, but I also have a knack."

"Oh." I'm not sure what to say. "That's nice."

"And yes, I am in demand." More twinkling of those deep blue eyes, and it reminds me again that this guy is famous for his charm and where it lands him—specifically into the beds of rich, beautiful women.

"Exactly." My reply sounds both pointed and not-at-all-affected by this dazzling package standing in front of me. I give myself some points for that. "Which is why I'm wondering why you're here."

He pauses, his eyes barely narrowing. "I'm overdue for a vacation. Your chariot awaits."

I blink at him, my smile almost lingering. This really is too much. The vision of him is literally blazing with way more big, rugged *manliness* than I can handle right now. "Look…Mr.—"

"Seriously?" He laughs, cutting me off. "Call me Colton. Like you did last night. I insist."

"Colton, this is—"

"Going to be a trip of a lifetime, I'm glad you agree." He goes over to the window where he gestures down the street. "I already got the RV."

"The what?"

"You're dealing with a Maddox here, so we're doing this in style, Sunshine. This baby has *all* the bells and whistles." His words hang in the air like a punchline waiting for laughter. Only, it doesn't seem like he's joking. Is this gorgeous, fresh-air-and-worn-leather-scented hunky playboy actually serious about a week-long road trip to California? With me? "This was the biggest one I could get without a Class A license. I don't have one because all I own are Shelbys, Lamborghinis, Corvettes, a Hummer and a Maybach. Oh, and the Maserati. And three Ducatis. And a couple of limos. I figured fuck the chauffeurs. I'm going to drive you myself."

Class A? Maybach? Ducati? Is he speaking English? My tequila-sodden brain is struggling. "Honestly…this is a terrible idea. We don't even know each other—"

"Sorry, beautiful, but it's a done deal. We shook on it. The RV is ready. Our itinerary is locked in. And you've got a wedding to get to and some asshole named Troy to seduce. So let's go. I'll meet you downstairs in ten. These good to go?" He gestures to my two open suitcases.

All I can do is stare at him, speechless.

Taking that as a yes, Colton bends down and zips up both suitcases—not without effort since they're so stuffed. Then he lifts them and heads back through the still-open door and down the stairs, lugging the behemoths like they weigh ten pounds each instead of more like sixty.

"Um…"

But he's already gone.

What in the actual hell is happening right now?

I go to the window and peer out, expecting a dilapidated Winnebago, like the ones you see midwestern families driving through Yosemite. But the vehicle parked outside does not look like an RV at all. It looks like a shiny, gleaming, luxury rockstar tour bus.

Whoa.

How did he manage to organize this since late last night?

Then again, he's a billionaire. I guess they can organize things faster than normal people do, maybe.

My head spins in protest and I grip onto the window ledge. I take some deep breaths, trying not to inhale the remnants of Colton's unfairly delicious cologne.

My forlorn little Toyota is in the actual shade of the colossal RV, looking almost relieved. If I leave my car behind, then I'll have to come back for it. Or I could sell it—not that it's worth anything. Maybe Sloane could take it and drop it off at a used car dealership for me.

Am I actually considering going with this? I must still be drunk, that's the only explanation.

I mean, my suitcases are already almost on the bus.

Wow. A whole week with Colton Maddox…in a luxury house on wheels.

I take a sip of coffee and watch him load my suitcases into an open side compartment.

He really is gorgeous. And so…muscly. He must work out a lot.

His phone rings and he answers the call. He gestures with his hand as he talks and I catch some of the conversation through the open window. *Because I'm overdue for a break, Cash, that's fucking why…that's none of your business…and that's also none of your business. Consider it a creative week if you must—which I also haven't had for over six months because I've been busy fixing your insider trading shit-show while you gallivanted around fucking Hawaii, remember? Okay…good. You should be.* Colton laughs, despite his obvious irritation. *Did you actu-*

ally just say something nice to me, brother? That might be a first. More low laughter. *Not if I see you first. Later, asshole.*

One of his brothers. Wondering why he's taking off for a week.

Why *is* he taking off for a week?

With me?

And is it totally crazy that a tiny part of me actually wants him to?

Okay, more than a tiny part.

It *is* crazy. But I do in fact need to get to the wedding by next weekend and this luxury bus will clearly be a lot more comfortable than my ancient Toyota. I wasn't entirely looking forward to the lonely roads and the divey motels along the way where drug dealers and serial killers probably hang out, as Sloane so generously pointed out.

I'm doing it.

To hell with it.

Should I tell Sloane? Probably not a good idea. I know for a fact my phone would be ringing off the hook if she knew Colton was here. I can practically hear her scolding me. *Do NOT in a million years go ANYWHERE with my playboy boss! Are you crazy? Yes, he's hot. Yes, he's in fact smoking hot, we can all agree on that. But do not befriend him! He is NOT boyfriend or relationship material AT ALL. He'll totally charm you because it's what he does and then the minute you think there could be something real there, he'll be nowhere to be found. It's always the same. Every freaking weekend I'm fielding irate phone calls and reading the headlines about how some heiress or socialite is broken-hearted, crying to whatever blogger will listen that she wants another night with him. This is a Code Red, Lila. DO NOT get on that bus!!*

That's the thing, though. I am most certainly *not* considering Colton Maddox as potential boyfriend or relationship material. Of course I'm not. He's providing a means of transportation, that's all. I'm not entirely sure why, but that detail is irrelevant right now.

What about the seduction lessons?

I shove that thought out of my head. That was obviously a joke told under the influence of copious amounts of very strong alcohol.

It's not like Sloane can be mad at me, once I tell her —after the fact. It's not *my* fault he's shown up here with a luxury tour bus. I know she'll forgive me once I arrive safely in Los Angeles and we can laugh it off as a random escapade that's now over.

With newfound energy I can only attribute to the double-shot of coffee starting to hit my bloodstream with gusto, I go into the bathroom and close the door. Then I run the shower, peel off my clothes and step into it. The hot water blissfully washes over my skin, rehydrating me by a single degree.

"I'll grab some more of these smaller bags and this sewing machine," Colton calls from the other room.

"Thank you!" I call back. "I'll get the stuff in my bedroom. I won't be long." Whatever. I'm too hungover to question this. For all I know, I could be dreaming this whole scenario.

Ten minutes is not long enough in any lifetime to get ready to go anywhere with someone as hot as Colton Maddox, but it's not about that, I remind myself. I'm not exactly sure what it *is* about, but I'm not in the state of mind to mull that over right now. So I put on a pair of cute jean shorts I made, with suede detailing on the side seams, and a fitted white t-shirt with a cheerful slogan about the demise of the patriarchy emblazoned across my chest. I leave my hair long, put on a little mascara and some pink lip gloss.

Then I pack the last of my stuff into my overnight bag and stuff my sheets and comforter into an oversized bag.

That's everything. If I decide not to come back—which I have—at least the apartment is empty.

By the time I check once more for anything I've forgotten and say a mental goodbye to my tiny studio, I hear Colton blasting the horn in an annoyingly rhythmical pattern. My neighbors are going to love me for that.

I close the door behind me, jogging down the stairs.

Which is most definitely a mistake.

I stop on the sidewalk, doubling over, contemplating gripping the sides of a nearby trash can. Jogging was a bad idea. Movement in general was a bad idea. And the last thing I need right now is for a billionaire to see me on the verge of being sick. *Please don't get out of the bus.*

"Need me to hold your hair and rub your back?"

Damn it. "No," I manage. "Please. I need a minute."

Maybe if I upchuck on the street, it would be for the best. Then he'll drive away in disgust and we can forget this whole crazy plan.

"Feeling sick?"

Didn't I just tell him I need a minute? But nope, he's still standing right there, grinning like all this is normal and like we're not complete strangers that are about to embark on a three thousand mile journey together.

He might be handsome, but I get the distinct impression I made a deal with the devil last night. No one should be this perky and charming and good looking after the amount of toxins we consumed last night.

I straighten up and the world spins. Colton notices me wobble. He holds my arm to steady me.

"You really have trouble picking up men?" he smirks. "I can't imagine why. Almost hurling all over a guy's shoes first thing in the morning is usually a real turn on."

I glance up into eyes that are all the colors of a summer day. "Okay, you can fuck off a little less."

Colton wraps an arm around my waist. "Careful, Lila, the last thing I need is a hard-on while I'm driving."

9

———

COLTON

"Can we please make that the last time we talk about your hard-on during this trip?" She blinks at me, with that same pouty little attitude that slayed me last night. Her silver eyes are light this morning, made brighter by the slightly bloodshot effect.

"Of course we can't. We have an agenda, if you recall from the pact we made last night. And I intend to follow through on every one of my promises."

Last night I was amped up by success, Moët and a spectacular sunset. I can admit the combination of Lila's gorgeousness and sass hooked me, but I couldn't help wondering very early this morning if it was a case of being caught up in the heat of the moment. If maybe I'd overdone it by offering to drive her all the way to fucking California.

But now, I can feel whatever hold she has on me

digging deeper, like those hooks are sweetly barbed with the kind of pain that feels…not just good, but better than anything has.

I don't know what the fuck is happening here, but if she's *this* fucking adorable when she's exhausted and hungover, I'm a goner.

Apparently not appreciating my early-morning sense of humor, Lila groans and mutters something under her breath, but lets me guide her towards the monstrous RV.

As she pulls herself up the steps, gripping the doorframe for support, she sways to one side and for a second I'm worried she's about to topple right back out again. I place my hand on her back to steady her, trying not to stare at how good her ass looks in those sexy little shorts.

"Easy there." I try to ignore the warmth that floods my entire body—especially one very hot, thick and overly eager part of it—at the contact.

Lila gasps when she sees the interior of the RV. The sound of her light inhale does fucked-up things to me. Especially since I'm practically grabbing her sweet ass in those tight Daisy Dukes.

Damn.

I *like* it, I realize. I love her awe. I like being the one who's inspiring it. It makes me want to give her everything I have, just so I can hear that amazed little huff.

I don't stop to think about the fact that I might possibly be losing my goddamn mind. I've never wanted to spend more than a few hours with a woman before and

I'm now planning a journey that will take at least a hundred and twenty with this perfect little stranger. By choice. *Because I'm fucking fixated.*

"Wow," she breathes. I wasn't joking about the hard-on, and the sounds she's making as she checks out the bus are getting me rock fucking hard.

I'm not going to analyze the fact that I've just rented an oversized and overpriced bus just to impress some admittedly-gorgeous friend of Sloane's, who I'm now planning to drive across the entire continental United States so she can meet up with her ex and supposedly seduce the fucker.

Cash interrogated me about why I'm taking a week off and about who I'm spending it with. If I told him the truth I would never live it down.

He knows I don't commit.

Then why are you standing here gazing at her like a lovestruck idiot?

Lila's Daisy Dukes have leather strips sewn along the sides. Must be one of her own designs, and the cowgirlish detail suits her. There's something a little bit untamed about her, like she has trouble fitting into other people's boxes and can't quite thrive when she's expected to. She told me last night she was from L.A. and it almost surprised me. I might have guessed Tennessee or Wyoming or something wilder than Venice Beach. Then again, L.A. is its own trip. Either way, I find myself looking forward to being the first one to show her Nashville. The times I've spent there have always been good ones.

The longest strands of her still-damp hair hang halfway down her back. The shorter strands are wavier this morning, framing her face with whimsical almost-curls. It's the cutest fucking hairdo—again, not something I'd usually stop to think about. Her tight t-shirt, with *Eat the Patriarchy* emblazoned in small letters right across her nipples, makes me bite back a smile.

Eat it? When can we start?

She's slim but curvy with long legs. She has the kind of banging body that any clothes look good on. The tight little outfit is messing with my fucking head.

Don't even get me started on her face. Her features are petite and devastatingly cute. Her cheeks are flushed and her mouth looks slightly puffy, and pink with lip gloss. Like a piece of candy-coated ripe fruit that's basically the most appealing thing I've ever seen in my goddamn life.

All these details combined are blowing my mind to an extent that's downright maddening. I know for a fact that I've never seen a more beautiful woman in my life. How is she not on the cover of every magazine? How did she just slip through all those cracks and end up alone and unguarded at a random Hamptons party? She seems too fucking *good* for randomness. Someone should be making sure she's okay. Someone should be making sure she's safe and taken care of.

Me.

I want to do that.

I don't even know what to do with the sudden—but as forceful as a runaway freight train—thought. It's such a foreign one, I do my best to dismiss it, but something rages in my psyche. *Troy wasn't up to that job. He let her go. And now you're actually going to deliver this beautiful girl straight into the arms of a clueless asshole who doesn't deserve her.*

Something is going to break between this moment and that one and I'm starting to hope it's not my own sanity.

Lila doesn't notice me staring. She's too busy checking out the bus. "This thing is *amazing.* It's nicer—and bigger—than any apartment I've ever lived in," she muses. "And it's on *wheels.*"

She sits on one of the two large leather couches, bouncing lightly as though to test it out. There are a couple of matching armchairs, a dark-wood coffee table, a flat-screen TV, lamps, and even a fireplace. She's mesmerized by all of it, giving herself a little tour. At the far end of the bus, an open-plan kitchen has stainless steel appliances, granite countertops and a kitchen nook with a table and seating area. Beyond that, a door opens into a full bathroom. Between the lounge and the kitchen, a staircase leads up to a second floor, which has another larger bathroom and a bedroom with a king-sized bed. I happen to know this because I spent a lot of time in the small hours of the morning googling like a fucking maniac.

She's already upstairs. "Oh my god!" I hear her squeal, which causes more blood to rush to my overly-enthusiastic cock. "There's a huge bed up here!"

All the better to begin your lessons, darlin'.

I force myself not to take those stairs by threes and begin Lesson Number One right now, dragging my brain into less X-rated territory. It might not happen. We might soon find that we don't click, I'll buy her a first-class ticket from Nashville to L.A. and we can both get back to normality.

Bullshit. You're more smitten than you've ever been in your wretched, serial-dating life.

It's because I've never found anyone I wanted to date twice, that's all.

Until now.

Fuck this train-of-thought argument going on inside my own head. It's like I just developed a full-blown addiction and my brain has no idea how to deal with it.

I need to calm the fuck down.

I sit in the driver's seat and turn on the engine. I've already got our route planned, the playlist organized and the GPS ready. Details I took care of while she was in the shower, to distract myself from visualizing rivulets of hot water gliding down her plush, naked body. Over her tight nipples. Down her stomach to her soft, sweet—

Fuck. I said calm the fuck down, not spiral into fantasizing about how hot the sex with her is going to be.

So I focus on the sleek dashboard. This machine is

growing on me. The windshield rounds the corners of the side of the bus to give better visibility and the two leather seats are what sold me on this RV—at 3 a.m., when one of my assistants (not Sloane, she was too wasted) finally got through to the owner of the dealership, who couldn't believe I was willing to pay his asking price.

The driver and passenger seats are huge, leather, they recline all the way and they have every kind of gadget known to mankind, including a massage feature.

Won't hurt to keep my girl nice and relaxed, I figured.

Would you listen to yourself? "Your" girl?

Yes. I made that decision last night. Around thirty seconds after meeting her. For one week, she's mine. I'm going to awe her, charm her, teach her and show her the time of her life.

And then what? Let her go? Hand her over to the dipshit?

I have three thousand miles to figure that out.

10

COLTON

"You ready?"

She's back in the kitchen now, opening cupboards and the fridge, which is stuffed full of food, Moët and bottled water. "Did you get all this stuff?" she asks.

"Affirmative."

"Can you stop saying 'affirmative,'" she laughs, mimicking my deep voice as she says the word. "What are you, the Terminator?"

"You can call me whatever you want, baby girl."

More laughter, and I'm even more beguiled by the sound than I was last night. "I can't believe you got more champagne."

"Hair of the dog, sweetheart. You'll want one later, I guarantee it."

"It would probably kill me at this point."

"I doubt that. Come on. Get your sweet little ass up here and buckle up. I've never driven one of these things before. Safety first."

Lila comes up to the front and takes her seat. The scent of her fruity shampoo makes me want to feast on her mouth, which is becoming a painful problem.

Especially when she smiles sort of insolently. "I'm going to ignore the 'baby girl,' 'sweetheart' and 'sweet little ass' comments, but only because you're saving me from a very long, bumpy drive. My Toyota's shock absorbers are totally shot."

"That thing belongs in a museum. How are you feeling? Any better?"

"Yes. Much better. The shower and coffee helped. Thank you for the Americano, by the way. My electrolytes feel almost fully restored."

"Glad to hear it, Sunshine." The banter between us is so easy it feels like we've known each other a lot longer than twelve hours.

With Lila safely sitting down, buckled up and appearing to no longer be about to hurl, my first job is maneuvering the RV out of this narrow street and out onto the open road without flattening anything or anyone. A girl I used to know once told me there's something very attractive about a man who's a good driver, and of all the things women have told me, for some reason that one stuck. I have no idea why my number one priority in life has become impressing the hungover little goddess next to me, but I have other things to worry about right now.

Gripping the wheel, I ease the RV backwards and forwards, attempting to get out of the space that suddenly feels way too small for the Goliath I somehow squeezed into it.

I murmur, more to myself than her, "This can't be any harder than driving a Zamboni, am I right?"

"A Zamboni? When did you drive one of those?"

"In college once. Just as a prank. We got hold of one and drew a cock and balls on the ice one time as a joke."

A sarcastic, "How hilarious."

I smirk at her. "It was, actually."

"You're about to hit the curb," she says helpfully.

"Thanks, co-pilot." Inch by inch, I ease the colossal machine forward, praying that I don't take out a mailbox —or worse, a pedestrian.

But once we clear the narrow street without causing a neighborhood crisis, it's not all that much different to driving a Hummer. I catch Lila's wide-eyed gaze and I give her a cocky wink, like I do this all the time.

"Well, that was nothing short of a miracle," she announces, as I get us onto a main road with what I hope looks like effortless ease. "I'm sure part of your sales-pitch last night was that you're a good driver."

"We're still alive, aren't we? Cut me some slack, princess."

She tilts her chin, like she has no intention of doing any such thing. "So far, yes, but the day is young."

"Come on, you have to admit this is far more interesting than the alternative."

"I'd be sleeping, so no." But I can tell she's having fun. There's excitement in her lightning-bright eyes. "So, if you drove a Zamboni, does that mean you played hockey?"

I glance over at her. There's something almost breathless about her question. "Four years for the Crimson, two as starting center."

"That's Harvard?"

I give her a mock-horror frown at the question. "Yes. Everyone in my family has gone to Harvard, for at least three generations. I wasn't allowed to even look at other schools, I had to maintain a solid A average, and if I so much as missed a single class, my father would—and so often did—threaten me with disinheritance. He barely put up with the fact that I was on the hockey team but overlooked it when I became captain my junior year."

"You must have been good. Did you ever think about going pro?"

"All the time. But Daddy-o again threatened to disinherit me if I didn't immediately give all my time, blood and guts to the family business as soon as I finished my degree. I wouldn't be surprised if he put a hit out on me to make sure he got his way. My knee got slammed between the boards and most of the Cornell defense. It got bent forty-five degrees in the wrong direction."

"Ouch." She winces at the thought.

"It took a few surgeries to fix it. And it pretty much guaranteed my hockey career was over. Of course my father was thrilled."

"How awful. I'm sorry."

"What, that my father was an overbearing tyrant or that I never went pro?"

"Both." Lila's watching me, like she's genuinely interested. There's empathy in her expression. And the clear absence of the grasping eagerness I'm so used to. It strikes me that Lila isn't here with me only—or at all—because I have a lot of money. She's not trying to *get* anything from me. It's sort of stark in the moment how much that detail has been a part of *all* the very-short-term relationships I've had.

I find myself craving more of this *realness* between us that's been a part of our conversation from the very first word.

"Hockey was the one thing I did that was completely mine," I admit, without really meaning to. "It had nothing to do with my name or any entrenched family legacies. I could take out all my angst and rage and disappointments on the ice. At the time, it helped."

"So you took your aggression out on the puck."

"Affirmative."

Lila laughs and bats my arm and I have never felt

such a sense of triumph. *I fucking love making her laugh.* "Well, Terminator, it's too bad you couldn't have made a career out of it, but it looks like you've done pretty well for yourself without hockey."

"I always knew it would have created a war between me and my father if I'd seen it through. When the accident happened, it almost felt like fate had stepped in." It's been a while since I thought about all that. The little angel is digging into emotional territory—places I don't usually go.

"It sounds like there were a lot of heavy expectations on you."

"You could say that." She doesn't know the half of it. "Are you a hockey fan?"

"Not really." She's gone cagey, and her gaze lands somewhere out over the scenery, like she's not really seeing it. She's clearly got baggage of her own.

So I dig a little further. "A hockey *player* fan?"

"Definitely not." Her answers are suddenly blunt and sullen.

"Interesting," I tease her.

"What's interesting?"

I've touched a nerve, obviously. "You went to UCLA?"

"Yes. How did you know that?"

"You told me last night."

"Right." She's embarrassed by the memory or lack thereof and twirls a long strand of her hair self-consciously. "Last night I gushed about a whole lot of stuff I should *not* have gushed about. I'm sorry about that. My oversharing knew no bounds. Tequila and champagne are clearly a lethal combination when it comes to obliterating self-control."

I shrug. "It was a good way to break the ice. I feel like we're old friends at this point, I know so much about you."

A light grimace crosses her expression. "A little *too* much."

"You must have gone to a few Bruins games," I fish.

"A few." She's still staring out the window.

But I'm not letting her off that easily. "We've got a long drive, honey pie. You might as well tell me what's rolling around in that pretty little head of yours because I'll keep interrogating you until I get *all* the dirty details you're clearly skating around. No pun intended."

Lila gives me a dismissive look, like she has no intention of telling me anything. And like she's starting to second-guess her decision to come with me.

But it's too much fun getting a rise out of her to relent. I lift my eyebrows, letting her know I'm not bluffing. "We've got five whole days together"—at least—"and I'm nothing if not persistent."

More eye rolling. But then, as though realizing I'm as relentless as I've promised, she gives me the short answer. "The guy I spewed about in far too much detail last night…he was a hockey player."

"Ah. The unrequited lover. That explains the mood. What's Troy's last name?"

She gently pinches the bridge of her nose. "Let me guess. I told you last night that his name is Troy."

"Sure did. Tell me his last name."

"No." Another huff. "I just said I'm *not* telling you. Is there something wrong with your hearing, Terminator?" She imitates me again, muttering in a deep voice, "Affirmative."

I can't hold back a low laugh. "Come on. I can google it. How many guys named Troy have played for the Bruins? Actually, it rings a bell."

"It does?" Cautiously, like she's horrified by the thought.

"Yeah. Now that I think about it, there was a Troy who played center for the Bruins for a while."

I can tell she *really* doesn't want to tell me, but we're in too deep by this point. And maybe she knows me well enough by now to know I'm far too thorough—okay, and nosy—to let this go. "Troy Beckett."

I glance over at her. "Troy Beckett. Yeah, I remember that name."

"Did you know him?" Her face is flushed and I fucking hate that it might be because we're talking about *him*.

"I didn't know him personally. But I knew of him." I almost don't say it. "He was famous for being the biggest douchebag in Division 2."

She sighs, folding her arms. "I knew I shouldn't have told you." She can't bring herself to look at me—or barely. Her mouth is twisted into a sultry little pout. I feel like kissing the pout right off her and showing her what a real man does. Namely, the opposite of ignore her. That this angel was *ever* ignored is a fucking crime. And one I plan on fixing so thoroughly she'll have no choice but to fall head over heels in love with me.

11

———

COLTON

"ANYWAY, IT HARDLY MATTERS," Lila murmurs.

"Of course it *matters*." I'm no choirboy, but there are so many things wrong with this equation, it's beyond infuriating. She loved him. She might *still* love him. *And he can't have her. He's not fucking good enough for her.*

I don't know what to do with my rage at the thought or why I feel like there's fucking fire burning through my veins.

So I twist the knife. "But you already know he's a douchebag, don't you, Lila? Because he never swept you off your feet like he should have. He never lifted you into his arms and carried you to bed like a fucking caveman because you're so damn beautiful there should have been no other choice."

She makes a scoffing sound, sliding me another half-surprised glare, but it's softer this time. "You mean like *you* would have? Give me a break."

I veer the RV into the right lane, signaling only after the fact. Someone honks at me.

"What are you doing?" She puts a hand softly on my arm and a zing of awareness shoots straight to my cock.

"Proving it."

"What? *No.* Colton, do *not* pull over. Are you crazy? Keep driving. I mean it."

I do, but I stay in the slow lane. Our gazes meet and the brightness in her eyes slays me a little more. *What the fuck are you even doing right now?* "I'll prove it to you right now if you don't believe me."

"Fine. I *believe* you." Not convincingly. Like she's just saying that to stop me from behaving like a lunatic. "Anyway, it doesn't matter, okay? It's in the past and you weren't there and I don't want to talk about it. Can't we just listen to some music or something?" She props her feet up onto the dashboard and I'm momentarily mesmerized by the sight of her bare, painted toes.

I have the most insane urge to lick her everywhere, to suck on her toes and feast on her softness like a starving man. I've never felt this fucking hungry in my life.

I realize I'm veering further, so I swerve us back into our lane, ignoring her white knuckles on the armrests.

"Isn't that the whole point of our trip?" I insist. "Aren't we driving three thousand miles so you can change this dipshit's mind about you?" I know I shouldn't be this much of an asshole, but I want to rile her. Who am I to have any say in any of this—and I have no idea why I would even want to, especially *this* fucking manically—but the whole topic is making my blood boil.

"All right," she seethes. "Pull over. Stop the car."

"Why? Are you going to be sick?"

"No! I just need some air. And a time out from the most relentlessly annoying person I've ever met. I *said* I don't want to talk about this!"

With someone else, this might feel like a full-blown argument. But it doesn't. There's a playful edge to it, despite the real emotion behind the things we're talking about. It's weirdly fun. It also feels a lot like very hot foreplay. "You told me last night that you don't want your heart to get broken for the second time. I think that also needs to be addressed."

"Okay, that does it. I've changed my mind."

"About what?"

"Driving with you. Just because I got drunk last night doesn't mean you have total license to delve into all my deepest emotions. Whether my heart is or isn't broken is, in fact, none of your business. And I don't think I can bear this for five whole days."

I could be wrong but I think she's bluffing. She's pissed off but she's also flattered. That I won't let this go. That I care. So I push her a little further. "You should have thought about that last night, princess, before you shook my hand and made a deal with the devil."

"Thanks for confirming my suspicions."

This makes me smile. She's one of the smartest people I've ever met, and the quickest. I can definitely rule out the two of us not clicking. We're sparring like we're long lost soul mates. "Just pretend I'm your therapist."

"As if."

"Come on, Lila, you didn't have any trouble telling it like it was last night."

"That's because I was three sheets to the wind, thank you very much."

"You're welcome." If it's half as much fun having sex with her as it is arguing with her—and it *will* happen—I'm going to be one happy bastard. "We're not stopping just so you can argue with me. It's my job to get you to your destination on time and I won't be able to do that if we pull over every time I annoy you. It would take at least a month to get to California."

I catch her biting her bottom lip, as though to stop herself smiling. "More like a year."

"That's my point."

She leans her head back on her headrest. The sight of her throat and her slightly parted lips hits me like a wrecking ball. *She's so fucking gorgeous.* "Has anyone ever told you you're incredibly infuriating, Maddox?"

"Once or twice."

At this she laughs, despite herself. "I'm sure. And the answer to your question is no, by the way. We're driving three thousand miles to go to my best friend's wedding. That's all we're doing."

"That's not what you said last night."

"God, Colton, can you please just let it go already? I don't want to hear the name Troy Beckett again on this entire trip, okay? He might not even be going to the wedding."

"Oh, he'll be there. I guarantee it."

"How do you know?"

"I just know."

She lightly smacks her forehead with her palm. "No, you *don't* know. You can't. End of story."

"I'll bet you five dollars he's there."

"No. As if I would bet you. Besides, *you* won't know if he's there or not. You're not going to the wedding."

"Most wedding invitations imply a plus one is welcome to tag along. I'm sure your *best friend* wouldn't mind. If the girl baking the cake can bring a plus one, I'm sure you can."

Her silver eyes flash and I love this. I *want* her to react to me. To *feel* me. To take out her passions and her rage all over me. Her soft voice is cool when she replies. "I would prefer to go without a plus one. I appreciate the ride—and I'm still not sure why you'd want to bother with all this—but it's just a ride. It's not an invitation to the wedding. I'm sorry, Colton, but I'm going alone."

I've spent a lifetime arguing with my brothers, and the past three years perfecting the art of convincing everyone I meet to do exactly what I want them to do, from employees to investors to watchdogs at the SEC. The adorable little goddess is hardly getting off that easily.

"You'll need moral support," I tell her. "Think about it. You're about to come face to face with the guy you've *saved* yourself for. For *years*. That's major. And it could go either way. I mean, I'm going to equip you with all the skills you'll need to guarantee success, but you mentioned last night that the guy already has a date, so you'll have to be ready for curveballs. I'm prepared to be your emotional support person in case this chick already has her hooks in, even if your best friend told you they're not exclusive."

Lila stares at me like she can't believe I just said that, and like she can't believe she told me all that, and also like she knows I'm winding her up on purpose. "Is there anything I *didn't* tell you last night?"

"Nope."

She shakes her head, mad at herself but mostly at me. "I don't need an emotional support person. And even if I do, I have Jessie for that."

"Jessie's going to be *busy*. Duh. It's her *wedding* night. She's not going to have *time* to be your shoulder to cry on. *I* will. Besides, I'm invested at this point, Lila. You really hooked me with your backstory last night and I need some closure."

She blinks at me, like she's seriously considering throttling me. "I can't believe a person can be this persistently and intentionally infuriating. I really can't."

"What can I say? I have three older brothers. I've turned bugging people into an art form—*and* supporting them in exactly the way they need to be supported, even if they can't see that right away. I persuade people to do things that are in their own best interests. It's a gift. Trust me, I can do this for hours."

Lila gives me a long once-over. "Well, *I'm* an only child, so your well-practiced techniques are useless on me. Like laser bullets bouncing off a fully-functioning Death Star."

"I like the analogy."

"And I refuse to take your bait again for the remainder of this trip. So I'll ask you nicely, one last time. I'll even humor you by taking your bet, if that helps. Once and for all, would you *please* shut up about Troy Beckett." Like the matter is now closed.

I pretend to mull it over. "If you take my bet *and* take me as your plus one, I promise I won't mention the loser who doesn't deserve you again until at least your first lesson."

This earns me a blush and full lips parted in a light O.

I do my best to ignore how fucking painful my life is right now because I have never, ever been this hard in my life as I ease the RV through traffic to take a left exit. "I'll take that as a yes."

12

"IF YOU'RE TRYING to embarrass me, you can't," I assure him, light defiance in my voice. "My embarrassment over this particular topic is all used up."

I'm talking, of course, about my long-ago crush—not the infamous *lessons* he keeps going on about, a joke he somehow still thinks is funny.

The man is a nightmare. A distractingly *hot* nightmare who just managed to casually drop into the middle of our argument at least three of the nicest things anyone has ever said to me. Between the hangover, the late night and the stress of recent weeks—not to mention the dazzlingly sexy and exasperating chauffeur—my head is spinning.

Colton glances over at me, taking note of the blush on my cheeks. His grin lingers before he turns back to the road. "If you say so, Sunshine."

But then he finally leaves it alone for a while and I thank my stars for small mercies.

Even after our bickering—or maybe because of it—the silence between us is surprisingly comfortable. He's playing some old school country music and it reminds me that I'm excited about where we're going. I'm finally going to *Nashville*, a place I've wanted to go for as long as I can remember. And I can admit it's nice to not be going there alone.

It's also nice not to have to worry about…*anything*, at least in this moment. I realize how heavy all the decision-making and trying-so-hard-24/7 has been lately. For an entire year, I've barely looked up.

For now, I don't have to think about which exit to take or what motel might be the safest option that won't break the bank. I don't have to be in charge of everything. I don't have to be scared.

Because I *have* been scared. For a long time. I work until I'm exhausted so I don't have to think too much about how alone in this world I really am.

Sure, I have Jessie and she's always been a rock to me, but she also has her mom and six cousins and the busy, hectic schedule of a person who has a family that's involved in her life. And now she'll have a husband. And a *baby*. There's Sloane, but it's not the kind of friendship where you'd call each other up out of the blue and talk about how worried you are about maybe not being able to cope with all the stuff you have to cope with.

I find myself taking a deep breath and exhaling it in that way you do when you're sort of overwhelmed with relief.

I hardly know Colton Maddox, but he already feels like a buffer against the harder edges of reality. Which is crazy.

I don't analyze it and I know it's very short-term, but right now it feels ridiculously good to just be…cared for, if it could be called that.

Watching him as he drives, humming along to a Waylon Jennings oldie, his forearms are muscular and hair-dusted as he grips the steering wheel. I can't help but notice that he's incredibly…*masculine*. Big and well-built. His hands are tan and strong-looking. His thighs, in his jeans, are sculpted and solid, filling them out like…well, sort of ideally. Like he's a living, breathing work of art.

His profile is somehow romantic against the backdrop of the colorful fall landscape. His jaw is square and his neck is corded. His thick hair—

"Damn, girl. You're checking me out like you want your first lesson now."

Here we go again with the smug smirk.

The man sure knows exactly how to push my buttons. "You can stop with the 'lessons'. There aren't going to be any lessons."

"Too late to back out, Bailey. We shook on it."

"You obviously rate your own sense of humor very highly, Maddox. You could get a side hustle as a stand-up comedian if the stock market ever crashes. But hopefully it won't because you might find you're not as funny as you think."

Colton bites back another smile. "I'll keep that in mind. Thanks for the tip, gorgeous."

"Anytime."

Even though he's clearly trying to ruffle every single one of my feathers—and I'm not entirely sure why—there's something almost comforting about squabbling with Colton Maddox. He's incredibly easy to be with. There's no awkwardness in our teasing banter, even though there probably should be.

It doesn't make sense at all, but I already feel like I know him better than most people I've known for years. I can't help feeling that we *click* in a way that's rare—even if he is without a doubt the most maddening man I've ever met.

"So, do you have business meetings in L.A.?" I ask him, reclining my seat. "You still haven't told me why you decided on this spur of the moment drive across the country."

He stares at my painted toes for a few seconds, until I almost remind him to keep his eyes on the road.

Colton ignores my question, concentrating on passing a slower car.

"Colton?"

"Yeah?"

"You have meetings in L.A.?" I ask again, in case he

didn't hear me over the music and the acceleration of the motor.

"Affirmative."

It's a joke that doesn't seem to get old and we both laugh, but something about the way he dodged my question makes me wonder if he's lying. And why he would.

"So," Colton says, pulling his sunglasses down over his eyes. "Since we've got all the time in the world, I want to hear the entire life story of Lila Bailey. Make it juicy."

"I already told you all the juicy parts last night. Sadly, that's as juicy as it gets."

"Are your parents still in Venice?"

I open one of the bottles of water already propped in the cup holders and hand it to him. Then I open the other one and take a long sip. "So we're getting real now, are we?"

"We've been real all along. Answer the question, please."

He's right about that. We have been real the whole time. We can't seem to help ourselves. "I never knew my dad. He and my mom had, like, a two-week relationship that ended before my mom even found out she was pregnant with me. I never met him."

"Really?" This is clearly shocking to him.

"Really."

"Do you know his name?"

"Yes. But he died a long time ago. There wasn't a lot to google. He was a drifter from west Texas. My mom said he had trouble written all over him but that he was so good-looking she went with it anyway. She said she fell head over heels in love with him but she knew from the very first minute that there was no way he'd stick around. And she was right. He stayed for a few weeks, then one morning he told her she was the most beautiful woman he'd ever met but that it was time for him to go. He walked out and she never saw him again."

"What?" An incredulous chuckle. "This story sounds made up."

"I wish it was."

"So your mother just…never heard from him again?"

"Nope. When she found out about me, she tried to contact him, but she had no phone number and no address. It was like he disappeared into thin air. And then one day I googled him, like I used to do from time to time, and there was a death notice. It was sort of a coincidence because he'd only died a few days before I googled him." I've never actually told this story to anyone in this much detail. But this is what I seem to do when I'm with Colton Maddox. So I keep going. "He was riding a motorcycle somewhere north of Kansas City and got hit by a sixteen-wheeler. The cops actually found a photo of my mom in his wallet with her name written on the back of it. So they called her up and asked her if she wanted his ashes. She told them to sprinkle them into the wind. It was where he was happiest."

Colton gives me a sympathetic but sideways glance. "That's unbelievable."

"Yeah. It is."

"And your mother? Is she still in Venice?"

"She died around two and a half years ago. Of a brain aneurysm. She was totally fine one minute and then the next minute she was gone. It was really sudden."

"Jesus. I'm sorry, Lila."

"I actually think it's a good way to go." It's something I've thought about a lot. "You're just living your life like you always have and then, bang, you're dead. The doctors told me she probably didn't even feel it."

Colton reaches for my hand and gives it a squeeze. "That's fucking rough, honey. I'm sorry."

I shrug, easing my hand from his, ignoring the flurry of butterflies that just took flight in my stomach at the contact. "What about your mother? Are you close with her?"

"She died when I was five."

I watch his face for a second. I wasn't expecting that. "I'm sorry, Colton."

"After she died, my father went into full-throttle asshole mode. I'm sure part of it was grief. He really loved her and she must have loved him too, fuck knows why. My brothers have said that all the good parts of him died when she died."

"Wow. That's…awful."

"Nothing was ever the same." Colton's voice has gone

huskier at the memories. He's almost completely lost the roguish playfulness that's usually so much a part of his personality. "We had a brigade of nannies for a few years but my father decided to send us to boarding school when I was seven. To keep us in line."

"You went to boarding school when you were *seven?*"

"Yeah. It felt like a prison. My brothers handled it better than I did."

I can see for the first time that Colton Maddox isn't *only* a happy-go-lucky playboy. Under that cocky exterior, he's got some deep emotional scars. No wonder he's afraid of commitment. Maybe his sense of abandonment still haunts him.

"Is your father still alive?"

"Nope, he had a massive heart attack a few years ago. We grieved for what could have been more than what was."

"Sometimes that's even harder."

He glances over at me and it's connective. "Yeah. It is."

"But you have your brothers."

"Yeah, I have my brothers. They're a pain in my ass but they're also my best friends."

"You're so lucky to have them." I don't say it, but what I'm thinking is, *you're so lucky you're not alone.*

Colton reads my thoughts easily. "You're not alone now, Sunshine."

His nickname for me lightens the tone of our

suddenly-very-heavy conversation. "True. For the next five days I get to bask in the fabulous company of the Terminator—and please, don't say it again."

But he does anyway. "Affirmative. And damn straight I'm fabulous company. I plan on showing you the time of your life, baby girl. You'll see."

Baby girl. There's something almost heartbreaking about the endearment. Because as gorgeous and fun as he is, even if he does have emotional layers I'm just beginning to learn about, he's still *Colton Maddox*. I've already outlined the long list of reasons why there will never be anything between us beyond banter and a road trip.

I recline my seat a little further. "God knows I need 'a time of my life'. I've been drowning in a sea of chiffon and Botox for an entire year. That's when I'm not waitressing and getting my ass pinched by old bankers who are so rich they don't have to worry about getting canceled."

His reply is surly. "That won't be happening anymore."

I'm bemused by the low tones of fury in his reply. "Yeah, that's because I'll be getting my ass pinched by old bankers in L.A. instead."

"I think we can probably come up with a better plan." Before I can ask him what exactly this "plan" might entail, he asks, "How long have you been in New York?"

"A year, almost exactly. New York Fashion Week is what everyone aspires to—even if some people in L.A.

won't admit it. So, after I graduated, I thought I'd see if I could make it happen for myself." I don't really want to lay out my whole sob story, especially since I already did that last night. So I keep it brief. "It hasn't really worked out the way I'd hoped."

"Why not?"

I contemplate him for a minute, in all his billionaire glory. The shirt that most likely cost more than I make in a month. The glinting Rolex. The gold chain that's no doubt 24 carat. The suntan he probably got from sitting out on his Fifth Avenue penthouse roof garden over-looking Central Park. Of course he wouldn't understand. "It just hasn't."

We're both quiet for a few seconds but then I hear his low laughter. "Nice try, sweetheart. Tell your friendly Terminator/therapist everything. I want detailed descrip-tions of every single one of your dreams. I want the whole vision. And give me some idea how you plan to get from A to B. I might be able to help you out. That's what Daddy's here for."

I let my head fall back, groaning lightly. Once again he's able to make me smile even though I'm actively trying *not* to give him the satisfaction. "You can be *either* the Terminator *or* Daddy. Not both."

"I can be everything you want me to be, baby. You just wait until our first lesson tonight."

"Oh my god, would you stop?" *And now I'm all hot and bothered. That intimate, wet, tingling thing is happening again, at the thought of what those lessons he keeps talking about…might feel like.*

"Spill," he orders me with mock sternness.

Oh, what the hell. I know he'll get it out of me eventually anyway because he seems to be very good at doing exactly that. "I don't have a lot of time to work on my own stuff because I work two other jobs. And my boss in the boutique isn't really looking for the kind of designs I make. They're a little too young for her clientele."

"Plenty of hip young women in the Hamptons," he comments. I try not to think about how many of them Colton knows personally. "Maybe you should open your own store."

"With the whopping three hundred dollars currently in my bank account? Sure." I immediately wish I hadn't said that. It must sound so pathetic to someone like him. "But yes, maybe I will, once I get a little more established. It's not like I can't promote myself on Instagram from L.A. I'll just have to work harder." The mere thought of it exhausts me.

"Where do you see yourself in, say, three years?"

I think about his question. "I don't know."

"Come on, you can do better than that," he insists. "What would be your dream scenario?"

"My own label, I guess. And maybe someone to help me with the marketing side of things, since it's so time-consuming and what I really want to be doing is designing clothes."

"Then we'll just have to make that happen," he says, like it's that easy.

"Sure we will." Just to humor him. As well-meaning as his questions are, he doesn't quite get that I don't live in his universe, where things magically fall into place because you have unlimited amounts of cash to throw at them.

"Who's your favorite designer?" he asks. "Your dream company to work for, as you build your own brand?"

"Ralph Lauren." I don't even have to think about it. "I watch all the shows of all my favorite designers and theirs are always the best. There's never anything I don't like in their lines. Their clothes all have that cowboy edge but the way they put the outfits together is so sophisticated. I can't even imagine what it would be like to work there. Maybe in my next life."

When I glance over at him he's grinning slyly at me. "What?"

"Nothing," he says innocently, his eyes back on the road.

This reclining chair is so comfortable, I curl onto my side so I can watch him. The music is soothing and the hum of the engine is hypnotic. My eyelids feel so heavy.

Colton winks at me and there's genuine feeling behind it that I don't like the look of. He's too gorgeous—and off-limits—to look at me like that. "Sleep for a while, co-pilot. I'll make sure we get to where we're going."

"Are you sure?"

"Affirmative."

I exhale a weary laugh. I'm bone tired, if I'm being honest.

"I've got you, Sunshine." The assurance makes my eyes sting for some reason. *He's got me.* And the comfort of him feels so damn good, I can't stop myself from drifting into a peaceful sleep.

13

My eyes blink open.

Low guitar music is playing on the sound system. The lights are dim and daylight is starting to fade outside the large windows. Neon lights blur with movement.

I see him then.

Colton Maddox.

We're still on the road. We're in a bus and he's driving me to L.A. We talked for hours and then I slept for what felt like a hundred years.

I sit up a little and he notices.

"Hey, sleeping beauty."

I'm a little embarrassed that I crashed out so hard. "How long was I asleep?"

"Maybe six or seven hours."

"What? Wow."

He grins at me with his full-wattage smile. *Damn.* "You were tired."

"I really was."

"Feel better?"

"Much better. Where are we?"

"Just outside Roanoke, Virginia. Only around three miles from our hotel."

"Oh. But why are we going to a hotel? We have an RV."

"That's mainly so we're comfortable on the road. Our RV, however, does not have a hot tub. Or a five star restaurant. Or a view out over the mountains. Or a bar."

It seems unnecessary. "But we have everything we need right here."

He takes the exit. "Get used to it, sweetheart. You're traveling with a Maddox now. We like to do things in style."

I guess it's not worth arguing with him. "If you say so."

"Oh, I say so."

I feel amazingly well-rested. "I can't believe I slept for so long. I haven't slept that deeply in a long time."

"Yeah, you were completely out."

Yikes. "Sorry about that. I was supposed to be your co-pilot. And keep you company."

"You did keep me company. You looked so peaceful and beautiful I almost crashed a few times because I couldn't stop staring at you."

I don't mean to blush from his flattery or kindness or his gentle joke or whatever it is. "Stop," I murmur. It's *this* side of him that will get me into deep trouble if I'm not careful.

He takes a right turn into a tree-lined driveway that leads into some kind of estate. There's a small, beautiful lake. Rolling meadows are dotted with trees in peak foliage, glowing red and orange in the golden dusk. In the distance, on a low hill, I can see a stone building that looks like a huge, upmarket castle. The windows are lit, giving it a grand, romantic appeal. "What is this place?"

"Our hotel."

Wow.

As we pull up, there's a fountain in the middle of the circular driveway, spraying rainbow-flecked water into the twilit air. A restaurant to one side of the castle has large windows and an extended deck with yellow umbrellas and a stoked fire pit. Well-dressed diners are eating by candle-light and enjoying the view.

"Are you sure we can—" I was about to say *afford this* —my default mode—but then I remember who I'm traveling with. And it suddenly feels very…uneven. Because *I* can't afford this and there's an unspoken offer here, that *he's* going to pay for everything and I don't know if I want that. "Colton."

"Yeah?" He pulls the giant RV into a side parking area where it takes up at least three parking spaces.

"I might stay in the RV."

He kills the engine, not even reacting to my pronouncement. "You are absolutely *not* staying in the RV, gorgeous. You're going to accompany me to our presidential suite where we'll be ordering room service, helping ourselves to champagne on ice and availing ourselves to the balcony hot tub. You should know better by now than to argue with the Terminator. Continued refusals will only get you thrown over my shoulder and carried inside."

I glare at him. "You wouldn't dare."

"Try me." His blue eyes glimmer with the challenge.

There's more to this than the bill, of course. There are a lot of logistics packed into that description. Sleeping arrangements, to begin with. Sitting in a hot tub with Colton Maddox. Getting *wet* and being completely alone with him. Not that we haven't been alone in the RV, but that's different. "I don't think it's a good idea."

"Picture it. All those people out there, enjoying their dinners on this beautiful night. And one wild woman, kicking and screaming as she gets carried to her luxury suite because she's so upset about being offered Michelin-star rated food, French champagne and a jacuzzi under the stars."

"Very funny."

"How about this," Colton says slowly, his voice low and laced with that smoky husk that makes the tiny hairs on my arms lift *and gets my panties wet. Help.* "We'll go to the room. We'll order room service because we've hardly eaten all day and I'm fucking starving. We'll sit in the hot tub because we've had a long day and it'll feel good. Then, if you want the room to yourself, I'll come down here and sleep in the RV. Deal?"

He holds out his hand to shake. I know better than to shake hands with this devil but I can admit his offer doesn't sound too awful. I *am* hungry. And my hangover is completely gone. And, now that he mentions it, a hot tub does sound…tempting.

At least he hasn't mentioned *lessons*.

And why is a small part of me wishing he would?

So I take Colton's hand, staring into his eyes, which are the exact same color as the darkening indigo sky. "Deal."

14

Sunday
Roanoke, Virginia

THE FOYER of the hotel is like something out of a French chateau but with over-the-top American details that scream *no expense has been spared so be prepared to spend shit- loads of money!* I dread to think how much a night in the "presidential suite" costs. At least it's not a honeymoon suite.

Colton checks us in, a uniformed man immediately appearing to take our bags.

I notice again that Colton Maddox is tall. And muscu- lar. We've been in the RV all day and it strikes me how… *beautiful* he is. How perfectly made and masculine his silhouette happens to be. Like a king who belongs in a castle like this.

I'm not sure why, but my heart is beating fast.

This is the most beautiful hotel I've ever seen. A wall of windows along the back of the building offers insane views of purple mountains and the molten orange slice of the setting sun, made even more spectacular by its frame of plush velvet curtains, the rows of glowing crystal chandeliers, and the Old World grandeur of the decorating choices, which are clearly made by a team of people who know what they're doing and also have unlimited budgets.

It's a glittering, perfect oasis that doesn't feel real. As much as Colton becomes one with the luxury, I can't quite suppress the feeling that I don't belong here. Maybe that's what happens when you grow up worrying about every penny you spend and you suddenly find yourself in a place where a single vase costs more than three mortgage payments.

Colton has them falling at his feet without even trying. He's both charming and aloof—a lethal combination that has all the women at reception swooning. His killer smile slays them…just like it's been slaying me for the past twenty-four hours.

It's the reminder I need.

Colton Maddox is a notorious heart-breaker, which Sloane never tires of gushing to me about.

A cute receptionist flirts with him as she hands him back his black credit card.

I can't even blame him. Colton's not doing anything

other than being himself. I already know he has this effect on every woman he meets.

Like me, for example. I agreed to this ridiculous escapade after a few drinks and a brief—okay, not that brief—conversation. And now look at me. Stuck with him for five whole days. Caught in a trap of trying to resist what feels like a real connection when he clearly tricks every woman into a similar haze of blind attraction, only to leave them "crying into their Bloody Marys by breakfast"—one of Sloane's direct quotes that for some reason resurfaces now.

It makes me wonder if we'll even get as far as L.A. together. There's no guarantee he won't bolt somewhere between Nashville and Vegas.

Chill out, girl. Enjoy the moment. It's better than the freaking Super 8. Have dinner with him, then politely offer to sleep in the RV, at which point he'll probably insist on being the one to slum it in the parking lot. You can toss and turn for a few hours on king-sized memory foam, wrapped in zillion-count Egyptian cotton. Then it's only four more days to go.

Colton walks over to me and I make a point of *not* marveling at how that white shirt shows off his tan and sort of tightens across his chest, showcasing his sculpted arms and the flatness of his abs. "Ready?"

No, I want to say, but I follow him into the elevator anyway. He pushes the button for the top floor.

"You okay, Sunshine?" Reading my mood, maybe.

But the elevator swooshes us up and dings before I

can think of an appropriate reply. *No, because what if I can't resist you? Yes, because this place is beyond amazing? Sort of, because I'm resolved to resist you but I'm still enjoying your hotness and your blazingly-manly company more than I want to admit to myself?*

We get to the room, and Colton opens the door into the huge suite, with floor-to-ceiling glass looking out onto a large balcony. Steam rises from the corner of the balcony, where the promised hot tub sits, taking full advantage of the view.

It's an unseasonably warm night but there are several of those outdoor heaters on the balcony glowing their warmth, and Colton goes over to open the folding steel-and-glass doors, doubling the size of the suite.

He walks out to admire the now-muted colors of the sunset, stretching his arms, which causes his shirt to ride up and expose the skin of his muscular back, his leather belt and his low-slung jeans.

Damn it. Yep, he's a literal demigod.

"So you weren't lying about the hot tub." I'm doing my best not to stare.

He turns and I quickly peel my gaze away. "I never lie about things as serious as a jet massage."

This was a bad idea.

I notice our bags have already been set just inside the —only—bedroom. The champagne has been popped, poured and returned to its ice bucket.

Colton goes over and takes the flutes, handing me

one. His eyes are lit by the darkness, somehow, like their blueness has taken on layers of inky, mysterious hues. "Relax, Bailey. Drink it. It's French. You already slept off your hangover. What do you think of the room?"

"It's beautiful. Very classy."

"Of course. What were you expecting?"

"Um…mirrors on the ceiling? A locked red room full of handcuffs and leatherwear?" *Why, Lila, why? Do NOT make jokes like that just because you're nervous.*

"Maybe wait until you get into the bedroom before you make your final judgement," comes his darkly amused reply.

I try to downplay my internal panic that he might not be joking. "If there's so much as a silk sheet, I'm out of here before you can say Professor Maddox." *Lila! What the hell?*

"I wouldn't do that to you, baby girl." Winking. "Not until lesson three, anyway."

Here we go.

I groan, taking my champagne out onto the edge of the balcony to fully appreciate the view—and so he can't see how much I'm blushing.

"What do you want to order?" He comes up behind me and my body *feels* his approach, warming intimately. *Oh god. I can feel my own pulse. Right there.*

"I-I don't mind." *Hold it together, Lila.*

"The filet mignon they do here is one of the best I've ever had." He leans a hip against the railing, close to me, reading the menu he's holding. He's a good seven or eight inches taller than me and probably outweighs me by two to one. The man is *built*.

It's not fair that he's put me in this situation, where he knows how hot he is and the effect he has. Can he tell that my panties are now saturated, clinging softly? "You've been here before?" I guess I shouldn't be surprised, and I make a point of *not* sounding breathless.

"One of our companies owns several chains of luxury hotels, including this place," he says, like it's no big deal.

"Oh."

"How about I order us a couple of steaks with all the fixings, some chocolate cake and maybe a fully-loaded platter in case we get hungry again later."

"Sure." My stomach growls loudly and I blush even more.

Colton's slow, lazy smile catches me off-guard. "I've neglected you. My girl is hungry."

My girl. "You definitely haven't neglected me. Anything would be fantastic." I don't tell him I've been living off ramen noodles for months on end. Or that I suddenly feel more ravenous than I ever have. Or that I often choose to buy fabric instead of food beyond the absolute basics because it's the only way I'll ever be able to create the line I'm working on.

While Colton calls the front desk to place our order, I check out the rest of the suite. The bedroom has a massive bed with mountains of plush white coverings and the bathroom is literally twice the size of my apartment.

Holy hell. Imagine living like this.

I splash some cool water on my face, staring at myself in the mirror for a moment. The lighting in this room is so much better than my apartment's bathroom.

I look…good. My cheeks are flushed and my eyes are bright. My hair looks shiny. The lack-of-sleep shadows under my eyes don't look quite as bruised as they have lately. I look almost… happy.

Not because of him, I insist to myself. *Because I'm on the road and it feels good. Because I'm going to Nashville and then Aspen and then Vegas.*

He's just a perk.

A hot perk.

A fun, hot perk.

A gorgeous, fun, hot perk who's really easy to talk to and who says things like "I've got you."

And who's off-limits because he's a walking heart-break-waiting-to-happen. End of story.

I go into the bedroom, plugging my phone in next to the bed, noticing there are a bunch of missed calls from Sloane and Jessie. I send them both the same text.

> I'm in Roanoke, Virginia! Just heading out to get some food. Don't worry about me! All is well!! I'll try to call soon

Sloane's reply comes through almost immediately.

How's the driving going?

It's good! No problems. How are you?

I don't want to lie, and the omission almost feels like I am, but it would be too hard to explain everything in a few texts and I'm definitely not up for a long phone conversation tonight. I'm fully aware of everything Sloane would warn me about—again—and I have no intention of going there.

I miss you already! Everything's fine except my boss has gone AWOL and taken a spur of the moment vacation, which his brothers can't figure out. They're taking bets. Did he mention anything about taking time off to you last night?

How to answer?

That's crazy

It's not a lie. It *is* crazy. And I'm still not sure why he's doing it.

Oh and guess what, I wore one of your tops to a charity lunch I went to today and everyone was asking where I got it

So I told them about you and they were all raving about your Insta. Have you checked your orders today?

Really? Wow. No, I'll check now

I've always taken care of my own orders but one thing I did manage to organize before I left New York was to get a small agency to handle my orders for me until I get set up in L.A.

I've got around fifty garments I've made that are available for sale, mostly unique pieces but also some that are copies of the designs I post on Instagram. One of those is the top Sloane bought from me after I wore it to meet her for a drink one night when she was out in the Hamptons for work.

Holy hell.

I've had ten new orders this morning, all of the same top, which is now sold out.

I made two thousand dollars today.

That's more than I've made in the past two months from my business.

Sloane! I can't believe it! They ALL sold!!!

Yay! Told you, you wild talent!! Some of them are influencers too so you should get a lot more orders within the next week or so. I told them to tag you and promote the hell out of you because

you're the sweetest

Omg. Thank you soooooo much, honey. Really ♡ I'll have to hit the ground running as soon as I get to LA

For a VACATION. You still might come back to NY

We'll see. Thank you, Sloane!!!!!! I have to go but I'll try to call in the next day or two. TYSM ♡

Of course, bestie. Be safe! And have fun. Don't do anything I wouldn't do

It's the first time I've ever had more than one order at a time.

I check my Instagram and do a double-take.

I have a *thousand* new followers. One of Sloane's friends—who has over 100K followers—has tagged me in a new post. She's wearing my top. *How cute is this! Follow @lilabaileydesigns #lilabailey #lilabaileydesigns #ilovethistop*

Holy shit.

I realize there are tears in my eyes because this—right here—is what I've been busting my ass for, for a whole year and for many years before that, with no breaks and not even a single day off.

It's working. Finally.

I hear Colton's phone ring from the other room. "Hey," he says, and I'm guessing it's one of his brothers from the deeply familiar tone he falls into when he talks to one of them. "I'm fine, thanks for asking…I already explained this to Cash…No, I'm not giving you details… I'm not telling you that, bro, so you can chill the fuck out." He laughs lightly. "It might…As I mentioned to your CEO early this morning, that's none of his business —*or* yours…Yeah, a week." Colton sighs dramatically. "Jesus. I promise you, I'm fine. Why is everyone freaking out because I decided to take a week off after two fucking years of not taking a single vacation? It's called spontaneity, Noah, you should try it sometime." Another pause. "Bets? Well, you can all fuck off." More low laughter. "I'm hanging up now…yes…okay, bro, you enjoy your night too. Later…I'm hanging up on you now…goodnight, shithead."

There's a knock at the hotel room door and Colton goes to answer it. The scent of delicious food hits me and my mouth waters.

I can hear the sounds of carts being wheeled in and Colton thanking the waiters, then the door closing.

"Lila," Colton calls from the other room. "Food's

here."

"Okay, I'll be right there."

I wipe my eyes and go into the main room.

The large dining room table is covered with plates and plates of food.

Steaks, a bowl full of crispy smashed potatoes, a gigantic salad, roasted vegetables, pitchers of sauces and dressings, a fruit plate, a fully-loaded antipasto platter, a chocolate cake, bottled water, a bottle of red wine and another chilling bottle of champagne.

"Wow," I gasp.

"Hope you're hungry, Sunshine." Colton contemplates me for a second. "Hey."

He closes the space between us and tilts my chin up to him with two fingers. His face is stunningly handsome, and being forced to stare directly at it shocks me a little. Even tired after a late night and a full day of intense driving—or maybe because of it—he's mind-numbingly beautiful. His blue-on-blue eyes are rimmed with dark lashes, blinking at me. I hadn't noticed it before, but he has a scar, a thin line across one cheekbone.

Colton uses a rough thumb to wipe an errant tear I hadn't noticed. The concern in his eyes…shouldn't be there. It's too caring. Too invested for what this is.

"You're crying," he tells me, his perfect eyebrows furrowed, like it's the worst thing that's ever happened in the history of the world.

I take a step back, wiping any other tears that might

have given me away. "It's nothing. I'm happy. I just sold a bunch of my garments—*ten* in one day—thanks to Sloane wearing one of them to an influencers' lunch. I really can't believe it. And dinner's on me."

"Dinner is not on you, gorgeous. Dinner is most definitely on me, but that's great news, Lila. Congratulations. It's a big deal."

"Thanks." It *is* a big deal and it's nice of him to say that.

A channel of something passes between us I'm not sure I want there. A feeling that we're on the same wavelength, when we shouldn't be. We've known each other for exactly one day. This is a very temporary…friendship? Road trip buddy camaraderie? *Four-night-stand I need to maybe enlighten me before I get on with my life?*

No, because you'd totally fall for him along the way and we all know he doesn't commit.

So what? It could be purely for educational purposes.

But what about Troy?

Troy is not an issue here! Why are we even talking about him? He's nothing and he never was. Even if your tequila-soaked subconscious pined for him last night to anyone who would listen like he was The One Who Got Away.

Ugh. This is way too complicated to think about when I'm this hungry.

"Come on," he says, "we're both starving. Let's eat."

Colton serves me up a heaping plate of food and pours us both a glass of red wine. We eat at the table outside on the balcony. The moon is full and the stars are out. Live music drifts up from the restaurant patio. "This is without a doubt the best food I've ever had in my life," I say, when we finally come up for air after eating most of the food and half the chocolate cake.

"The chef is French and very highly rated. It was one of the reasons we bought this hotel. We offered him a total refurbishment of the hotel, the wine list of his dreams and a ten-year contract. He's been awarded two Michelin stars since then. People come from all over the world to stay at this hotel just for the food and the wine."

"Wow." What a world he inhabits.

I feel myself relaxing into the moment, in a way I haven't in a long time. I don't feel so exhausted, after my extended power nap in the RV. I'm excited about my business. If it keeps growing, I might be okay. I might be able to work on it full-time, and the future seems unusually bright tonight. The good food and obviously-incredibly-expensive wine has a calming, luxurious effect. And Colton is so easy to be with, I almost forget about all the potential minefields of the next few days and weeks. Everything, in this moment, feels sort of perfect.

But then Colton pushes back his chair and grabs the bottle of champagne from the ice bucket. "And now I'm getting changed and meeting you in the hot tub, baby girl. I have no intention of breaking my word. I made you some promises last night and it's time to deliver. Get ready for your first lesson."

15

"Are you coming in, or what?" he calls from the balcony. "Don't make the Terminator come in there."

"I'm *coming*, Mr. Impatient," I call back. I protested, of course, but he keeps insisting *we shook on it*. Like whatever we agreed on is now carved into granite. I vaguely remember shaking his hand at one point last night, not realizing that I was entering some kind of my-word-is-my-bond *pact*. I mean, he filled me in on a few details on the drive but I can't actually remember all the intricacies of our conversation. Or his promise. All I know is that it involves the *lessons* we keep skirting around. "Just give me a minute. I need to find my bathing suit."

"Need help with the ties?"

"No, I do not need help with the ties. It doesn't have ties."

Digging around in my overnight bag, I pull out the

white bikini I packed specifically for topping up my tan in L.A., and cringe. It's easily the tiniest piece of clothing I own and was packed with zero intentions of hanging out in a fancy-ass suite with an almost-stranger under a rare super moon (I only know this because someone mentioned it on Instagram).

I wiggle into my bikini, trying to adjust it for maximum coverage. Which doesn't help at all. My boobs aren't huge but they're big enough and basically on full display except for two tiny strategically-placed triangles. And the bottom piece isn't exactly a thong but might as well be.

Oh, what the hell.

I'm from *L.A.*, for god's sake. People wear this kind of thing all the time and I don't have to feel self-conscious about wearing a bikini. Even if I *am* practically naked.

And I refuse to be nervous about a ridiculous pact I may have made while mildly intoxicated.

All I have to do is call it off. Easy.

Or not.

Yes, I can. And I will, of course. I'm the master of my own destiny and I feel like enjoying this beautiful night without over-analyzing every goddamn thing, for once.

So I grab my phone and head back out to the balcony.

To his credit, Colton's head is tilted back as the bubbles fizz up around his shoulders, and his eyes are closed.

I set my phone on the raised beam next to the hot tub and lower myself into the water. The warmth swirls around my body and I let out a light moan. "Okay, you were right. This is amazing."

His eyes barely open and there's a smirk behind his expression. His slightly too-long wet hair flicks and curls around his ears and down the top of his manly neck sort of deliciously. "I'm rarely wrong. You'll come to know this about me."

"Your humility is one of your best qualities. Oh, wait, you don't have any of that. Never mind," I tease, settling across from him.

"Careful, Sunshine. We're in close quarters, and I'm not above splashing."

I laugh and trail my fingers through the bubbles as I lean back against the jets, letting the water relax me.

Colton hands me a glass of champagne and I clink it against his, savoring the contrast of the cool liquid on my lips when the rest of my body is so warm. "This is the life. I like hanging out with you." I say it in a bantering way, but it ends up feeling sincere.

"I like hanging out with you too."

His reply has a hot edge and at the same time is more genuine than I know what to do with. My heart skips a beat. I feel the gentle pulse, centering between my thighs and in the peaks of my nipples, which feel warm and hyper-sensitive.

He rests his muscular arm along the edge of the hot

tub and I notice then he has a tattoo of a tiger along his side. "Told you this would be better than the RV."

"I like the RV. But this is nice too. Thank you for bringing me here."

"My pleasure."

The moon and the stars really are something out here in the foothills of the mountains, with almost no light pollution to dim them. "Did you know it's a super moon tonight?"

"Yeah, I read something about that."

"It's supposed to be good luck."

"I'd say it's definitely good luck." Lazily. Taking another sip of his champagne while the bubbles play around his tanned, broad shoulders.

He's got a tantalizing dusting of dark hair on his sculpted chest. *God. He's, like, seriously cut.*

"So, is it true?" he drawls.

"Is what true?"

"Your confession from last night."

"Um." *Damn it.* "Which one?"

"The whole pure as the driven snow thing."

Oh. That. I sink a little lower in the water.

The smirk is back and it annoys me, that he's making fun of me now. "There's nothing *wrong* with it, Bailey. It's a good thing."

"Easy for you to say. It feels more to me like I've wasted my life."

"You haven't wasted your life. You've waited for the right person."

"No. I waited for the wrong person." I wish I hadn't said that. I really do *not* want to get into the old tired unrequited crush territory right now.

Colton's quiet for a few seconds and I'm glad. Maybe for once he'll let it go. But then: "How are you planning on seducing the fucker?"

His sudden low fury as he says the word catches me off-guard. It's almost like he's…jealous. But that would be ridiculous. "I have no intention of seducing anyone and I'd prefer to talk about something—*anything*—else. The sky is so clear," I point out hopefully. "Look how many stars you can see."

"What if you get to the wedding and he's there and you find all those old feelings resurface? Then what?"

"Yay, we're back to my least favorite topic." I give him a look I hope will stop him from obsessing about this again. "I don't have old feelings and I don't want to talk about this."

"If you don't have feelings then why do you cry about him every time you get drunk?"

"Oh my god. I *don't*."

"Well, you sure fucking did last night."

I set my glass of champagne on the edge of the hot tub. I'm very close to getting out. I've explicitly asked him at least ten times not to keep fixating on this incessantly. The one thing stopping me from storming to the only bed that we still haven't discussed who's sleeping in is the fact that I'm not wearing any clothes. And Colton's eyes definitely aren't closed now.

"And now you're driving clear across the country to see him again. You can't tell me you're over him."

"Do we really have to do this again? *God*, Colton." Here he goes again, getting under my skin like he's so good at doing. "I'm completely over him, thank you very much, and *all* I'm doing is going to my best friend's wedding, like I've already explained a gazillion times!"

"You blush whenever you talk about him."

"I do *not* blush!" Fuck it, he *is* like a goddamn therapist—if the devil was a psychoanalyst. "You know what, fine, Colton. Let's unpack the entire scenario in the excruciating detail you seem to crave. *If* I get there and *if* all the old feelings resurface, which I highly doubt they will because it's been a long time since I even thought about him and I've absolutely moved on, then…I'll talk to him. I'll gauge the situation with the information I have available to me and the emotions driving me in that moment—and I already *know* what the emotions will be because I've been feeling them for more than a year: that I'M. OVER. HIM. And I'll confirm that when—*if*—I see him at the wedding and then I'll get on with the rest of *my* life. Get it? *My* life."

"What if he offers to take you back to his hotel after the wedding?"

"He won't. He's bringing a date."

"What if he ditches the date and wants you instead?"

"I'd say no, of course."

"I don't think you would. Admit it. You're still in love with him and you'd jump into bed with him at one click of his fucking fingers."

I take my half-full glass of champagne and I throw it in his face.

In shock, I stand there in the hot tub for a few seconds. I can't believe I just did that. I've never done anything like that in my life.

Colton blinks his eyes, his eyelashes spiked with moisture. Little jewel-drops drip down his face. He hasn't moved. His grin isn't exactly amused and it isn't exactly dark but something in between. Like a lion who smiles before it's about to devour its prey. "Good girl, Bailey. You just broke through one of your barriers. Reacting is good. It's how you get over things."

"I shouldn't have done that. I'm sorry. I'm going to go out to the RV now."

"Let's finish our conversation first."

"It's already finished!"

"There's nothing wrong with being in love with him." *Damn him. He's absolutely relentless.* "Maybe he's changed his ways and this is the timeline that was meant to be all along."

I roll my eyes. "I think we both know that's not true." Patiently: "I'm not in love with him. At all. I'd completely forgotten about him until Jessie called me.

Last night's gush was just a knee-jerk reaction to an old scar."

"Exactly. A scar you never dealt with."

I realize I'm standing, with my hands fisted on my hips, exactly where the level of the waterline is. Nice. I'm practically yelling at Colton Maddox with my barely-covered breasts on full display, no doubt bouncing with my indignation. I don't want to give him the satisfaction of watching me stomp away like he's won, so instead I sit down into the water again, letting the jets attempt to soothe me. I sigh deeply, pretending he hasn't affected me as much as he does.

Why do I always indulge him? And how is he able to dig out my deepest wounds and darkest confessions so easily?

I lean my head against the padded rim and let my eyes close.

"Maybe you just want to find out what it's like, and he's the only one you've ever thought of like that. So your subconscious is fixated on a ghost who never actually existed."

My eyes open a fraction so I can peek at his face. Which is staring at me like he knows he's right. I'd never thought about it like that. "I guess that's a possibility."

"I'm not going to top up your drink again until after I make this suggestion, but I'm going to see the agreement we made last night and raise you."

"I have no idea what you mean."

"You said you didn't know how to seduce a man—which is bullshit, by the way. But you were practically in tears because you feel insecure about your lack of experience." *Sweet baby Jesus.* "So, when you asked if I would teach you—"

"Wait a minute." I hold up one palm. "*I* asked *you?*"

"Implored might be a better word."

I let my hand rest over my eyes for a second, but I spread my fingers so I can still see him. "Now you're just torturing me for fun."

"You deserve it, Sunshine."

"I guess that's fair," I admit begrudgingly. I'm still shocked by my overreaction. "I just threw a glass of champagne in your face."

"At least we're in the hot tub."

Neither of us can hold back our laughter.

"I'm sorry," I tell him again.

"I deserved it, baby girl. I was trying to get a rise out of you."

"It worked, Maddox."

"Don't overreact to what I'm about to say."

Now I'm curious. "I can't guarantee anything."

"I promised I'd show you how to seduce a man and that I would lay all your insecurities to rest, which I plan on doing thoroughly—"

"I'd like to strike our agreement from the record book, counselor. You are no longer beholden to the oath. Let's just forget—"

Colton slides over to sit next to me, covering my mouth with his hand and splashing water over me with the movement of his body. "Negative, Bailey."

God, he's even bigger up close.

"What are you doing?" I murmur against his hand.

"Let me finish." Sternly. It's a command, like he's finally lost his patience with me.

I give him a muffled, "O*kay*."

He takes his hand away, but not entirely. His thumb brushes across my bottom lip and his other hand wraps itself around my hair, pulling only enough to let me know I'm fully at his mercy. His sapphire eyes are fiery with challenge. "A part of you thinks you might still be in love with someone you haven't seen in a long time who never loved you back, because you have nothing to compare him to. Which is something you need and something I can provide."

I blink at him, sort of obeying him, for once. And possibly only once. Because his warm, solid thigh is flush with mine and my brain can't quite compute what he's offering. He's also without a doubt the most physically beautiful—and strong, and warm, and *hard*—human being I've ever been this up close and personal with.

"I promised you the time of your life," he growls.

I blink again.

"Let me fucking give it to you."

16

"Lesson one," he growls, "is a kiss." He seems furious, still gripping my hair so I can't move. He's so freaking *strong*. And mean. *And gorgeous.* "Show me how you're going to kiss the guy you want, Lila. Make it good."

"*No.*" Now he's just being a bully.

"Do it."

Fine, then. If he wants a kiss I'll give him a goddamn kiss. I'll fucking bite him.

We're glaring at each other and he releases me *just* enough so I can get closer. I want to piss him off and provoke him, like he always does to me. I want to make him *feel*.

I touch my tongue to his scowling, perfect mouth, licking his plump bottom lip, which still tastes like champagne.

God.

He tastes so good.

I lick him again, pressing my lips gently against his.

The feel of his warm, wet mouth against mine is beyond electrifying. My body comes to life, like someone just plugged me into a hot, pulsing current. My barely-covered breasts brush against his hard chest and the contact of my nipples against his skin jolts searing sensation straight to my pussy, which feels slippery and hot.

I nip at his lips gently, savoring the fiery danger of this.

Be careful, girl. He's going to make you fall in love with him like you've never fallen. This is a different league, a different animal and a different universe to anything you've ever experienced.

"Good girl. Surrender to how much you fucking want me, baby. Use me. Fucking feast on me like you know you want to."

He's so damn cocky. And *so* damn delicious. With one taste of him, my inner sex goddess has suddenly roared to life and she is *hungry*.

I wrap my arms around his neck and kiss him for real, letting my tongue slide deeper, tasting more of his drugging flavor, of French champagne and dark spice that's all Colton Maddox. He tastes like lust and magic.

The sound he makes is somewhere between a growl and a groan, and the deep purr of it drives me crazy with need.

I want him. I want everything.

Colton's iron-strong arms pull me closer. His tongue tangles with mine as he takes my mouth aggressively.

I'm on his lap now and—*holy hell*—I can feel the *huge* granite-hard ridge of him underneath me.

Oh my god. He's so freaking big.

His tongue sinks deeper into my mouth and I suck gently. "Fuck, you get me hot. My wild little innocent virgin."

"Shut up, Maddox."

I gasp as I feel his gigantic length press between my thighs, where a bloom of teasing pleasure makes me gasp. This tidal wave of sensation is only the beginning, I can feel that. *I need more.* I crave him like I've never craved anything in my life. And I know for a fact I'll give Colton Maddox anything he wants if he'll only *get me there.*

Anything.

As if on cue, my phone dings with an incoming text. And another one.

"Ignore it," he commands. "No interruptions during lessons."

But I peek at my phone anyway because it's right next to us on a raised beam next to the hot tub. The texts are from Sloane.

I can read them from here. I don't think Colton can, because my phone is at an angle behind him.

Noah said they're tracking Colton's geo-location to see who's going to win their bet. He's in Virginia. Near Roanoke. And I just got this strange feeling that…I'm sure I'm imagining things

YOU TWO AREN'T TOGETHER, ARE YOU??????

Lila, please reassure me. DO NOT EVEN THINK ABOUT IT, GIRL!!!!!

THAT WOULD BE A HUGE MISTAKE!!!!!!

HE IS THE KING OF HEARTBREAK!!!!!!!!! He'll rip your heart out and eat it for breakfast!!!!!

Shit.

She's right.

He *is* the king of heartbreak. She's described all the headlines to me in excruciating detail.

And now I know why he's earned his title.

It would be so very easy to fall for him.

He tastes so damn good. He feels like carnal ecstasy, as though every cell in my body is on fire from his effect. And it's only been one kiss. Imagine how hard I'd fall if I *did* give him everything?

Can I do this without getting broken into a thousand tiny pieces?

I can.

You can't. You're already half in love with him. If you let him

cash in your V-card, it'll break your heart to watch him walk away and straight into the arms of his next supermodel conquest, like you mean nothing to him. Like you never did.

No, it won't. I hate him. He's a jerk and a bully.

You've had some of the deepest, most meaningful conversations of your life with him. You've told him more than you've told your best friend. You've laughed more in the past 24 hours than you have in the past 24 months.

It doesn't matter.

Of course it matters.

Damn it!

I pull away from him. My heart hurts because I don't know if I can do this *only* physically. He's too gorgeous. We *click* too much. I don't know if I'm strong enough to separate orgasms from falling in love.

You can at least try! You're so close!

I climb off of him, sliding over to the underwater seat a few feet away from him. "I can't."

"You can't what." Pissed off. He picks up my phone, where the texts are still lit up. "Those fuckers."

I take my phone from his hand and I climb out of the hot tub.

"Lila—"

"Goodnight, Colton. I'm going to bed." I don't bother bargaining with him for the bedroom. I'm not schlepping out to the parking lot in my bikini. I'm on the verge of tears and I don't want him to see me crying. He'll think I'm crying over him and I'm not.

I'm crying because he's fun and hot and I don't *want* to love being with him as much as I do. I don't want to be so crazily turned on by him that it feels like a new addiction I'm scared I won't be able to break after only one taste.

King of Heartbreak, you can add one more to your fucking score card.

I text Sloane because I don't want her to worry about me all night.

> He offered me a ride because he has business in LA. IT'S JUST A RIDE. NOTHING IS GOING ON. Please don't worry about me. I promise I'll call you soon

Okay, it's a small white lie but I've fixed it now. I resisted him and I'll continue to resist him because she's right about him. I caved a little bit tonight but I won't make that mistake again.

> Oh shit. Honey, please please please be careful. He's dangerously hot and absolutely non-committal. DO NOT BE FOOLED!!! I hope you're ok. CALL ME xx

How am I going to survive four more days?

17

COLTON

I'M TEMPTED to call Noah. They're fucking *tracking* me? Even worse, they're discussing it with fucking *Sloane*? I realize Noah probably knows nothing about Sloane's connection to Lila. Or that Lila even exists.

Deep down I know they're probably doing it because they're worried about me. Taking off for a week with no explanation is very unlike me. I've *never* taken off with no explanation. I tend to be the one who keeps in touch with all three of my brothers on a daily basis.

It doesn't make me feel any less like punching my fist through a wall right now.

She's so damn beautiful.

How can anyone be *that* stunning?

My cock is so hot and hard I'm in physical pain. I have never in my life been as turned on as I am for Lila Bailey.

Since the minute I saw her, my cock has become a heat-seeking missile aimed directly at her while at the same time I'm trying to control myself so I don't freak her the fuck out. I don't *want* to be constantly hard for her. I find myself genuinely wanting to get to know her. She's gorgeous. Smart and sweet and fun to be with. Turns out it's a mind-blowing combination I've never seen all poured together into such an appealing cocktail of a human being before.

It's almost like she's perfect.

I *looked* for flaws. I *wanted* to find at least one, but no goddamn luck. As far as I can tell, Lila Bailey is flawless.

Which is fucking with my head. Not to mention my engorged cock that has only one thing on its mind. *Getting inside. Pumping her full of hot cum until it's spilling down her thighs.*

Jesus H.

I just don't know how anyone can be *that* ideal.

Yet here she is.

For the past day I've been walking some twisted line between agony and ecstasy. I'm mesmerized by everything about her. The puffy pink pout. Those silver eyes with their long lashes that blink at me whenever I piss her off. Which is every five minutes.

Her hair is soft and wavy and cut into those layers that frame her face.

Her *body,* all curvy and lush in that little white bikini just about blew my fucking head off.

And now she's mad because my meddling brother and pain-in-the-ass assistant can't mind their own fucking business.

Sloane and I are going to have to have a little talk. Sloane has obviously been telling Lila I have a reputation as a commitment-phobic man-whore who loves to break women's hearts.

Which isn't true at all.

It's not *my* fault they're all grasping and needy.

I can't control the fact that the falling-in-love mechanism in me is broken, which I blame on my dumpster fire of a role model. I'm not capable of connecting with anyone on the kind of level that would allow me to love someone like that and I *know* that about myself. I've accepted it and I decided a long time ago—instead of worrying about it—to make the most of the parts of my personality that allow me to have a good fucking time. So what.

I *tell* people that, right off the bat, so this whole myth about me being the "King of Heartbreak" is fucking bullshit.

I climb out of the hot tub, not bothering to grab a towel.

I get inside and I can hear the shower running in the master bathroom.

Fuck.

She's in there, naked, warm water running down her sweet body. She might be crying. I could tell she was on the verge of tears. But it's too soon for me to go in there for any of the ten thousand reasons I want to.

What if she's crying over him?

I'm already resolved to do better than the asshole we're on our way to see. The loser who *did* break her heart without ever giving her the time of day. And she's fucking dreaming if she thinks I'm not coming to the wedding with her to protect her from the fucker—which I'll convince her of by the time we roll into Malibu.

I won't be making the same mistake.

I think about going down to the RV but there's no way. Not when the most beautiful woman I've ever seen is here. I'll sleep on the floor if she doesn't want me in the bed. She might need me for something. I might still be able to catch a hint of her dizzying scent.

There are two full bathrooms in this suite so I use the other shower, turning it on to as cold as it will go.

The icy jets do nothing to dull the pain. I need some relief or I'm going to lose my goddamn mind. I take my painfully gigantic hard-on in my fist.

Her mouth, so soft. So hungry. The hot little virgin wants it. The way she squirmed against me, her pussy warm and wet under that slippery little bikini. It would have been so easy to slide it to the side, to ease inside that tight little heaven on earth—

I come in jolting bursts so intense it's almost unbearable. I have never come so hard in my life.

But it does little to dull the lust that rages in me like a fever.

I pull on some boxers and go to the door of the bedroom. She's in bed now and the lights are off.

So I walk over to the far side of the bed from where she's curled up facing the windows. "Lila?"

"Yeah?" She turns to glance at me. Moonlight catches the silver of her eyes. Dark strands of her long hair curl over the pillows.

She's so damn pretty.

"You okay?"

"Yeah. Just tired."

"I'm getting in. I don't want you to be alone. Okay? It's a big bed. I'll stay on this side."

"Up to you." She turns back toward the windows.

She's not going to argue, at least, but there's a cool edge to her reply. I get in, lying on my back, resting my head on a bent arm on the pillow. I pull the sheet up to my waist.

We're both quiet for a while.

I know what she's thinking: that she's made up her mind. She'll ride this out, but the kiss was a mistake she doesn't plan on repeating.

It's surprisingly easy to come up with a way to make everything up to her—whatever she thinks she knows about me. Because I *want* to. The need to do whatever I have to do to make her *happy* is burning in me along with my new obsession.

"You're going to like tomorrow night's hotel even more," I tell her, my voice low. "I booked us the penthouse suite at the best hotel in Nashville. It's got a view of the river but it's directly around the corner from Broadway. And one of my favorite Nashville bands is playing tomorrow night. We'll have dinner at a rooftop bar and then we'll go dancing."

Lila turns, facing me, curled up on her side with the duvet wrapped around her. She looks so vulnerable, so incredibly young, with her scrubbed-clean face like a fallen angel's. She's so beautiful I wonder if I'm dreaming her. "Okay."

She's still mad, or sad, or some combination of both that I can't fucking handle. "I got tickets for us, too, to go watch George Strait, Chris Stapleton and Lainey Wilson at the Ryman tomorrow afternoon. They're only letting a few people in. They're going to be warming up for a fundraising event they're doing the following night, but by then we'll be halfway to Aspen."

"Really?"

"Yeah."

"I love Lainey Wilson."

I'm breaking through a little. "How do you feel about helicopters?"

She blinks at me. "I hate flying."

"So that's the reason for the road trip, instead of just jumping on a flight to L.A."

She nods. She's so fucking cute I'm literally dazzled by her. "George *Strait*? Like, *the* George Strait?"

"The one and only."

"Chris *Stapleton*?"

"Affirmative."

There it is. Her gently exasperated smile.

"It's snowing in Aspen," I tell her.

Her eyes glimmer in the moonlight.

"We can take the gondola up to the restaurant at the top of the mountain. I've rented us a ski-in condo further down. With a hot tub on the deck and a snowmobile we can take down to the resort."

She's watching me. "Wow. You sure know how to… *arrange* stuff."

It's a good sign, that I've managed to revive a fraction of her sass. You can't be sad and sassy at the same time, I figure.

"Colton?"

"Yeah?"

"Why are you doing all this?" she whispers.

I turn onto my side so I'm facing her. I think about making a joke to try to make her laugh but instead I hear myself telling her the truth. "I don't know. I think it might be because you're the most beautiful girl I've ever seen and I can't actually believe you're real. I want to spend time with you and get to know you."

She's still watching me, her little white teeth gently sinking into her bottom lip, which fully revives my hard-on. I ignore it.

"And the more time I spend with you the more beautiful you get. I don't know how you do it, Sunshine."

Lila's quiet for a few seconds. I wait for her to say something. "Did anyone ever tell you you're dangerous, Maddox?"

"I think you're the one who's dangerous."

Softly: "Well, I think you're *more* dangerous."

"Well, all I'm going to be doing tonight is staying right here, watching over you while you sleep so you don't have to worry about anything."

Her silver eyes are inky and soulful. "Stop doing that."

"Doing what?"

"Saying the nicest things anyone's ever said to me."

"You can ignore Sloane, by the way. She thinks she knows everything about me but she doesn't. She doesn't know what drives me."

"What drives you?"

It would sound cheesy as fuck to say it, but the only word that comes to mind in the moment is…*you. You've become the only thing I can see. I'm fucking obsessed with you. And all I've had is one taste.*

This sudden addiction feels more feral than anything ever has. Like everything suddenly has meaning and it's all magnetized toward this little moonlit goddess with her smooth skin and her wild curls and the light bruises under her lightning-bright eyes.

I have no idea what's happening to me but whatever it is, it's *fucking* sure of itself.

I'm going to ease those bruises and fix everything that's ever felt broken.

18

Monday
Roanoke, Virginia

AND SO WE KEEP GOING. Colton orders us an early room service breakfast that could feed several armies and I pack some of it up for a picnic for lunch.

We're on the road by seven and I'm amazed by how well-rested I feel. Once we finally got to sleep, I slept *so* deeply.

Almost like his promise to look after me in the night allowed me to let go of all the things that usually keep me awake.

Don't get used to it, girlfriend.

Colton and I talked late into the night, about our favorite movies, books we've read, our favorite restaurants in the city (I only have one, but he knew it), Netflix series we've watched (he's hardly seen any; I watch stuff in the background when I sew), and some of our favorite artists and bands.

Colton puts on some country music and tells me he's educating me on all the good stuff.

"Why does a New York billionaire know so much about country music?" I ask him.

"I started listening to it when I was stuck at boarding school. I think I could relate to the yearning in it. At that time I was yearning for stuff too."

"Even billionaires yearn, who knew."

"You don't get to be a billionaire in the first place without wanting something pretty fucking badly, Sunshine."

"I guess that makes sense. Are you CEO?"

"I'm COO."

"What's the difference?"

"A CEO—that's my brother Cash—sets a company's vision, culture and brand identity. My job is to make sure the vision is realized."

"How do you do that?"

"I make sure operational efficiency is optimized and that we're being as productive as possible with the resources we have."

"Oh. Sounds complicated."

"It would be if I didn't know what I was doing. Luckily, I do. The business probably would have failed without me."

"That's nice that you're so humble about it," I tease him.

"The boardroom and the bedroom are two places that have no room for humility."

"Is that right?"

He glances over at me. "Yes, it is right, Miss Bailey. Which I'll be demonstrating to you very thoroughly tonight. And I know exactly what to do with that sassy little mouth to keep it quiet, so watch out."

I try to bite back my smile. And I don't bother protesting.

Because I've made a decision.

I'm going to close off my heart and I'm going to have a wild love affair with Colton Maddox. I'm going to play along with his lessons—in fact I'm going to insist on them. I'm going to allow him to enlighten me and I'm going to cash in my V-card, once and for all.

I want him to be the one.

I suddenly feel very much over Troy, maybe because Colton is…well, Colton. Even if it's only going to last a few days, our connection feels *real*, and that alone is enough. It's a detail that's somehow life-changing. It eclipses everything else.

Plus he's gorgeous.

Obviously good in bed.

Extremely well-hung.

I mean, I could feel how freaking *huge* he is. It's intimidating.

But what the hell. When in Rome and all that.

The kiss was—without being dramatic about it—the most intense thing that's ever happened to me in my life.

I want more.

I want to *feel*.

I want to follow those cravings he so easily inspires and see where they lead me.

And I want it as hot and dirty and sweaty as possible.

So I mentally lock my heart into its little steel fortress and throw away the key. Or at least stash it in an air-tight compartment for now.

For better or worse, closing off my heart is something I know how to do. My father left before I was born, my mother died before I could say goodbye and the one guy I ever thought I might have loved strung me along for years but gave me nothing.

I can do it again.

I'm going to have *fun*, starting now. That's what I've decided. I'm going to throw all caution to the wind and make the most of a rare opportunity that will soon end.

He promised to show me the time of my life. So that's exactly what I'm going to have.

19

Monday
Nashville, Tennessee

I'm COMPLETELY CHARMED by Nashville from the minute the city skyline comes into view.

"Look, there's the Batman Building!" I point out. I've watched online video tours of Nashville online. It always looks so cool and colorful, and the reality is even more vibrant, with a cowboyish, gritty edge.

"Welcome to Music City, darlin'," Colton grins at me.

We drive straight down Broadway and even though it's only mid-afternoon, the place is already pumping. The street is packed with people dressed like they're going to a rodeo. Music is blasting from the open doors and windows of the many, many bars. It's so loud you can *feel* the bass notes. "I wish I had some cowgirl boots," I say, more to myself than to Colton.

I'm wearing one of my own dresses, hand-sewn. It's a babydoll style, off-white with white flowers I embroidered by hand and a lacy hem that comes to the middle of my thighs. It's cute and comfortable. And it would look good with cowgirl boots.

Colton swerves the RV over to the curb so suddenly I grip my armrests for dear life.

"What are you doing?"

"Buying you some cowgirl boots. There's a boot store right there."

"You can't park here."

"Watch me, Sunshine. Come on." He kills the engine, jumps out of his seat and unclasps my seatbelt, pulling me by the hand down the steps of the RV and out onto the street, like it's Christmas morning or something and he can't wait to get started. Then he pulls a roll of cash out of his pocket and peels off a hundred dollar bill. To a passing couple who are probably in their sixties, he says, "I'll pay you a hundred bucks now and two hundred when we get back if you'll sit in this RV for twenty minutes and honk if a parking cop comes. We need to buy some boots."

"Sure thing, buddy," says the husband. His wife nods enthusiastically. They look wholesome and trustworthy.

Colton pulls me into the boot store—which has more cowboy boots in one place than I've ever seen.

"Wow," I murmur.

"What size are you?" Colton asks me.

"Seven."

We find the aisle with the sevens and, right there, the very first pair that catches my eye, is the perfect pair of cowgirl boots. They're brown suede with little white flowers stitched all over them. I pick them up and I do what I always do. I look at the price.

$3,850.99. "You've got to be kidding me," I mutter. Even with the money I made from selling my garments yesterday, I don't have nearly enough. As if I'd spend all the money I have in the world on a pair of cowgirl boots anyway.

"Try them on," comes the command.

"They're too expensive," I tell him, and I start to put them back.

"Try. Them. On." Jeez. Bossy much? Colton takes them from my hands and he kneels down in front of me, holding one of the boots for me to slip my foot into.

Looking down into vivid blue eyes, I give him a look. But I obey him anyway, because these boots really are to die for.

They fit me like a glove.

And they're the most comfortable boots I've ever had on my feet. The heel is the perfect height. I pace up and down the aisle in them to try them out and Colton watches me with a strange, mesmerized look on his face.

A saleslady has joined us. She's dressed in full head-to-

toe Nashville regalia. "They're absolutely adorable with that dress," she says.

They really are.

"We'll take them," Colton tells her, handing her his credit card. "She'd like to wear them now."

"Sure thing, sugar."

"Colton—" I splutter.

"Oh, let him, sugar," the saleslady laughs, waving away my protest. "Never stop a man from buying you the perfect pair of cowgirl boots. It's a cardinal rule here in Music City."

"You heard the lady, Lila." Colton winks at the saleslady conspiratorially, like they're in this together.

"But—"

"No ifs, ands or buts about it, sugar." I guess she calls everyone sugar. And she's already ringing them up. "Those boots were made for you."

They kind of feel like they were.

"Let your husband treat his beautiful wife," she scolds me. "It's the least he can do."

"Oh, he's not—"

"Hell, if *my* husband offered to buy these for me, I'd do anything he asked. And I mean *anything*."

Colton's trying not to laugh. "Did you hear that, Sunshine? *Anything*." His comment is too low for her to hear. But *I* hear it.

Before I know it, the boots are bought and paid for and we're back out on the street.

Except I feel different now. My feet are unbelievably comfortable, this is my favorite outfit I've ever worn, and the world just got a whole lot more…*glittery.* No one tells you that wearing the perfect pair of cowgirl boots makes you feel like you're living your very best life.

Or maybe it's Colton Maddox who's making you feel that way.

Colton gives the couple guarding our RV another two hundred bucks—plus a tip—and soon we're headed back down Broadway. The whole excursion took less than fifteen minutes. *And cost more than four thousand dollars.*

"I'll pay you back," I tell him.

"It's my treat, darlin'."

"The Terminator has morphed into Blake Shelton," I comment dryly.

"Affirmative." In a southern accent.

"Oh my god," I groan, but we're both laughing like it's the funnest joke we've ever heard.

Colton somehow manages to maneuver the huge RV around the corner and into the space in front of the hotel, which has blue flags with guitars on them and large tropical plants out in front of it.

A valet is waiting for us. Several men in uniforms are ready to carry our bags. I already know that people jump to attention whenever Colton Maddox turns up on their doorstep. I guess having a *billion* dollars to throw around will do that. But it's hard to get used to.

We get to our suite on the top floor and once again, it's ridiculously luxurious. The sliding doors are open to take in the view of the swanky patio and, beyond it, the river. A welcome basket full of food is on the table, along with a bottle of champagne on ice. There's even a polaroid camera with a little note saying, *record your memories!*

"Who *lives* like this?" I murmur.

Colton comes over to stand close to me, towering over me with his six-foot-whatever frame. He takes a long lock of my hair and twirls it around one finger. "You do now, sugar."

For four more days. Don't get used to it.

He's so big. So burly and toned and *built*. His face, with its scar across one cheekbone, his whiskers darkening his square jaw, his azure eyes rimmed with thick lashes, has become familiar…and I love this. His face is the most sublime thing.

There's heat behind his eyes and also tenderness. The intensity of both makes my heart skip a beat. "Thank you for the boots," I say softly. "I love them."

"It's the least I can do for my beautiful wife."

"Very funny."

An uncharacteristic note of…longing, maybe, or regret crosses his expression, but then it's gone. "We better keep moving if we're going to get to the rehearsal at the Ryman before they finish. You ready?"

We go to the theater where the Grand Ole Opry spent so much of its history, and we watch literal icons warming up for tomorrow night's show. The whole experience is surreal. It's freaking *George Strait* up there on the stage. I feel like I'm living in a dream.

After the rehearsal, Colton takes me out to dinner at a rooftop restaurant where there's live music and some of the best food I've ever eaten. We talk and laugh the whole time.

I don't allow myself to think beyond four days from now. He's *too* easy to be with. *Too* smart and funny. *Too* sexy as all hell.

I see the way other women stare at him. And no wonder. The man is a big, sexy tomcat.

Yes. A big, sexy tomcat who will be back out there in the wild in a matter of days.

But I can't help noticing that he doesn't seem to notice any of the many beautiful women who ogle him. He's completely focused on me.

Colton takes me to see his favorite Nashville band at a little hole-in-the-wall bar that's right on Broadway. Memorabilia covers the walls and there's a cozy Americana vibe. We order two-dollar Pabst Blue Ribbons and drink them straight out of the can—mainly because that's all they serve.

When the band starts playing, Colton pulls me onto the dance floor. "Do you know how to do the two-step?"

"No," I laugh, trying to stop him from pulling me into the small crowd of people who obviously *do* know how to two-step, but it's no use.

"I'll teach you."

As if the man wasn't already perfect enough, he's also a seriously good dancer.

Dancing with Colton Maddox in that little honky-tonk bar with lively music being played by some of the most talented musicians I've ever heard perform…it's downright magical. It might be the most fun I've ever had.

A slow song comes on and Colton pulls me into his arms. The lighting is low except for the neon signs in the window and the low spotlights on the musicians. Colton has moved us toward the side of the dance floor now. My body is pressed up against his dizzying hardness. He's hard…*everywhere.*

Right here on the dance floor.

I'm so inexperienced with this kind of thing, it shocks me. *He can just walk around like this? And dance like this?*

Apparently so. Our gazes lock. I blush because it's incredibly intimate. Having his giant…*erection* pressed up against my stomach as we dance. I have no control over the reactions of my body. My nipples bud as they rub lightly against his chest. I can feel the soft pulse of my heartbeat *there*. In the exact same place where I felt him press against me last night, where all my newfound wildness seems to be centered.

I've never felt so cherished as I do right here and now in the middle of this packed dance floor surrounded by people I don't know with Colton's arms around me.

And I'm tired of demure, unrequited bullshit. Colton

Maddox is too hot to let anything go fucking unrequited. I can see in his eyes that he's noticed the change in me. He can read the decision I've made.

His smirk is hot. "My little Sunshine girl is ready for her next lesson."

"We did shake on it, Professor."

"Yes, we did." The smirk gets darker and his hands slide further down to grip my ass. He presses me tightly against him and his cock gets even harder. *Woah.* "And you have a lot to learn."

So we're really doing this.

Last night I got scared…of *feeling* too much for him. Now I want to feel everything. Who knows if I'll ever get another chance. Having sex with Colton Maddox will be like summiting Everest when you've never even climbed a foothill. But at least I'll *know*. It's a gift I'm going to give myself after living a lonely life for so long.

And, *wow*, he really is hard. *I want to make him harder.* "I must not be *that* bad at seducing a man if you're already…" I can't bring myself to point out the obvious.

"Already what?" He grips me and presses his rigid length into me. "Hard as a fucking rock?"

Oh god. I can feel every throb and every ridge.

"Why are you so hard, Professor?" I whisper in his ear, letting myself tease him. Our constant banter is getting dirtier.

"You know why. Because you're so fucking sexy. Come

on, baby, get me even harder. Let's see if you can improve on last night's kiss."

I don't rise to his taunting. The only rise it's getting out of me is that I'm turning into a puddle right here on the dance floor. "You didn't seem to mind it last night."

His sneer is promising me as much as I can handle. "I sure didn't mind how fucking good you tasted." He leans closer. His tongue licks my earlobe and he gently bites it until I squirm. "Or how wet your pussy was when you writhed all over my big cock, you little minx. I bet it's all wet and ready for me right now too. I bet you're wondering what it's going to feel like when I eat you like a fucking berserker and make you come so hard you can barely remember your own name."

I feel my eyes widen. If I'd thought I was being coy, he just upped the ante.

I can't believe he just said that. But now that he mentions it, yes, I am wondering what that's going to feel like.

This isn't like me at all but…I nod.

"Don't be such a fucking cocktease, Bailey, or I'll have to take you over my knee."

I blink up at him. "And then what will you do?"

He leans close to my ear. "Spank that sassy little ass until you're pink and wet and ready for me."

Oh.

Colton holds my face with his hand and he kisses me.

This isn't the careful introduction he allowed me last night. This kiss is hungry and full of lust. His mouth devours mine and his tongue tangles with mine, tasting me in intimate thrusts.

He kisses me like I belong to him.

His strong grip forces me to grind in a barely-there rhythm against his giant cock. My pussy feels swollen and soft, like it's been dipped in warm honey.

"Surrender, baby girl. Submit to me. You know you need it. Do exactly what I say and give me everything I want."

Against his mouth, I whisper, "*I want you.*"

20

COLTON SLOWLY BREAKS THE KISS, like he's addicted to the taste of it. But then he slings his arm around me, guiding me out the door. "Well then, Sunshine, that's exactly what you're going to get. Let's get the fuck out of here."

As soon as we get out onto the street, Colton lifts me into his arms, carrying me through the loud, high-on-life crowd.

All the way to the hotel.

He kisses me in the elevator. And down the hall to our room. When we get into our room, he kicks the door closed and sets me down on my feet next to the bed.

Taking his time, he pulls a large armchair closer to the bed and sits on it, knees apart, burly arm slung over the arm of the chair in a way that's very…*male*.

So I'm standing in front of him as he sits there like a

king checking out a new member of his harem. I feel naked already. *And so wet my panties are clinging sort of distractingly.*

"Our pact was for me to teach you how to seduce a man. So that's what you're going to do."

This is a different Colton Maddox to the one I'm used to. The playfulness has turned dark and menacing. Now, he's pure dominance.

And I feel not only playfully submissive but also like I might *die* if he doesn't touch me again. My body is on fire. I feel beautiful and hot and supremely alive. My inner sex goddess is determined to get exactly what she wants—and what she wants is that massive lust wand Colton Maddox is packing, which is practically busting through the button-fly of his jeans like he stuffed a fat anaconda down there.

I want to provoke him, like he so easily does to me. "Yes, Professor Maddox."

His glare is stormy. "Take off your dress."

It doesn't matter that I've never done this before. I want to tease him and torture him. Even though I'm a beginner, I know exactly how to do it. By slowly, temptingly giving him everything he wants.

I'm naturally shy when it comes to this sort of thing, so I *use* my shyness. Almost demurely, I pull my dress up. Over my white lace panties, which are mostly sheer and are now bunched into a thong because the thin fabric is wet, clinging to my pussy, which feels slippery and tingly and so *needy* I feel like I'm going mad with it.

Even more slowly, I ease the hem of my dress higher. I'm wearing a white lacy bra that matches my panties. The fabric has its work cut out for it, since it's thin and stretchy with no wires and my breasts are full. I know he can see how how tightly budded my nipples are.

I pull my dress over my head and drop it onto the bed.

"Holy fuck," Colton growls, his voice husky with awe. "It's a crime for you to wear clothes."

I move closer, standing between his spread knees. "Can I touch you?" I whisper.

"No. Don't be so fucking easy, Bailey. Make me work for it."

I bite back a smile because his Dom voice is a little like his Terminator voice. And I know why he's grumpy. His cock looks so big and constricted by his jeans, it's clearly painful.

Right now my femininity feels like a superpower. "First you tell me not to be a cocktease and then you tell me not to be easy. Which is it, Professor Maddox?"

"You can stop with the sass unless you want detention."

I play innocent. "What happens in detention?"

"You get that smart mouth stuffed full so you stop talking so much."

Now he's giving me ideas…

"Pull that lace lower so I can see those ripe little nipples. They've been teasing me since the second I laid eyes on you, begging me to suck on them until they're all pink and juicy."

Yikes. My pussy clenches at his dirty talk and it feels… *so good.*

I obey him coyly. I lower the lace over my nipples, until the bra is pushing my breasts up and together.

His eyes darken. "Fuck, Sunshine. Look how fucking gorgeous you are." He drinks in the sight of me for a few seconds, then he says, "Feed them to me."

I know he's trying to make this dirtier than I can handle. He *wants* to test my limits and see me blush.

But I'm tired of my limits. And I don't want to give him the satisfaction of winning this game.

So I stand between his spread knees and I do it. I lean over him, offering my nipple to his sneering mouth.

Holding my eyes with his own, he laves his tongue over the sensitive underside, taking my nipple gently between his teeth.

I moan.

"That's my good girl. You *love* it when your man worships you, don't you, Sunshine."

Your man.

He pulls my nipple into the hot fire of his wicked mouth. *God.* The suction of his mouth sends warm currents of pleasure to my core, where a light throb is gaining momentum.

"Damn, you're a hot little thing. You've made a real mess of your panties, baby girl. Are you ready to take them off and show me how wet your pussy is for me?"

I don't care about anything except *feeling* him. My body is so ravenous it hurts.

"Take everything off except the boots. Those are staying on."

I accept his challenge and then some. I swirl the moisture he made with his mouth over my nipples with my fingers, playing them. I gasp a little at the sensation. "Your tongue felt *so* good," I whisper, watching his eyes. I take off my bra and then I slowly, provocatively, ease my panties down, stepping out of them.

"Jesus, Lila, what are you doing to me? How can anyone be so fucking perfect?"

I'm not sure what to say so I wait for his next command.

Colton takes my hand. Slowly, he touches my fingers to my pussy, swirling them through the moisture. I'm so sensitive *I think I'm about to come.*

But before I can, he guides my fingers to his mouth and he sucks them clean.

Holy hell.

"I'm going to release the beast now, baby," he says huskily, "because I can't take this anymore."

Colton unfastens his jeans, taking himself out.

Sweet Jesus.

He's *so* turned on. His cock is rigid...all the way up

his stomach. It's all engorged and hot-looking. The head is slick with moisture.

I'm riveted by the sight of him. I'm also mildly concerned about how it's going to...*fit*, when—we're probably beyond *if* at this point—we get to that part, but at the same time, I've never seen anything so mouthwatering in my life.

"Get onto the bed. Crawl on all fours until you reach the pillows. Show me what you're offering me. Make it fucking good."

Okay, wow.

But I *want* to show him. I want to drive him crazy with lust.

So I do it. I crawl onto the bed, looking behind me to see him stroking his big cock.

I crawl to the end of the bed and I lay back on the pillows.

"Touch yourself," he growls. "Let me see my meal. Get that sweet pussy nice and ready for me to feast on."

I'd laugh if I wasn't so freaking horny.

So I let my hands slide down my stomach, touching my fingers to my slippery softness. "Like this?" I exhale as the warmth rises under my own touch. "I'm *so* hot and wet, Professor." I kind of feel like I'm acing my lessons.

"*Fuck.*" Colton stands and pulls his shirt over his head. It's the first time I've seen him without a shirt on and not submerged in water. He's so beautifully made, so broad across the shoulders with sculpted muscles. The tattoo of a tiger on his side winds around his torso gracefully.

He lets his jeans and his boxers drop to the floor.

Wow.

His eyes are darker than I've ever seen them. He looks big and mean and dangerously aroused.

But still, I want to *own* him. I want to ignite him and play with my own power. To somehow push him further than he's ever been pushed.

"You know this is all yours, don't you, Maddox?" I say sweetly, dipping my fingers barely inside. "Yours. All soft and ready for you."

Colton crawls onto the bed and crouches over me. "You're dangerous, Sunshine. And so fucking beautiful it's killing me. Lay back now so Professor Berserker can give you your prize for being such a good student."

21

OH.

Colton licks my mouth, dipping his tongue and kissing me hotly. But he doesn't linger. He moves lower, feasting on my nipples hungrily. Making a mess with his mouth and leaving me sore and sensitive.

Then he licks his way down my stomach, forcing my legs wider and holding them with his iron-strong grip.

I squirm because he's so close now I can feel the hot strikes of his breath. *Okay, this is crazily intimate.*

He kisses me.

And this is a whole new kind of education. Because he wasn't kidding about the berserker thing. He's greedy and downright debauched. His mouth is everywhere, tasting and feasting with insatiable gusto. His rough fingers skate and prod, pressing into me, dipping in and out. Opening me like a flower. His fingers curl as his mouth closes around my clit, sucking strongly, and I cry out.

A tidal wave of pleasure overwhelms me, peaking and breaking in hot clenches that wrack through my body, milking Colton's fingers as his mouth feeds.

I completely lose myself in the excruciating bliss, moaning his name as I writhe in surrender.

I have never, ever imagined the kind of pleasure Colton Maddox has just given me. "*Mine*," he murmurs. And he's still playing me, more gently now but no less insistently.

The rushes start again and are somehow even higher this time. His thumb glides over my clit in a silky, relentless rhythm as his tongue delves with sublime pressure.

I shatter all over again. I can feel my inner muscles squeezing as he tastes me.

It lasts a long time.

When I finally resurface, I feel like a different person. A calmer one. A happier one. One that knows that rapture like this exists. The endorphin rush goes beyond physical into something close to spiritual.

After he kisses and licks me for a while, lazily, like he's not quite ready to disengage, he crawls up my body and lays next to me.

I love how blue his eyes are. How his thick dark hair is in wild disarray.

"Cole?" I don't even mean to give him a little nickname. My brain isn't fully functioning.

His slow smile kills me. "Yeah, baby girl?"

"Thank you." It sounds weird but I kind of mean it. He's just changed my life. "Now I know what I've been missing out on."

"You're welcome, darlin'. Thank *you*. Now I know what heaven on earth tastes like. You're going to need to get used to me doing that a *lot*."

I touch my hand to his chest and I notice then that his —*wow*. I'd almost forgotten about his…situation. Which has clearly gotten even more painful. It's freaking *huge*. And dizzyingly hard. It's very…wet. Like it's leaking. And extremely hot-looking.

I wasn't expecting to be so…*hungry* for it. My inner sex goddess feels insanely greedy, like she wants to rub herself all over it and claim it as her very own.

"I think I'm ready for my detention."

22

COLTON

I'm ADDICTED, it's as simple as that. She's so gorgeous and *she tastes so fucking good*, I'm having trouble dealing with the extent of it.

She's slim but curvy in such a feminine, luscious kind of way, all I can do is stare. And taste. *And feast.* Which I do until she's crying my name and coming hard. I can't remember ever being this fucking happy.

I've dated a lot of women, but always on my own terms. Relationships are something I've avoided like the plague. Mainly because the one that shaped my life was fucked up on so many levels, it put me off completely.

After watching two of my brothers fall ridiculously hard, I was *glad* I was immune to that kind of bullshit.

But now, I suddenly get it. I could hardly stand to be in public with her. Dancing in the bar with other men near her, I felt like a goddamn wild animal. A hungry, feral tiger who knows exactly what it wants. An alpha beast who will kill anyone who gets in my way.

If I'm losing my mind I don't care.

Never in my life have I thought about killing another man until one of them glanced in the general direction of Lila Bailey.

The thought of her breezing out of my life on Saturday morning—and possibly straight into The Asshole's arms—might in fact threaten my sanity.

It's. Not. Fucking. Happening.

I only hope I don't kill that fucker at her friend's wedding.

The need and greed I feel as I feed on her pleasure is almost more than I can handle. I'm surprised at myself, at how much I *love* the sound of her moans as I prolong her orgasm and make her come again.

Once the ripples have calmed and she's totally spent, I climb up and lay next to her. Her silver eyes are blood-shot, her make-up lightly smudged. I've never seen anything so devastatingly beautiful in my life as this girl's stunning face.

I'm obsessed with her.

"Cole?" she murmurs. My brothers occasionally call me Cole. My mother used to call me Cole. I like the sound of it coming from her, so soft in her angel's voice.

"Yeah, baby girl?"

"Thank you. Now I know what I've been missing out on."

Her expression is dazed and blissed-out. Enlightened. Could it be possible that she's never come before? Surely not. Even virgins must have toys. But something about the way she says it makes me think that maybe my little sunshine girl is even more innocent than she lets on.

"You're welcome, darlin'. Thank *you*. Now I know what heaven on earth tastes like." Truer words have never been spoken. "You're going to need to get used to me doing that a lot."

She notices then how out of control my fucking hard-on is. Besides the agony of it, I hardly even care about getting my rocks off right now. I'm so mesmerized by all the layers of her beauty, all I can think about is *her* pleasure.

Lila's long eyelashes blink at me, "I think I'm ready for my detention."

I don't immediately get her meaning.

You get that smart mouth stuffed full so you stop talking so much. That's what I'd said to her.

There's shyness in her, but I can see the fire in her eyes. My girl has a taste for the devil.

I crook an arm behind my head, laying back so she can get used to me, to use me however she wants to. "What's on the menu?"

"I want to…kiss you." She can't take her eyes off my raging hard-on. Fair enough, the thing's a fucking monster on steroids. "Can I?" All angelically.

"The teacher's pet gets whatever she wants, honey pie."

"I don't really…know what to do."

I can't help but exhale a low laugh. "Of course you do. Help yourself. Whatever you want, it's all yours." She could get me off by blinking at this point, but I'll go along with it, since that's the game we're playing. "Don't be scared of it, baby girl. Go ahead and touch. Put your soft mouth on me."

She feathers her fingers along the ink of my tattoo. "I like your tattoo." Then down my stomach, more boldly now. To the crown of my cock, where I'm practically overflowing. She swirls the wetness.

I can't bear how good it feels.

Fuck fuck fuck.

"Like this?"

"Take it in your hands." My command is deep and rasped. I'm about to lose my mind.

She's careful, and her hand eases around my thick length. She's exploring, getting a feel for the hardness of it and the weight. I groan as another gush of pre-cum soaks her fingers.

"Can I taste you?"

"Only if you're prepared to get very, very dirty."

She's shimmying down my body. She's so small, so petite. She rubs her naked breasts along my cock, sliding her body over mine.

Holy mother.

She kisses me, licking her tongue along the slit at the head of my cock, teasing lightly, then wrapping her lips around me. She sucks gently on the tip, pressing her tongue to the underside.

My head falls back. "*Oh, fuck.*"

"Is this okay?"

"It's fucking perfect." I feel like I'm strung up on a torture rack of ecstasy. "You're a natural, baby. That's a good girl. Keep going, just like that."

She likes my praise. She's kissing me and suckling on me like I'm a sugar-coated popsicle. I can barely handle it. The pleasure is astounding. The wet, tugging pulls of her mouth paint my cock with red-hot fire. Each languid stroke of her tongue, each kiss, only compounds the pleasure-pain.

I grab fistfuls of her hair to keep her there. Pushing her further onto me. "Take more of me."

She's obviously inexperienced, struggling to find rhythm. It's this combined awkwardness and *eagerness* that's about to undo me. The little minx is greedy for my big, spilling cock.

Her fingers explore, and her tongue strokes me as she takes me deeper.

"*Oh fuck, baby.* You feel too fucking good. You're going to make me come. Are you going to be a good girl and drink everything I give you?"

I'm trying to warn her. She can still back out if it's too much for her. Instead, she takes me deeper, gripping harder.

My orgasm erupts. My cock jerks violently in her mouth as I come very, very hard. She doesn't pull back. She's *swallowing*, drinking as much as she can take, but there's too much. It spills down her chin and over her hands.

It looks dirty, what I'm doing to her. Her, naked except for those sexy little high-heeled boots she's still wearing, covered in my cum. She's licking me now. Kissing me. She's full of my seed and I *love* this. It's inside her. Nourishing her. Becoming one with her. I'm a part of her now.

I'm breathing hard, trying to recover from the most intense orgasm of my life. I pull her up to me and hold her in my arms. I wipe her mouth gently with my thumb, kissing her lips. "Sunshine girl," I murmur. "You're so beautiful."

She's tired now and her eyes blink closed. She's sated. Sticky and perfect. I'm so fucking in love with that drowsy, still-sassy smile. "How do you think my lesson went, Professor Maddox?"

"I think you get an A plus. An A plus plus plus plus plus times a billion."

Her smile lingers. "I like drinking you," she whispers, already half asleep.

Where did you come from and what are you doing to me?

This girl *owns* me, just like that. And there's not a damn thing I can do about it except fight like hell and do whatever it takes to prove to her that she's mine.

23

Tuesday
Nashville, Tennessee

"Rise and shine, gorgeous. Our flight leaves in an hour —and before you say no, I'm going to cure your phobia with champagne and orgasms. You need to trust your all-knowing guide and guru."

I open one eye a fraction. This bed is so comfortable. I slept *so* deeply. "Go away."

"Nice try, Sunshine. I ordered room service." I feel the bed move as he sits next to me, propping himself against some pillows. I sneak a peek and he's freshly showered, wearing jeans and a button-down white shirt with the sleeves rolled up. It's not fair for him to be so hot this early in the morning. "I brought you coffee."

"'*Guru*' is pushing it a little, don't you think?"

"People have referred to me as a guru before." He sounds offended by my skepticism.

"When?"

"When I make them lots of money, that's when."

"If you think I'm getting on a plane, you're dreaming."

"Sit up and drink your coffee. We'll discuss this as soon as your brain has rebooted."

The coffee smells good. It's the only reason I obey him.

He helps me lean against several uber-soft pillows and he hands me a steaming cup of black coffee, just the way I like it. "Thanks."

It's only then, as I feel the stickiness of my hands and my chin, that I remember.

Holy shit. I gave him a seriously horny blow job last night and he came all over my face. I drank as much of him as I could, in lusty mouthfuls. That was right after he gave me three orgasms in a row. With his mouth.

I mean, there's no point being embarrassed. In fact, I feel…reborn. To be perfectly honest, I feel better than I ever have in my goddamn life.

I take a sip of coffee. He's even added half a sugar.

"Your hair looks like a bird's nest," he comments. "A very sexy one."

"You're in a good mood this morning."

"Of course I am." I swear his eyes actually twinkle. "Now, hear me out. I chartered us a Gulfstream because it was too short-notice to get one of ours from New York. If we drive, we'll have to stop for a night in Nowheresville, Kansas. It's a twenty hour drive. Or, we partake of the king-sized bed in the luxury jet I've booked us, get served lunch on the way and arrive in just under five hours. Then we get two nights in Aspen instead of one."

As if.

"You're going to love Aspen," he adds.

"I can't."

He's not deterred at all. "Did you know that your chances of dying in a car accident are roughly one in a hundred and seven? Your chance of dying in a plane crash are one in eleven million. And private jets are even safer than commercial jets because they have to adhere to stricter safety protocols and they have fewer touchpoints."

"Is that true? One in a hundred and seven?"

"The RV is a veritable death trap compared to the Gulfstream. Plus you're going to be busy having more orgasms so you won't be paying attention to us being off the ground."

I blink at him, ignoring the orgasms comment for now. I'm more concerned with the being off the ground part.

"You were prepared to drive across the country alone in an ancient Toyota that barely runs, Bailey. Let's be a tiny bit realistic about what the safer option is here."

I barely shrug. I wasn't aware of those statistics. And

he's right that my Toyota's odds of breaking down along the way were extremely high. Definitely higher than one in eleven million.

"Is that a 'yes, guru, I'm considering taking your very sound advice and I'd rather get to Aspen in five hours instead of twenty'?"

I take another sip of coffee. "It's a maybe."

"Why are you scared of flying?"

It's a good question. "I don't know. I've never been on a plane before. It just seems scary to be way up in the air like that."

"So you have no actual reason to be scared."

"That *is* an actual reason. It's unnatural. It's a metal tube that propels itself through thin air at high speeds."

"So's a Toyota."

"Except for the thin air part."

"You can't *crash* into air."

"You can crash into the ground!"

"You can crash into the ground when you're *on* the ground. Or you can crash into a wall. Or a tree. Or another car."

His argument is annoyingly persuasive. "But all my stuff is in the RV."

"Not anymore. It's now on its way to the jet that's waiting for us at the airport."

"You probably shouldn't have assumed that I'd fly when I told you I don't fly," I point out.

Colton places his coffee cup on his bedside table.

Then he takes mine from my hands and puts it next to his.

"I wasn't—" I squeal when he dives under the covers, pinning my legs down—and apart—and starts licking my pussy. He's so freaking *strong*. And heavy. I push at his head and try to squirm away from him. "*Cole*. You can't just *do* that."

"*Mine*," he murmurs, nuzzling me, circling my clit with his tongue.

I almost surrender because he feels so damn good, but he stops and pulls the covers back over his head. His hair is messed up and he looks playful and sexy as all hell.

He props his head on a bent, brawny arm, his other hand still resting high on my thigh. "Have you ever had an orgasm before last night?"

"I...that's personal."

This makes him smile. "So's drinking mouthfuls of my hot fucking seed, Sunshine. And with gusto, I might add. Tell me. Have you?"

I don't want to admit this, but I can't bring myself to lie to him. "No."

He shakes his head a little, genuinely astounded. "My poor little angel girl. That was your *first* orgasm? And second and third?"

"Yes. I just said that."

His chuckle has an incredulous edge to it. "Haven't you ever heard of a handy little invention called a vibrator, Bailey?"

"Of course I have. I didn't…I didn't want to get my first orgasm from a…piece of plastic."

"Why not?"

"I don't know. Call me a romantic."

"What were you waiting for?"

I can tell by the look on his face the exact second he realizes what the answer to that question probably is.

"Fucking *Troy*?"

"No. Of course not. Anyway, Colton, you can't get mad about that. It's actually none of your business."

"I'm not *mad*, Lila. I'm sad. For you. Actually, you know what? I'm glad. I'm not just glad, I'm over the fucking moon. Because the better man got to you first. I'm glad you waited. For *me*."

"So am I."

It's absolutely true. But that doesn't change the fact that Colton and I are just having some fun. For three more days. That's all this is and we both know it.

You don't know it.

I *do* know it. Because my heart is locked away from him.

I refuse to fall in love with him.

I completely and totally refuse to fall in love with how fun he is and how easy he is to talk to, like a long lost best friend I never knew about. And I absolutely refuse to fall in love with how easy it is for him to send me spiraling into orbits of insanely beautiful pleasure with a few flicks of his goddamn tongue.

Or that his fucking hot seed—as he insists on calling it—feels like it's given me superpowers. I feel so healthy and energized I hardly know myself.

And we haven't even gotten to the Main Event yet.

We're sort of glaring at each other now, but we're used to this. We're constantly pissing each other off, but there's an edge to it. Like we're having fun pissing each other off, so we keep doing it because it's…turning me on.

"Do you want more coffee before you get up?" His question is gruff but with a man-version of patience behind it that's more than a little endearing. "Because our plane is waiting for us—and do *not* say no until you've at least seen it and talked to the shrink I brought in."

"Shrink? What shrink?"

"She specializes in the fear of flying and she's waiting for us at the airport to talk to you if you're still unsure once we get there."

"That's…very thoughtful of you."

"If you need a shot of whiskey or tequila or something a little lighter I've also got mimosas. A chef has prepared brunch for us, which is being loaded onto the plane as we speak. And did I mention there's a bedroom with a king-sized bed?"

"Yes. You did."

One of his eyebrows is cocked. "So? Is there anything I haven't thought of that you need?"

"Can I take a shower first?" Am I really considering

throwing my old phobia out the window at the first offer of flying private to Aspen with a sexy billionaire? Apparently yes.

"Take all the time you need. Put on one of your slinky little outfits and we'll catch the limo that's waiting downstairs to take us to the airport."

Wow.

"You're going to love Aspen."

24

———

I THANK Dr. Norton and climb out of the limo, where I just had a twenty minute session with her to address my "issues." On the way to the airport I told Colton it wasn't necessary for me to talk to a psychiatrist, but when I turned white as a sheet as soon as the plane came into view, he insisted.

"If I can take the edge off your fear, then that's what I'm going to do," he said. "That's what I'm here for, Sunshine. No arguments."

Meeting with shrinks in limos on the tarmac? Having your pilot wait until your therapy session is over before he fires up your private jet? This is seriously a next level lifestyle.

Colton's waiting for me, leaning up against the *other* limo, arms folded. Looking surly. Not even reading his phone. Just waiting there. Even with the scowl, he looks mind-numbingly gorgeous, with his big, buff body, his aviators and his dark, windswept hair.

For I second I wonder if he's mad that I've held us up. But he carefully loops a muscular arm around my shoulders and I realize his mood is all about…him being worried about me. Something about this unease in him etches itself into me. Like there's a permanence to the mark it leaves.

How am I going to heal from all these marks he keeps branding me with once he's gone?

"How was it?" he asks.

"It was helpful."

"What did she say?"

"She told me to remember that anxiety isn't the same thing as danger. I'm safer at 40,000 feet than I am on the ground."

"As I've already said." Cockily. But there's something almost sweet about his concern. "*I* should be a shrink."

Despite my nerves, his unashamed arrogance makes me smile. "Maybe we should go talk to Dr. Norton about your overinflated ego," I tease him.

"No need. My ego's perfect just the way it is."

This makes me laugh. "Of course it is."

"You're good to go then?"

I take a deep breath, looking up at the admittedly very shiny and brand new-looking plane. "Let's do this. I've been ordered to embrace the discomfort."

"I'll make sure you're too distracted to worry about it, baby girl. You can trust me."

Here he goes again with the saying-the-nicest-things-while-still-being-grumpily-gruff-and-totally-hot. It's my weakness. "She did say my fellow fliers can help me cope with anxiety during the flight by avoiding my triggers."

Colton lifts me into his arms and starts carrying me toward the steps of the plane. "There's only one trigger I'm interested in. And since I'm your *only* fellow traveler, I'm going to make sure your trigger gets so much attention you end up in the fucking stratosphere."

"Metaphorically speaking, I hope."

"Orgasmically speaking."

Oh.

It strikes me again that there haven't been a lot of times in my life that I've felt so incredibly *cared for*. At all. My father bailed. My mother didn't have time. My friends are my friends but they have their own lives.

Colton Maddox makes me feel like I'm the most important, most beautiful person in the world.

It's a heady feeling.

And one you definitely should not be getting used to.

I can't help wondering if he makes all his girls feel this way. I have to make an effort not to let the sting behind my eyes become tears.

Maybe I'm just emotional because I'm so wildly out of my comfort zone. I'm boarding an actual *airplane*.

Holy shit. And what an airplane it is.

It's like something out of a Kardashians Instagram post. There are oversized leather seats next to the windows and a built-in table with two flutes of mimosas freshly poured. Through the doors of glass-fronted cabinets, I can see platters of food, ice and cold drinks.

Colton sets me on one of the seats next to the window and buckles me in, sitting next to me.

A man's voice comes over the loudspeaker. "Welcome aboard, Mr. Maddox, Miss Bailey. Flight time through to Aspen is four hours and forty-nine minutes. Skies are clear and it should be a smooth flight. I'll ask that you fasten your seatbelts for take-off. Once we're airborne and the seat belt sign has been turned off, you can help yourselves to the platters and meals our acclaimed chef has prepared for you. Over 700 movies are available on our entertainment system, and there's a super-king bedroom suite and full-sized ensuite with luxury amenities for your convenience. I'll let you know when we're beginning our descent into Aspen. Until then, sit back, relax and enjoy the flight."

Colton hands me the cocktail. "Drink it. It'll calm your nerves. And it's more fun than sleeping pills."

I don't argue. I take a sip. It tastes so good and I'm so nervous I end up drinking all of it.

As the jet engines are spooled up, the noise gets louder.

I give Colton an anxious glance. He's cool as a freaking cucumber.

Colton takes my hand, weaving his fingers through mine. "Easy, Sunshine."

We're rolling forward! I squeeze Colton's hand so hard I'm surprised he doesn't complain.

"Good girl. You're okay. Think of it as freedom. You're fully alive, like a soaring eagle taking flight. You've never been more powerful than you are right now."

I watch the blurred landscape. We're going so fast now and we lift off the ground—"Holy shit, we're in the air!"

"That's the idea, baby."

We're over some buildings now, getting higher.

"Cole," I gasp, because it's actually…*amazing*. We get up to the clouds and then we go *through* the clouds and from here they look all fluffy and surreal, like a giant layer of white cotton turned pink and silver by the sun. "*Look.*"

His grin is…beguiled.

"Isn't it *beautiful?* Colton, you're not even looking at it." He's still watching me.

"It's not as beautiful as what I'm looking at."

There's a ding as the seat belt signs overhead turn off.

Colton unbuckles his seat belt and then mine.

He lifts me into his arms and carries me into the bedroom, closing the door behind us and lowering me onto the bed. The look in his eyes is wolfish. "The professor needs his fix," he says. "It's time for your next lesson, darlin'. I can't wait a minute longer."

"Yes, Professor Terminator Shelton," I giggle, because

I just chugged an entire glass of mostly-champagne mimosa and I *do* feel free and powerful up here above the magical pink clouds. I feel like I've conquered my fears and also like I'm a little bit in love—temporarily, of course. He's so damn gorgeous all I can think about is running my fingers over his chest that's straining against his buttons and running my fingers through his thick hair. "What are you going to teach me today?"

"I'm going to teach you what it feels like to have a man go literally out of his mind crazy for you. You'll learn that once you get a taste of something real, you're ruined for anyone who doesn't have fucking time for you."

If I wasn't so high on life right now—literally—I might get mildly offended by that. I know who he's referring to, of course.

But it's impossible to get offended because he just told me *he's crazy for me.*

But by next week he'll be gone and you might never see him again.

Then why is he using words like "real"?

The thought brings back that sting behind my eyes and I can't stop it this time. A single tear paints a line down my face.

He holds his weight above me with his strong arms.

"Tell me. What could possibly be making the most beautiful girl in the world cry?"

"You are." *Because you're going to break my heart, I can feel it.*

But we're here now. We have today. And right now that feels like enough. I'm in this fancy space-age bedroom 40,000 feet in the glittery blue-sky air with a hot billionaire. I'm going to let myself enjoy the moment.

"Are you scared?" His face is very close to mine and he's dazzling me.

Why do I get the feeling he'd turn the plane around and take me back to the RV if I asked him to? "No. It's not as scary as I thought it would be."

"Then what's wrong?"

I let my fingers glide through his hair, gazing into the bluest eyes I've ever seen. I love the colors of him and the textures. The strength and the heat of his big body. "Thank you for bringing me here. Even if we never make it to Aspen or the Grand Canyon or Vegas, this was the best trip I've ever had. I just wanted you to know that."

Colton smiles gently. "We're going to make it to Aspen, baby. And the Grand Canyon. And Vegas. Then L.A. Then back to New York."

Back to New York. I let it slide. "Okay."

He kisses my face. He kisses my eyelids softly. My tears wet his lips.

My tears seem to have struck something in Colton, some animal desire or protective flare. There's a new edge to his kisses. Something in him has turned, and there's a new desperation and a heightened ferocity to him that makes my heart beat faster.

"I like the dress."

I'm wearing another one of my own designs, a pink floral shirtdress with a flouncy short skirt and flared detailing on the three-quarter sleeves. "Thanks."

"Take it off or I'll rip it off."

Jeez. Not wanting him to ruin it, I peel the dress over my head. I'm wearing a lacy pale pink push-up bra and a matching g-string.

"Are you *trying* to drive me fucking insane, Bailey?"

Coyly, sort of, because I am. "Maybe." I made my decision and, after last night, I can admit I want Colton Maddox more than I've wanted anything.

Colton unclasps my bra and peels off my panties. Roughly, like he's lost his mind a little. And like he's completely forgotten about our lessons—or he's given up pretending. He pulls his shirt off and unfastens his jeans, releasing his huge, glistening cock.

Woah.

Even though I've already tasted it—and then some— it's hard to get used to the sight of so much...*maleness.*

With his fingers, he draws circles around my nipples, teasing them. Pinching, pulling and playing them until each squeeze sends a current of need deep into my body. He's rough and it's almost painful. He licks me, biting lightly, drawing the sensitive bud into his mouth, increasing the pace and the suction, until a melting warmth starts to build in the core of my body. It feels *so good.* He moves to my other breast, feeding there like he's hungry, drawing with his mouth until the melting warmth inside me gets hotter. And deeper. And higher, reaching a crazy peak and then tumbling over it. I moan as the pleasure-surges clench voluptuously inside me, over and over.

Holy hell. He just made me come…so easily.

He starts kissing a line down my stomach. His tongue dips and teases which makes me squirm but he holds me down and roughly pushes my legs apart, kissing me, licking into me. Greedily. In slippery glides. *Everywhere.* "Fuck, you're beautiful," I hear him murmur. "You taste so fucking good."

His mouth fixes onto my clit and sucks in deep draws. My body goes limp. The pleasure, where his mouth is latched onto me, becomes everything about me. It's centered there, radiating in slow-moving waves. His fingers are using the moisture, sliding inside me, pushing the pleasure deeper, stretching me and compounding the bliss as the suction of his mouth milks me in a beautiful rhythm.

He's so *dirty.* One of his fingers slides wetly in a *very* secret place as his other fingers slide deeper inside me and his mouth tugs more strongly until all the sources of pleasure converge in a tidal wave of beauty that shatters me. My pussy clenches tightly around his fingers as he sucks and licks and plays until it blows my mind.

He's so damn good at this.

I'm writhing against his mouth. Wave after wave of pleasure throbs hotly throughout my entire being. I hear a low sound and realize it's me, moaning his name.

After the waves calm and I can actually form words, I whisper, "Cole. Cole. Come here."

He takes his time, kissing my clit, causing another deep ripple of bliss. Then he kisses his way up my body, taking his time, laying himself over me.

I weave my fingers through his hair. *I need him so much.* I grab onto him and hold him. I'm riding some crazy rush and I need him to anchor me.

"You're okay," I hear him murmur. "I'm here. I'll take care of you."

My soul drinks in his words even though I don't want it to. "Cole?"

"Yeah?"

"I want it to be you. Here. Now."

There's emotion behind his blue-on-blue eyes. Not just lust, but fire. I can read his jealousy, because even though I didn't mean to, we've wandered back into…the reason I waited.

"I'm on the pill," I tell him.

He blinks at me. Frowning. "Why?"

"Why?"

"When did you start taking it?" Like he's mad about it.

I don't want to admit it. "Just…like, a few days ago."

"You went on it in case *he* wanted to take you to bed." It's more of an accusation than a question.

I hate that the thought had crossed my mind. Once. Maybe twice. But that wasn't *really* the reason. Either way,

I don't have to feel bad about that. I hadn't even met Colton yet. And I don't want the nothingness of my past to ruin this moment. It's not about Troy. It's about Colton. "No. I went on it because I'm about to turn 24 and I thought it was overdue. In case I met someone. Some day. Which I was obviously hoping I might, eventually."

His eyebrows are furrowed and I use my thumb to gently smooth away his anger.

"And now I have. And even though he's only my guide for one week, he's really hot." I kiss his perfect lips. "A little ornery, maybe, and *very* full of himself...but I want it to be him."

"Is that right." Still grumpy.

"Yes. And...I just wanted to let you know that...it's safe." My doctor told me the pill is effective from the day you start taking it.

"There's nothing safe about you, Lila Danger Sunshine Bailey. You're the most dangerous person I know."

25

"Am not," I say.

"Are too."

"Why am I dangerous?"

"Because you're more beautiful and sexy and off-the-charts hot than I can fucking handle."

Damn it. Why does he have to be so sexily gruff and say such nice things to me all the time? "Does that mean…you will? I want that to be my next lesson."

Colton glares at me, like I've offended him. "You want me to fuck you right now, with no condom?"

I bite my lip. "I mean…you can use one if you want. I guess it's the safer option, considering we—"

He holds me down, pinning my body underneath his.

His hot—*enormous*—cock slides against my slippery, still-pulsing pussy. I gasp, because the pleasure wave is still waiting there, getting ready to crash all over again.

"You want me to take you now, just like this?"

God, he's so close. His cock is pressing against me, *opening* me. "Yes. Yes."

"You better be sure, baby girl, because if I fuck you without any barrier between us, I'm going to come inside you. There's no way I'm pulling out of this tight little juicy heaven on earth once I'm home. I'm going to want to pump you so full of my hot cum you'll be overflowing with it. Is that what you want?"

Yes. I want him. *This* is the way I want to remember him.

I can feel his engorged length throb against my clit and it's almost enough to tip me over the edge again. *Almost.*

I squirm against him trying to get more of him but he's too strong and too heavy.

"*Please*, Cole." The slow, slick glide of his cock is so beautiful I feel emotional again.

"I've never done it bareback before."

This surprises me. And I don't know why I'm so freaking happy about it. Okay, I do know why. Maybe I *am* special to him. I ignore the echo of Sloane's warning. *He'll rip your heart out and eat it for breakfast!!!* "Never?"

"Never." He shifts his weight, and the head of his cock slides against me, barely *into* me.

"*Oh.*"

It's so freaking thick. Even though I'm *very* wet and

he's hardly even inside me at all, there's a hot, stretching burn.

Now I'm wondering if this is even possible. Maybe he's too damn big.

"*Cole*," I whimper.

"Come on, Bailey, don't cry about it. Take it like a good girl. If you want my big cock so bad, then fucking work for it. It'll hurt at first but you won't care because you'll be coming so hard you'll be crying with pleasure and the best kind of pain. Beg me for it if that's what you want, you little minx. Say it. Say, 'Cole, fuck me hard with that big cock until I'm crying because I'm so full of it and it feels so fucking good.'"

Oh god. "*Do it.*"

"Say it."

"*Fuck me, Cole. Please.*"

"Good girl." He's adjusting me, roughly pushing my legs wider. "Wrap your legs around me and hold on tight."

He pushes his gigantic bulk against me, opening me as he grips me. He's so strong I think he might leave marks on my skin but I don't care. I want him to.

"Is this what you need, baby girl?" He softly bites my neck. "Daddy's giant cock?"

A giggle escapes me and he's laughing too but I'm also moaning because his thickness is forcing me to take more. I feel dizzy with the overwhelming pleasure-pain. The wave is starting to build again, and this time it's even stronger. Higher. More forceful. Full of gliding friction and deep, star-flicked heat.

Colton drives deeper. And I'm not laughing anymore because there's a sharp pain as he thrusts hard.

He just broke through.

He pushes further, more aggressively now. Deeper. And deeper still.

God. How much more is there?

My body's resisting him. *He's too freaking big.*

"Cole," I whimper at the hot, stretching demand.

"Relax, baby girl. Let me in."

I struggle a little, trying to free myself of the feeling of being split wide open. "*Cole. You're too big.*"

"You can handle me, angel. That's my girl." He pushes my legs even wider, settling deeper with a forceful thrust. Cole's soft-edge grunt hums with a note of finality and I know that he's fully inside me now.

It's uncomfortable, this extreme fullness of him deep inside my body. It's too much.

I ease forward a little, and back. I can feel the huge thickness of him barely slide out. But then he thrusts again, even deeper, and I moan.

God. I can feel every vein and every ridge, rubbing against some insanely sensitive trigger inside me.

He does it again.

We both groan.

His hands are on my ass now, gripping me as he continues this rhythm, pulling back, then pushing deep until the melting wave of pleasure-pain is a tsunami riding a crazy-high crest.

"*You feel so fucking good, Sunshine. Like heaven on earth. Come for me, baby. Let me feel you.*"

He thrusts again and it tips the wave over an impossible peak, crashing over me. The clenching spasms of my body squeeze Colton's massive cock in a luscious rhythm, and I can feel the deep throbbing pulse of him as he surges and comes. He's growling my name. The jets of his liquid heat set me off again, my inner muscles working him, over and over.

It's a while before either of us can move. We're dazed and entwined. Our bodies are locked in a rippling bond. He kisses me lazily, his tongue caressing mine, his body still deeply, wetly inside me. My arms and legs are wrapped around him. To keep him there.

I love him.

I wish we could stay like this forever.

My perfect little Sunshine girl, he whispers.

26

Tuesday
Aspen, Colorado

By the time we land in Aspen, I feel like a completely different person.

I've conquered my fear of flying.

I'm definitely no longer a virgin.

Colton Maddox came inside me three times.

I'm very sore and I feel used and punished in the best kind of way.

I have bruises from his punishing grip and I'm still high on my multi-orgasmic endorphin rush.

And I feel like I've been reborn as a golden phoenix who's not only beautiful but invincible. It sounds overly dramatic, but no one tells you that overflowing with a sexy, feral man's hot *seed* happens to be extremely empowering.

We took a shower in the luxury suite. Colton fed me delicious food from the platter that had been prepared for us and we drank more champagne.

The flight was smooth and I was thankful for that. Or maybe I didn't notice the bumps because Colton and I were making our own turbulence. The landing was slightly terrifying, but by then I was too satiated and content to worry about it.

Another limo picked us up at the airport and brought us into Aspen. Which is the most beautiful place I've ever seen. The golden leaves of the silver birch trees have mostly fallen now and an early snowfall looks like diamond dust has been sprinkled into it. Everything glimmers.

The village is quaint in a way that's rustic but screams extreme wealth.

Since it's much colder here than it was in Nashville, Colton insists on stopping in one of the village's shops, where he buys me a brand new to-die-for long suede coat. And since he insisted I can't wear my cowgirl boots in the snow, he bought me another pair that matches my new coat. They didn't even have price tags.

I'll never get used to the luxury—which is a good thing, because I *can't* get used to the luxury. Once Sunday rolls around, it's back to studio apartments and ramen noodles for me.

Our condo in Aspen is the most spectacular yet. He carries me over the threshold.

I've noticed it's a thing with him. He always carries me when we're entering any new accommodation we happen to be staying in. "Why do you carry me?"

I think he's gotten even more handsome since we spent an incredibly connective four hours in bed on the flight. *He looks like he's mine.* His hair is slightly messed up and he looks healthy. Full of vigor and vitality. His color is high across his cheekbones and the bridge of his nose, like he's been out in the sunny fresh air all day. His eyes are vividly azure. "I'm superstitious."

I laugh. "About what?"

He just smiles and sets me down on my feet. "You, Sunshine."

"This place is incredible."

The condo is a swanky log cabin style that could be straight off the set of Yellowstone.

Mountains rise in the distance outside the floor-to-ceiling windows. The white ski trails are clearly visible. Dusk has painted the sky pink and, along the ridge, a deep lavender.

Wide wooden beams criss-cross along the vaulted ceilings and there's a massive stone fireplace. A fire crackles cheerfully.

Two men dressed in uniforms deliver our bags to the bedroom. One of them offers to take my coat. The other hands us menus from the resort's restaurant and asks us if we'd like a drink.

"Just some water, please," I say. I feel like I've run a marathon this afternoon.

Colton glances through the menu. "Two filet mignons, a bottle of your best Bordeaux and anything else Miss Bailey wants," he tells the waiter.

"Filet mignon sounds perfect."

As soon as the waiters leave, Colton's phone rings. He's ignored a lot of calls during this trip and so have I. We've barely been able to placate our respective friends and family by sending a lot of *everything's fine, I'll call you as soon as I get a chance!* texts.

"I better take this one," he says. "It's Noah and I've missed at least twenty calls from him."

"Of course. You should talk to him. I'm going to go check my messages too."

"Noah." Colton opens the sliding doors and walks out onto the balcony, but I can still hear their conversation. I go into the bedroom to give them some privacy, but they have loud voices.

"You're in Colorado now?" Noah asks him.

"Still tracking me, huh? Yeah, I'm in Aspen."

"I had to talk Alexander out of coming to get you. He's worried you're losing your mind."

"Why, because I'm taking a vacation for once in my life? Yeah, that's real lunatic behavior."

"It's more about the way you just randomly took off

like that. And then refusing to take everyone's calls for days on end. You're not cracking up, are you, brother?" There's genuine concern in Noah's voice.

"I guess it depends on how you define cracking up," Colton drawls.

"So," Noah eases into it. "Sloane told us about the— direct quote—'cute, gorgeous AF and incredibly talented' friend of hers you offered to drive to L.A. because you have meetings out there. I think we all know there's no business in California that requires urgent meetings. We work for the same company, in case you've forgotten."

"Fuck, you people are nosy," Colton grumbles.

"Only because we care." Noah says it almost jokingly but the sentiment there is clearly real.

"I can find business-related things to do in L.A., Noah." *Okay, so he didn't have business in L.A.?* "And yes, I'm traveling with someone, if you must know."

"Five days with one chick? On a *bus*? That's an all-time record for you, by at least four days."

"We flew from Nashville. And so what. I'll spend five days on the road with whoever I fucking choose to, bro. Is there anything else I can help you with?"

"Who's the girl?"

Colton doesn't answer right away. "She's an up-and-coming designer." It's…a nice way to be described. *Up-and-coming.*

"Are you *dating* her?" Like this possibility is beyond shocking.

"I'm spending a few days on the road with her, as I've already explained. We're going to a wedding this weekend."

"Whose wedding?"

"Jesus Christ, Noah. Her friend's."

"When are you coming back to New York?"

Colton sighs. "After the wedding, obviously."

Obviously.

Of course he is. Actually, we haven't agreed yet on whether he's coming to the wedding or not. It would clearly be a terrible idea. And an even worse idea if—not if, *when* and *because*—he's heading back to New York, possibly as soon as Saturday night.

Never to be seen again.

It's the reminder I need.

I'm not in love with him. I can't be, a) because my heart is safely locked away, and b) because this was always *only* about having an adventure and taking him up on his offer to educate and enlighten me. Which he has abso-lutely—and very thoroughly—done.

With no strings attached.

That was our deal. Our *pact*.

My phone vibrates. It's almost like Sloane has a radar. Or maybe she's with Noah right now.

Might as well get this over with. I close the bedroom door. "Hey, Sloane." I put her on speaker and lay back on the massive bed. The bedroom has the same spectacular view of the mountains as the living room.

"Finally, she answers her phone." Sloane pauses, like she's bracing herself, before she asks me the question. "So…how's it going? Are you okay? Where are you?"

"Aspen."

"Aspen. Wow. Are you still traveling with Colton?"

There's no reason to lie. She already knows. "Yes. Just until we get to L.A."

"How did this even happen? When did you two decide to suddenly hit the road together? And why didn't you *tell* me?"

"I'm really not even sure how it happened. It just… happened."

"Break it to me gently. You're not…" She can't bring herself to say it.

But *I* can. Fuck it. I'm a sophisticated, independent *non*-virginal, up-and-coming…person. So what if I had sex with a hot billionaire. I'm allowed to. "Yes. We are. We did. And now I understand what all the fuss is about. But I'm not stupid enough to expect anything more from this, so don't worry about me getting heart-broken, okay? It's all good. We agreed. It's just sex."

"*What?*" I can hear Sloane clutching her metaphorical pearls. "*Oh my god!*"

"Sloane. It's *fine*. I'm good, I promise."

"Are you in *love* with him?"

"What? No. Of course I'm not. Why would you even ask me that? I took all your warnings to heart and I'm purely in this for the hot sex."

"Ew. Oh my god, please don't describe it. He's my *boss*."

"Fine. But I told you I wanted to cash in my V-card and now I have."

"Lila, I can't believe this! That absolute *monster*, taking advantage of you like that! Are you okay? Is he being… *nice* to you?"

Nice? "Yes. He couldn't have been nicer." Not exactly true, but whatever. *Actually, Sloane, he was a fucking beast who's so well-hung, so good in bed and has such a filthy mouth I thought I'd died and gone to heaven. At least three times.* "Sloane, I *chose* to be here with him. We're two consenting adults. He hasn't done anything wrong and neither have I, okay?"

"Okay. Okay. You're right." She regroups. "I'm going to try to look for the silver lining here. At least you're being realistic about the part where it's only about the sex."

"That's all it ever was. For both of us. We made a deal."

"You poor thing. Talk about baptism by fire. My innocent little Lila with that *animal!* I should never have brought you to that party. I know all too well what he's like. I mean, I love him as a boss, but…I just hope it was good for you, honey."

"It was." *So good I feel like I've sprouted wings.*

"I guess, when you think about it, this is kind of perfect. Now you can meet up with your old crush and you'll radiate confidence. You won't be pining and he'll pick up on your new vibe. He's bound to fall in love with you on the spot and you'll live happily ever after. You can file this little chapter into Lessons Learned."

You have no idea. "We'll see." Her comment makes me realize that I haven't pined for Troy Beckett in…three whole days. I feel completely, totally over him. "How are things in New York?"

"Fine. But I miss having you here already. Last night I went to a fabulous show with those friends of mine, the influencers, who are now obsessing over your outfits. Have you had any more orders?"

"I haven't checked. I've been——"

"Don't you dare say 'busy' or I'll lose it."

I laugh. "Okay, I won't. I'm checking my orders now." *What?* "Oh my gosh. *Sloane.*"

"What's wrong?"

"I have 927 orders."

"Holy shit."

"How am I supposed to fill *nine hundred and twenty-seven* orders? It'll take me *years* to sew nine hundred garments."

"I think that's what staff are for, sweetie. It might be time for you to hire some help."

"I also have a message here from…Eleanor Jaeger. It says here she's the——" I can't believe what I'm seeing.

"She's the what?"

"She's one of the executive design coordinators for Ralph Lauren. It says they're impressed by what they've seen on Instagram and they want to interview me for a job."

Sloane's scream is piercing. "I *told* you you'd get your break! It was only a matter of time! Now you *have* to come back to New York!"

My head is spinning.

927 orders? Ralph freaking Lauren?

I can hear the banging noises of room service trays being wheeled into the living room. I realize the door of the bedroom didn't latch and has swung open.

"Sloane, I have to go, but I'll call you soon. What day is it?"

"It's Tuesday night."

That gives us tonight and three more nights.

"Are you going to reply to Ralph Lauren?"

"Of course I am."

"What are you going to say?"

So maybe I'm not moving back to L.A. for good after all. "Depending on how the interview goes, if they offer me a job, I'm going to say yes."

27

―――――

"Cole?"

"Mmhm?"

We're sitting by the fire. We just finished dinner. Yet another of the best meals I've ever eaten.

I'm curled up next to Colton on the couch, sipping a glass of French red wine he poured me and gazing out at the view of the purple mountains and the starry night sky. We haven't bothered turning on the TV or anything else. The view is too beautiful.

Being with Colton is so different to my usual life. So unfamiliarly comfortable. I remember thinking he was like a buffer against reality and the feeling only compounds itself the more time I spend with him. "Remember how I told you my favorite designer is Ralph Lauren?"

"Yeah."

"Well, believe it or not, I got an email from them today."

"Yeah?" The casualness of his reply answers my question before I even ask it.

"You don't by any chance know anyone there, do you?"

"I've been to a few of their shows. I get invited to a lot of fashion shows for some reason. They tell me I liven up the front row."

"With your killer sense of humor?" It's a petulant thing to say and I didn't really mean for it to be, but I'm picturing Colton flirting with gorgeous supermodels and A-list celebrities and a little devil in me wants to bite him.

He narrows his eyes at me. His slow smile is more like a sneer. "Something like that."

"You didn't happen to…like, mention me to anyone, did you?"

He crooks a burly arm along the back of the couch behind my shoulders and I stiffen a little. "One of their design coordinators invests with us in a minor account. She emailed me this morning for an update."

I wait for it.

"I might have mentioned a young designer people are raving about."

At least he's honest about it. And, obviously, it's not a terrible thing for him to have done. But still. It feels like he's playing with my life, in more ways than I can handle. "I kind of wish you'd asked me first."

"All I said was that a couple of my assistants and their friends were going crazy over your designs and she should check out your Instagram."

"You said that?"

"Yeah. What's the problem?"

"The *problem* is that she emailed me today and she invited me to interview for a job. In New York."

"And?" Like he can't see the problem at all.

"Don't you think you're taking some major freaking liberties by doing that?"

One of Colton's eyebrows lifts and his grin is annoyingly entertained. "Liberties?"

"Yes. Liberties."

"I wouldn't consider it a liberty. I'd consider it a seed."

"Seed?" Of course the word makes me blush because every now and then I can still feel trickles of *his*.

"Of possibility. Most people would be happy to get a job interview."

"I'm not most people. And I am happy." It's times like these that his uncut smugness rubs me the wrong way. "But you can't just take over my life like this."

"I'm not taking over your life."

"I don't want *you* to get me a job. If I get a job, *I* want to be the one to get *myself* a job."

"I didn't know if she'd contact you or not. I just pointed her in your direction. I can't sell your clothes if she doesn't like them. Looks like she liked them."

Why am I even mad about this? I'm over the moon

about the potential of the job offer, but something isn't sitting right about the whole thing.

Maybe because everything's so easy for him and he's making me feel like I'm losing control.

Of my heart. Of my body. Of my future. Because all of them want to entwine themselves around Colton Fucking Maddox.

And they can't because he's a commitment-phobic playboy who sits in front rows at fashion shows and who I've been warned about over and over and now he's doing it in slow motion.

He's breaking my heart.

He's not even remorseful about any of it in the slightest.

He mimics my frown. He looks so good doing it I hate him even more.

"Poor Bailey," he purrs, pouting like I am, taking my glass from my hand and setting it on the giant coffee table.

He gently but forcefully lays me back on the couch and pins me down with his weight.

"Don't," I snap.

"Don't what?" He's unfastening his jeans and crawling down my body.

And damn him, I'm already wet because he's so damn big and hard and he's pushing my dress up. And I'm not wearing panties because I lost them somewhere along the way of cashing in my V-card in the Mile Freaking High Club.

"Don't do things like that without talking to me about it first."

"All right, Sunshine." *Oh god.* He kisses my pussy, open-mouthed, licking into me. But he takes little breaks as he talks to me. "Chill, baby girl. I would have asked you but you were meeting with the shrink." Another *really* lewd lick. "I got the email and I remembered that you happened to mention that working at Ralph Lauren would be your dream job. And Sloane and her entourage had been talking about your clothes." He sucks on my pussy with such messy, greedy gusto, I'm about to come already. "So I used my contact to get you an in. I didn't *get* you the job. *You* still have to do that, which you no doubt will, with your talent and your sassy gorgeousness. So stop fucking overreacting." The stubble of his face scratches against me as he eats me in lusty mouthfuls and the tidal wave is starting.

But then his mouth is gone and the heavy weight of him is on top of me again. He pulls my knees high and wide as he moves, and the thick, wet head of his cock pushes into me.

I moan because I'm so tender but I'm *almost* coming. It's sitting there, a sure thing, just waiting for the tiniest push.

It's like he knows this. He holds himself still, denying me, staring down at me, his hair falling over his forehead, his eyes as dark as the night sky.

"'*Don't*?'" he whispers, withdrawing his slippery beautiful thickness just a fraction.

"Okay, *do*," I whisper back, gripping him. Trying to pull him closer.

"Do what, Bailey?"

"*Fuck me, Maddox. Fuck me hard with your big fucking cock.*"

I can hear his low chuckle turn to a growl as he drives all the way to the hilt. I cry out. The pain is too intense. But the pleasure is already there, being coaxed higher and higher by his deep, hard aggression. It erupts through my body in an explosive rush. The cascading spasms are too much. I'm moaning with ecstasy, my body tugging at the length of him until I can feel the violent beat of his release and the warmth of him pulsing deeply into me.

He presses his savage groan into my neck. "*Mine.*"

28

———

COLTON

Wednesday
Aspen, Colorado

THE PRINCESS IS in a mood and so am I.

I'm in a mood because even though I've spent most of the past 24 hours fucking her—more than I should have, considering she was a virgin yesterday morning—I can't get enough.

I spent the night worshipping her. Coming hard because she's so damn responsive and her tight little squirming body pulls pleasure out of me like nothing I've ever known. I kissed her like a lovestruck lunatic until I was fully revived, then did it all over again. I lost count of how many times I spent myself inside her.

Of course I would never in a million fucking years have considered doing that in any normal situation. Lila

Sunshine Danger Bailey—and holy fuck, is she dangerous—is a Code Red emergency.

I would never have trusted another woman if she'd told me all sweetly, *I'm on the pill.*

I'm a hot, well-hung billionaire. I've heard that one before.

But no, of course I didn't take any other precautions, because I'm so fucking manic to get inside this girl and pump her full of my overflowing cum, it's almost like I'm *trying* to knock her up.

Then she'd have to stay with me.

What the fuck am I even thinking right now?

If she's knocked up and gets a job offer in New York, which I'll make sure she does, she won't move back to L.A. She'll move in with me.

Jesus Christ.

I force myself to get a grip.

I can handle this.

I *have* to handle it.

I refuse to lose my mind over one sassy little nymph, no matter how gorgeous she might be.

I finish making her a latte on the European coffee machine. I put some whipped cream on it, as requested, and take it into the bathroom, where she's up to her neck in the bubble bath. She's sore. I pushed her too far. So I ran her a bath in the jacuzzi tub and carried her in, carefully lowering her into it, making sure the jets were getting the pressure points between her shoulder blades at just the right angle.

Her silver eyes are soulful, but still with that saucy little attitude behind them, and slightly bloodshot from not getting enough sleep even though she slept in until after nine.

"One latte with whipped cream for the most beautiful girl in the world."

The sassiness is my weakness, like a hook that sinks deep into my beating heart and refuses to let go. But the soulfulness is my fucking Kryptonite. I can deal with the kittenish anger. Any inkling of vulnerability in this girl has me on my fucking knees.

I'm *trying* to tone it down. But it's no use. One blink of those long eyelashes and I'm whipped like nothing I've ever known.

It's a problem, and one I'm going to need to deal with as soon as we get to L.A.

Until then, I'm going to shower her with praise and presents until she's smiling again. Because her smile is like water on parched fucking earth and I have no idea why.

I set her latte on the tray next to the tub.

"Thanks." She's still miffed about the job thing, and that's fine. She'll get over it. I made her reply to the email while I was running the bath to tell them of course she'd love to interview. She obeyed, barely even grumbling about how I'm trying to control her life.

"Drink your coffee. Then I have some things to show you."

"What things?"

"You'll see. It's a surprise."

She eyes me, and I can already see that she's curious enough to almost forgive me my sins. She takes a sip of her coffee. "Is it still snowing?"

"No, it stopped. The sky is clear now. It's a beautiful day out there, but cold. We're going to take the snowmobile through the village and up to the gondola. We'll ride up and there's a restaurant at the top where we can get lunch."

"Really?" Her eyes light up and it does weird fucking things to me. Like I'm addicted to her excitement. I want to make her happy like I want to fucking breathe.

How did I become so wildly obsessed with this stunning girl? So easily? So fucking uncontrollably?

She finishes her coffee and I wash her hair for her, running my hands through the silky strands. I'm fascinated by the wave in it, the long layers that cascade over her perfect breasts.

I massage the soap over her nipples, squeezing them gently, but I don't linger. They're already pink from my relentless need.

My job right now is to pamper her, not overwhelm her. There's nothing I want more than to feast on her again and take her back to bed, but I've already forced a punishing pace. What she needs right now is comfort, luxury and gifts.

I rinse her hair. Then I hold out the towel for her. "Come on. Time for your surprise."

She's uncharacteristically obedient, climbing out of the tub onto the bath mat. Her wet, naked body is ludicrously beautiful, but I ignore my painfully omnipresent hard-on, which morphed into a superhero on steroids the minute she walked into my life.

I dry her and wrap a plush white bathrobe around her, tying it. I take the brush and, as carefully as I can, brush it through her hair. She watches me do this in the mirror with an expression that's hard to read. She almost seems…awed. Accepting. Drinking it in. She likes it when I take care of her like this. Which means that's all I'm going to do from now on.

"There." I put the brush back on the marble counter. "Are you ready for your surprise now?"

"I don't know what surprise you're talking about."

"That's the thing about surprises, Sunshine. They're surprising."

I guide her out to the living area. The huge dining room table is piled high with food that was delivered while she was in the bath. It's also piled high with wrapped boxes.

"What *is* all this?"

"An early Christmas. Open them."

"These are for me?"

"Of course they're for you. Who else would they be for?"

"Why are you buying me presents, Maddox?"

"Because you like presents. Stop being all demure about it. Just open them."

I serve her a plate of the food as she opens them one by one and—fucking hell, I'm a goner. Her delight is so adorable, I don't even know how to describe what it does to me. My chest aches, like there's not enough room in there. My heartbeat feels hot, blazing with obsession.

"A snowsuit?"

"There's a lot of snow out there."

"It's so cute." She holds up the silvery-white one-piece snowsuit. She unties the robe and drops it, stepping into the snowsuit. With nothing underneath. *Fucking hell, just kill me now. I can't with this girl. She's too damn gorgeous.* She zips it up. It's one of those tight ones. It hugs every curve and then some. "I look like an astronaut."

"A very sexy one."

"Thank you, Cole. I love it."

She opens more of the boxes. There's a silver-white ski jacket to match the snowsuit, for an extra layer of warmth. There are matching gloves, a hat with fur trim, a scarf and fur snow boots.

"Colton, this is so over the top. You can't just *buy* me all this stuff."

"I can and I have. Open the last two."

She opens the smaller one, holding up the diamond

tennis bracelet with wide eyes. "*Maddox.* Are you kidding me?"

"Do I look like I'm kidding?" I almost point out my raging hard-on, but then I remember I'm supposed to be ignoring it. "Here, let me put it on you."

"Is it…" She doesn't finish her question. She's too busy staring at the glimmering diamonds, set in white gold, that are now circling her slim wrist.

"Of course it's real, Sunshine. Who do you think you're dealing with here?"

"A crazy person? You buy *diamonds* for your girls?"

I shouldn't be offended by the question, of course, but I am anyway. "I only buy diamonds for one girl." I don't know why I suddenly hate the sound of it so much. *Girls.* "Open the last one." It's the biggest box.

When she realizes what it is, her eyes pool with tears. She rips off the paper. "You got me a *sewing machine*?"

"Not just any sewing machine. They told me it was the best one on the market. It's computerized. You can do quilting, embroidery, whatever you want. You can even sew through leather with that bad boy."

She throws her arms around me and kisses me.

"Easy there, tiger. If I'd known a sewing machine was going to get this kind of reaction, I would have bought one days ago."

Tears wet her cheeks. "My sewing machine is so old, I can't even make half the things I want to make because it keeps breaking the needles."

"Well, this one will be able to handle anything you throw at it. It's got extra heavy-duty needles and all the latest technology. It can do anything you want it to."

She wipes her tears. "I didn't tell you this, Cole, but as of this morning, I have *1,283* new orders."

I play along, pretending to be surprised, but the door was open. I overheard her telling Sloane about it. I also heard her tell Sloane that what we're doing here is only about the sex. Which is the other reason I'm in a mood.

I should be fucking *glad*. It's a dream scenario. The gorgeous little virgin on the pill wanted to cash in her V-card before getting on with her life. I can get my fill of her and then I can get back to normality.

My problem is, *I don't want fucking normality if she's not in it.* "Fuck, baby. That's impressive."

"I have no idea how I'm going to do it."

I push her a little further on the subject, because it's a big deal and she's been holding out on me. "Why didn't you tell me that?"

"Because I'm nervous I won't be able to do it. What if I can't? Even if I hire people, it would take months. I just never expected it to blow up like this and I've been trying to figure out how I'm going to make it work."

"How long does it take you to sew one piece of clothing?"

"At least two days. Sometimes more."

"How long would it take with the new sewing machine?"

She considers this. "A day. I could do most of them in a day, if I work all night."

"You're going to want to get all the orders filled within a month, to keep the momentum going so they can post on Instagram or wherever, which will lead to more orders. That's how you'll grow the business. So, if you have 1,283 orders, that means you need 43 workers. At least. Let's say 50. You teach them and you give them the blueprints for the designs. The machines will take the guesswork out of it. You'll hire ten more people to package, send, track the items and deal with billing, social media and so on."

She tilts her head. "*Fifty* dressmakers? And each would need their own sewing machine? Plus ten more employees?" Like I've just suggested she fly to the moon in her new astronaut suit.

"Good thing you know a guy who's always looking for promising small businesses to invest in."

A little furrow appears between her lightning-bright eyes. "*You* want to invest in my business?"

"Of course I do." I don't deserve her. But I want her more than I know what to do with. Suddenly everything makes sense to me. My years of operating business logistics have led me to this moment. This is something I can do for her better than anyone else can. "If you want me to."

"But, Cole…"

I hold a finger to her lips. I know what she's going to say: we're temporary. What I'm proposing isn't. "I can help you. But it'll be on your terms. You call the shots, and I make sure those shots hit their targets. You can start setting things up and looking for the right people as soon as we get back to New York." She doesn't immediately protest the New York detail—or the *we* detail—so I keep going. "Eleanor Jaeger might even have some ideas. *If* you get the job, that is, which you will. They must have studios or factories or something, right? They might let us rent some space or utilize some of their resources. We can present them with a business plan and show them we're not fucking around. They might even consider a collabo-ration with you, if that's something you would consider. She owes me a favor, so I'm sure she'll at least give us a meeting."

"What…favor?" Her jealousy is so fucking cute.

"I made her a lot of money this year. Like, a *lot* of money."

Lila's expression is so hopeful and her face is so stun-ning, it's physically painful to stare at her. I have never, ever seen anything so beautiful as this girl.

Am I fucking in love with her? Is that what this is?

She blinks up at me. "Do you really think it could work?"

"It will work. I'll make sure of it."

"Thank you, Cole," she whispers. "For believing in me."

"Of course I believe in you. You're the only thing I *do* believe in."

I don't even mean to say that, but it's true. When it comes to falling in love—which I never, ever thought I was capable of—she's the only one who's ever made me believe it's possible.

Not just possible.

I am. I'm madly, deeply, head over fucking heels in love with her.

So this is what this feels like.

I kiss her and she opens to me, her tongue gliding silkily along mine. My soul feels like it's on fire and my cock thickens hotly, but if I take her to bed now we'll never get out of it. And we have things to see.

"Oh no you don't," I murmur. "You're not luring me into bed again, you dirty girl. We're going snowmobiling. You wanted to see Aspen, so that's what we're going to do."

She's already wearing her other gifts so I put on her hat, her scarf and her gloves. Then I lift her into my arms and carry her out the door.

29

ASPEN IS BUSTLING AND SNOW-DUSTED. It looks more like a movie set than an actual place. Everything is so picture perfect, it doesn't seem real.

I'm riding on the back of the snowmobile, my arms wrapped around Colton's chest. I lean my head up against his back as we drive right through the center of town, heading toward the mountain.

I let my hand slip lower, down his front. And lower. Fingering the huge ridge of him through his jeans. Even with my wool gloves on, I can feel him thicken.

I *love* getting him hard. I love that he can't help himself from reacting to me. I love that he's at my mercy. Most of all, I love that we're so connected and in sync. As we get further up the mountain and closer to the lifts, I let my hand just rest on his swelling warmth.

He feels so good.

I'm allowing myself to go with this for the week because it's impossible not to and it feels like I'm living inside a dream when I'm with him. But I don't know how to feel.

He's famous for his charm, I knew that from the beginning. He lures women into bed and no wonder it's so easy for him. The man is impossible to resist.

Does he give *all* the women he dates so many presents?

Does he buy them their dream gift? A state-of-the-art sewing machine that will make their lives ten times easier?

Does he give them diamonds?

I only give diamonds to one girl.

But…can I trust him?

Does he offer to put money—potentially a *lot* of money—into *their* businesses?

Does he tell them they're the most beautiful woman in the world?

Does he come inside them all night long?

He told me that part was a first for him, and I believed him.

But I wish Sloane's warnings weren't playing on a looped reel inside my brain. *He'll totally charm you because it's what he does and then the minute you think there could be something real there, he'll be nowhere to be found. It's always the same. Every freaking weekend I'm fielding irate phone calls and reading the headlines. This is a Code Red, Lila. DO NOT get on that bus!!*

Yet I did get on that bus. And it does sometimes—who am I kidding, *all* the time—feel like there could be something real here. And sweet Jesus, has he charmed me.

Today is Wednesday. We have three more nights together. And then what happens?

I'm dreading Saturday for ten different reasons.

Colton pulls up next to the gondola and kills the snowmobile's engine. "The gondolas are so cute." Little floating rooms suspended by a thick wire that goes all the way to the top of the mountain.

"Cute?"

"Yes. Cute."

Colton's still in some kind of a mood. We didn't really argue, like we so often seem to do, but he's intense and surly. Maybe it's that giant hard-on that never seems to go down, even though we made love *a lot*. All night long, we were connected in one way or another, feasting off each other's pleasure like we're addicted to it.

It's like he's gone a little crazy with it. Trying to get his fill before Saturday, maybe.

Because all of this is going to crash and burn three days from now. I'm prepared for that—or at least I'm trying to be. I'll give back all the presents, I'll go to the bank and get a loan if I can, and I'll do my best to get myself a dream job.

And I'll kiss my heart goodbye.

But at least I have hope. That's the biggest gift Colton

Maddox has given me. He's reminded me that good things can happen and sometimes they even do.

Plus I'm wearing the cutest snow bunny outfit in the world (and nothing underneath), I have real diamonds circling my wrist and I got laid so thoroughly by a billionaire beefcake last night, I'm still floating from all the orgasms.

"Don't be so grouchy, Maddox."

"I'm not grouchy."

"You are."

"Just get in the gondola, Bailey."

It's not overly busy because it's mid-week and early in the season. We're the only people in line.

A lift attendant opens the door of a gondola for us and we climb in. Then we're sealed in and airborne and it's the coolest thing. There are cushioned seats on both sides and two poles to hang onto. It's like a bubble, with windows offering views of the resort below us and the mountain rising above us. "These things are heated?"

"All the better to get you naked, Sunshine. Time for your next lesson."

"I thought I graduated. You know, with the unprotected sex-a-thon all night long."

"Nope. You've still got a lot to learn. Take off the astronaut suit. And hurry up, we've only got twenty minutes."

He's sitting on one of the benches. He unfastens his

jeans and takes out his big, heavy…manhood. No surprises, it's already hard as a pillar of steel.

"Jesus." I giggle, feigning shock—at least it's *partly* feigned. "Is it me or does that thing just keep getting bigger?" *He's really freaking hard.*

"Your fault, you little cocktease. Take it off."

This is our game. And the man is a devil who gets me wet without even trying.

The sight of that thick, glistening cock turns me into a raving nymphomaniac, every time. "What if someone sees us?"

"So what if they do. You're mine, the whole world might as well fucking know about it."

I feel so good, so luxurious and so damn turned on, I want to please him and drive him even crazier. I take off my ski jacket and my boots, and shimmy out of my snow bunny outfit. Until all I'm wearing is a pair of socks. I leave those on, so my feet don't get cold. Playful, I twirl around one of the poles.

I like being naked when he's mostly fully clothed. It makes me feel so feminine but also powerful, the way his eyes get dark with need. The gondola's heated, but there's still a cool edge to it and my nipples are pink and tightly budded. My skin feels cool but my pussy feels warm and so wet, a trickle of moisture wets my thighs.

"You're a naughty girl, teasing me and getting me this fucking hard."

"I'm sorry, Professor."

"I'm going to need to punish you for this, princess. You need discipline."

"How are you going to punish me?" I ask innocently, twirling again, feeling freer and more alive than I ever have.

"Lay face down on my lap and find out."

My pussy contracts lightly, making me dizzy with desire, and I do as I'm told. Because I want to show him how turned on I am. I crawl over him, face down with my ass up. His rough hands position me, widening my knees as I arch my back, so I'm fully exposed to him.

"Fuck," he rasps. "How did my little almost-virgin get so wet?"

"I'm sorry I'm so wet, Professor," I coo.

Colton groans as he rubs the moisture over the sensitive flesh of my pussy, wetting the secret cove of my ass, delving into the wetness until I'm moaning and squirming. "You drive me insane, Danger girl. Do you know how fucking crazy I am for you?"

He slaps my pussy gently and I whimper because the light pain warms into a deep, blooming pleasure.

He does it again, pushing his fingers inside me to tease the wave higher. I'm *out of my mind* with need.

I lift to him, wanting more, but he's rubbing me, skating his fingers over my clit, spanking it again, until I'm so close, all I can do is writhe and beg. "*Please.*"

"My angel loves being punished, don't you, you sweet

little dirty girl. But I want my big cock inside this juicy pussy when you come. Get up here and ride me like a good girl."

I don't even hesitate. *I need him.* I straddle him and he aggressively guides his hard thickness into me. I'm wet but still sore.

It hurts as he drives himself deeper, gripping me hard. I ease myself up, sliding onto him, taking more of him. He's too thick and I bounce and squirm as he fucks me hard until he's fully, deeply inside me, watching my breasts jiggle as I pleasure him for all I'm worth. It's different from this angle. He feels bigger. Even deeper.

Cole is almost panting, groaning each time I grind against him and squeeze him with my body. "*Fuck, baby. My straight A little fuck bunny is so good at taking my big cock.*"

"*I'm coming, Cole.*" The sweet-hot ache is laced with shards of desperation.

The clenching spasms of my release are luscious and wild, milking his thick shaft lovingly. Cole's growl is feral as his cock bucks and throbs inside me, forcing me to ride him and take it all. I can feel the pumping jets of his liquid warmth and they set me off again into long, lush waves of pleasure. I'm overcome, not just with physical ecstasy but with raw emotion. Tears wet my face.

"*Lila,*" he's gasping. "*Lila.*"

My arms and legs are wrapped around him and I'm

kissing his perfect mouth. I'm confused about how to feel and yet not confused at all.

I can't love him. I locked my heart away.

It's the clarity of it that hurts most of all.

Somehow, the beauty and intensity of our lovemaking has broken the cage.

30

Thursday
The Grand Canyon, Arizona

THE NEXT DAY, we take a helicopter ride to the Grand Canyon. I've become used to feeling awed over the past few days, but the color of the sky is electric with a faraway thunderstorm. The deep chasm of the canyon is all colors of earthy red, with the blue-green river winding its way through, like it's been doing for six million years, carving deeper and deeper.

I'm sitting on Colton's lap in the helicopter as the tour guide explains that we're now at the South Rim. The Grand Canyon is 277 miles long, with an average width of ten miles and an average depth of one mile. The Native American Hopi tribe considered the Grand Canyon to be a gateway to the afterlife.

I've never seen anything as awe-inspiring as this place. It makes me feel small and inconsequential and temporary. In a good way. In a way that reminds me that life is short and sometimes you have to make sure you're making the absolute most of it.

If you don't, you'll find it's suddenly six million years later and you've missed your chances.

I decide to jump headfirst into my business, no matter what it takes. No matter how much it costs or how much help I get. If Colton's offer doesn't stand by Monday morning—because there are at least ten wrecking balls that are rolling toward Saturday afternoon and I have no idea which one will hit the hardest—I'm doing it anyway. Even if I fail, at least I'll have tried.

The past year has been a disaster because I was giving too much of myself to things I didn't want. I was acting out of desperation. All it did was to make me more desperate.

I'm not going to continue making the same mistakes.

I'm done waitressing.

I'm done working jobs I loathe.

I'm done yearning for people who aren't worthy of me.

Colton Maddox is the worthiest person I've ever met. Pleasing him, teasing him and loving him is so easy.

For one week, I'm losing myself in him. Beyond that, I have no idea what will happen.

Either way, I'm grateful. I'm glad it was him. I'll never

regret the three most magical days of my life so far. And I'm determined to allow that magic to infuse the rest of my life with positivity, even if Colton isn't a part of it.

His arms are slung around me, his hard warmth underneath me. I'm high on life. I'm hardly even nervous to be flying. The view is the most beautiful I've ever seen.

And we're on our way to Vegas.

31

Friday
Las Vegas, Nevada

THUD.

Thud.

Thud.

I'm trying to figure out why a jackhammer has been implanted inside my skull.

Because you did two tequila shots again in that casino after winning four thousand dollars at a slot machine.

That was after drinking at least four glasses of champagne because people kept offering them to us and we were having so much fun.

Why, Lila, *why?*

The waiters were wearing togas and everything looked like a Roman palace.

That's the last part of the evening I actually remember.

Damn it. I *swore* I'd never to do this again.

Colton's lying next to me in bed. He's on his stomach, his arm slung around a pillow, the sheet low across his back.

Those wide, tanned, sculpted shoulders really are a work of art, I can't help noticing. I love his ink. His dark hair's a glorious mess. I can tell by the evenness of his breathing that he's still asleep.

Thud.

Thud.

I need some Tylenol pronto. And enough water to drown a camel.

Once Monday morning rolls around, young lady, you are not touching alcohol for a month.

Agreed.

I get to the ridiculous marble and gold bathroom and close the door. I should be used to this by now, but this hotel room is our most luxurious yet. Our bed even rotates. I vaguely remember spinning around on it last night. Jumping on it.

Jesus, Lila. You need to calm down.

The thought of spinning around makes my eyes water and my stomach lurch.

Oh no.

I barely make it to the toilet in time, hurling not just once but twice. It's mostly liquid. Alcohol, hopefully. I don't remember eating dinner. All I remember is that they were serving endless free drinks at the casino and I obviously partook in the debauchery like it was going out of style.

Damn it.

I actually feel a little better now.

I flush the toilet, wash my hands, rinse out my mouth, take two Tylenol, drink two glasses of water, brush my teeth for around ten minutes, pee (realizing only then that my thighs are still wet from Colton's overflow), decide to take a shower and—

Wait a minute.

What the hell?

What the hell is this on my finger?

The biggest, shiniest diamond ring I've ever seen in my life.

Oh my god.

I'm getting flashbacks now.

We wandered down the strip, laughing.

There was a wedding chapel.

And a Tiffany's.

He bought me the biggest ring they had.

Wait.

We got married.

No.

No no no no no no no no no no.

Holy shit.

We got married.

32

"Colton Maddox."

I'm standing next to the bed, one fisted hand on my hip, the other hand held out so he can see the monstrosity we're dealing with. I'm wearing some slinky negligee but I couldn't care less about that.

He opens one eye. "Mornin', Sunshine."

He sees the ring then, and rolls onto his back, crooking a muscular arm-porn bicep behind his head. "Oh, shit. That's right. We got married last night." He laughs.

"You're *laughing*? This is not funny at all."

"It's kind of funny."

"Could you be serious for one minute, please? We can't be married."

"Well, I think we are." He holds up his own hand and,

sure enough, he's got a gold band on a very important finger. "Yep."

"I can't believe this!" I try to pull the heavy, glinting ring off my finger. "It's *stuck*."

"Maybe it likes where it is."

"Come on. Get up. We're going back down there and we're going to get a refund for the rings and get them to annul the marriage." I try to calm myself down. "We were drunk. I'm sure this kind of thing happens all the time in Vegas."

"I think I remember them saying there were no refunds."

"Oh, Jesus. This is a disaster! We'll at least tell them the whole thing was a mistake, then. I'm sure it's very straightforward."

"Didn't they say you have to go to a judge for something like that? And that there are only a few reasons why a judge would agree to annul a marriage, like if we were related or if you were underage. We signed something."

"We did?"

"I think so."

"Colton! How can you be so blasé about this? We need to go down there right now and deal with this! I'm sure there's some kind of change-your-mind clause. You're a cocky billionaire take-charge COO. I'm sure we can figure it out. Get up."

"I can't."

"Why not?"

He points to the sheet, which has created…a gigantic tent over his massive hard-on.

I roll my eyes dramatically. "Is that all you ever think about? Seriously! We have bigger things to deal with right now."

"Bigger than this?"

"*Colton.* I mean it."

"I can't help it. It's morning. And I'm a married man. Come here, wifey."

"Stop it. Are you really not even *concerned* about this? We got *married* last night, Colton."

"And thoroughly consummated the marriage. You were a wild *animal* last night, Bailey. Holy hell. No one would have guessed you were an innocent virgin only days ago. I must be a fucking good teacher."

"How can you act like this is all a big joke?" I sit down on the bed, distraught. "I can't believe we got *married*. We hardly even know each other."

"Bullshit. You know me better than anyone ever has."

"That can't be true. We met less than a week ago."

"What a week, though, right?" I hate that the tone of his deep voice is sincere. And that the way he's looking at me is sort of…genuinely tender. And also sort of…fiercely devoted. In a way I've never known. "It's been the best week of my life, Lila."

I don't want to admit this to him because it feels raw and uncontrollable, so I whisper the words so they don't break my heart. "It's been the best week of my life too."

Colton takes my hand, fingering the gigantic diamond. "I think we knew what we were doing last night."

"I think the tequila knew what it was doing last night."

"The tequila tunes into your subconscious. Our subconscious minds made the decision for us. Just like they did last weekend."

Lila, you are out of control. "I don't know. Tequila and I aren't on speaking terms right now."

"That's what you said last time."

I fall back onto the bed, slinging an arm over my eyes. "I know. I'm an idiot."

Colton moves, displacing the sheet. I peek under my arm to see his engorged, *huge*, angry-looking erection. "Or a gorgeous evil genius who has me so tightly wrapped around her sweet little finger I can't breathe, see straight or get my fucking hard-on to deflate, one of the two."

"I just don't know how you can be so casual about this."

"There's nothing casual about my hard-on, baby girl. Come here and let me make love to my beautiful wife."

"Stop calling me that."

"It's true. You are my wife."

"Don't get used to it."

Colton pulls me up onto the pillows, spreading my legs and crouching over me. *Damn it.* He knows his colossal, seeping manhood drives my inner sex goddess insane. He *knows* I can't resist him.

He licks my pussy. "Look how ripe and juicy and fucking perfect my wife is." Climbing up my body, he slides his thick cock into the tight wetness, all the way in. Pulling out only a little to drive deeper, the hard, swollen ridges of him rubbing slickly against all my most sensitive triggers.

One thing I can't deny is that our souls click and our bodies *fit*.

This is crazy. Obviously, we'll have to do something about the ridiculousness of this sham Vegas wedding. We can't be married. We can't *stay* married. Real Life begins again tomorrow.

But right now all I can see and feel is stars.

33

Saturday
Las Vegas, Nevada

My eyes blink open.

A few low lamps are still on and the neon lights of Vegas paint the dark purple walls with flashes of color.

I need to pee.

A digital clock on my bedside table reads 3:21.

Colton doesn't stir as I climb carefully out of bed so I don't wake him.

Damn it. I've fully lost my mind. We still haven't dealt with the fact that we *got married*. Instead, we ended up once again fucking like rabbits and falling asleep in a blissed-out love nest, entwined, kissing, sweaty and fully sated.

My body aches in places I didn't even know I had

muscles. My lips feel puffy from his kisses. My nipples are tender and sensitive from his greedy hunger. My cheeks and my thighs are sore from his rough beard. And the soreness on my thighs stings a little from the trickles of moisture.

Once again Colton Maddox has filled me up with his *hot seed*, as he loves to describe it. Once again I'm bruised and used and overflowing with it.

It reminds me.

Holy shit. I forgot to take my pill.

Today.

And yesterday. I remember taking it the day before that.

Shit shit shit!

So much has been going on and everything's been crazy and I've only been taking them for less than two weeks *and I completely forgot about it.*

I'll take one now. Does it matter if you skip a day? Or possibly two?

My god, Lila, you fool. What the hell's wrong with you? Have you completely lost your mind? Are you so overcome with one hunky, well-hung, sweet-and-dirty-talking devil that you not only freaking drunkenly marry him but now—

No. My period's due any day and I'm sure it's too late in my cycle for one missed pill—*two*—to make a difference.

I'll google it. I'm sure it's fine.

Please be fine.

As I make my way to the bathroom, a glow in the low light catches my attention. Colton's phone has lit up. On the table. As I'm walking past it.

I shouldn't snoop, of course. But I can't tear my eyes away.

A text has just come through.

> I miss you so much. I can't stop thinking about our night together, you beast. Please call me back 💋

From someone named Kara.

My stomach swoops horribly.

It's not the only text.

I scroll further.

> Where are you? I've tried calling you like 20 times but your phone must be turned off. Pleeeese call me. I love you so much 🤍

From Bianca.

I love you?

And a bunch of texts from someone named Jemma.

> Colton Maddox, CALL ME

> You can't leave me like this!

> It was tooooo good, baby

> Please don't make me beg. You better call me back xx

There are more.

Many more.

Dozens of missed calls. A few from his brothers, but most of them are from women.

Celeste.

Olivia.

Five more from Bianca.

Another text comes through from Jemma but it's blurry now.

I can't say Sloane didn't warn me.

DO NOT EVEN THINK ABOUT IT GIRL!!!!! THAT WOULD BE A HUGE MISTAKE!!!!!! HE IS THE KING OF HEARTACHE!!!!!! He'll rip your heart out and eat it for breakfast!!!!!!

What have I done?

34

COLTON

Saturday
En route to Malibu, California

"We need to talk about tomorrow."

"What about it?"

We're in a helicopter, on our way to L.A.

And I'm running out of time.

She's been uncharacteristically quiet this morning. Possibly because we're on our way to the wedding, which starts in a matter of hours.

"You'll need a place to stay in New York and I want you to stay with me. I want you to move in with me." A week ago's version of me would have run for the hills if anyone had suggested I invite a woman to move into my apartment. But this is the new and improved version of me. The one who's so in love with this sullen little angel—my *wife*—I hardly recognize myself.

I didn't *plan* to get married, of course I didn't. Especially on the fly in Vegas. I was drunker than I should have been (but not *that* drunk). And when I saw that chapel and that Tiffany ring, wild horses couldn't have dragged me away.

When I got down on one knee and proposed to her right there on the Vegas strip, people cheered. She laughed.

And she said yes.

None of it makes one iota of common sense. But common sense is rarely on the menu in Vegas. And when the girl on your arm is wilder than fantasies you never could have dreamed up, things are bound to happen.

"I already have an apartment," she says, gazing out the window.

"In the Hamptons. And it's the size of a broom closet. You need something in the city."

"I'll start looking for something on Monday."

"I have five bedrooms, Lila." I mention this because she's obviously in a huff about something. Our hasty wedding, probably. Which, in the colder light of Saturday morning, was a fucked up thing to do. I have no remorse whatsoever—which is even more fucked up. The only downside I can see is that she seems to have a lot more remorse about the whole thing than I do. "You can have your own wing. You don't even have to see me if you don't want to."

"Who gets to sleep in *your* room?" There's a sassy bite to her softly-spoken question.

"You, obviously." This has always been the issue between us. *Other women.* Who don't exist. "What's with the attitude?"

"What *attitude*?"

"I'm not sure what I did wrong this morning, angel girl. You liked me last night." I try to take her hand but she slides it away. I notice she's taken off her wedding ring. "Where's your ring?"

"In my bag."

"Why are you mad at me?"

It's easy to see that she's debating whether to tell me or not.

"At least tell me what my crime is so I can get on my knees and grovel."

Quietly, still refusing to look at me: "Maybe you should take someone else as your plus one."

"What's that supposed to mean?"

"Bianca. Or maybe *Jemma*. I'm sure *Kara* would just love another date."

Fuck. "You read my texts?"

A sulky pout and more staring out the window. "I woke up in the night. Your phone was lighting up. You're obviously a popular guy. But of course I already knew that."

"How far did you happen to scroll back, Sunshine, because if you did you would have noticed that I didn't reply to any of those texts. And if you go past yesterday you'll notice there are none. Because I delete them."

"It hardly matters to me. You do you."

"'You do you'?" I exhale a disbelieving laugh. "Sure. Okay. I'll do me. But just so you realize, *doing me* involves possessively escorting you to your friend's wedding before taking you into my bed to ravage you all night long because by then I'll have gone almost twenty hours without fucking you and I'm already wondering how I'm going to get through this entire wedding without tasting your sweet little pussy. And making my *wife* come all over my tongue like she loves to do."

She almost winces at the word. "You're a barbarian."

"Professor Berserker, at your service."

She rolls her eyes, but the light blush on her cheeks tells me she's remembering that particular lesson.

"What do you want me to do, Lila? Apologize for relationships I had *before* I met you?"

"No." Petulantly.

"Am I expected to be a fucking psychic or something? Here, let me pull my crystal ball out my ass and read you the future. I'm really good at it."

"I don't expect you to read the future." Even more petulantly.

"Then what *do* you expect?"

She squares her shoulders a little and gazes down into

the desert. "I expect you to get on with your life and I'll get on with mine. We both knew this was a road trip and nothing more."

Ouch. "Nothing more? What about crossing off every single thing on your bucket list? What about conquering your fear of flying? What about Aspen and the helicopter ride and all the *lessons*? What about losing your virginity and having non-stop raw dog sex for days? What about drinking lusty mouthfuls of my hot cum and crying my name when you were coming so hard on my big fucking cock? What about getting *married*? None of it *meant* anything to you?"

"Of course it did. But that doesn't change anything. I didn't expect this to last. I knew it wouldn't before we started. We both did. We'll just have to figure out how to have this ridiculous marriage annulled, and as soon as possible. It was a mistake, obviously. A foolish, drunken mistake." Her eyes finally meet mine and the sadness in them is like a fucking spear through my goddamn beating heart. "It's okay. People make mistakes all the time."

I pound my fists on the arm rests. "It's not okay! It's far from fucking okay. And it wasn't a mistake."

She frowns at my outburst. "Why are you acting like this?"

"Acting like what? Like it *means* something to me? Because it *does*, Lila. It *means* something. In fact, it means everything." Weirdly, it suddenly does.

But little Cold Heart over here doesn't even hear me.

"It means we had a good time. Which is now almost over."

"Fuck that, Sunshine. It's not over. Not for me. And not for you either. I *know* you. I know more about you than most people you've known for years do, admit it. You're my *wife* now."

Her eyes are wide, but then her resolve clicks back into place. That same shield she held in place when we first met. I was able to break through it, with fun and lust and hot sex. But reality is now knocking at our door, and she's bolted that motherfucker back into place. "Just because a cheap Vegas wedding certificate says we're married, it doesn't mean we actually are, in the true sense of the word. We both know it's a joke. I'm sure with all your connections and your m—" She stops herself from saying *money*. "…*connections,* you'll be able to fix it."

I grit my teeth, forcing myself to get a grip. "I don't want to 'fix' it."

She glares at me. "Well, *I* do. You can't be married to me against my will."

"You signed the paper just like I did, baby girl."

"Can't you just admit that we got drunk and it was a foolish thing to do and that we need to undo it?"

"No."

"You know what, Colton? I've made up my mind. I don't want you to come with me to Jessie's wedding. It's not a good idea. I want to be able to focus on her and I won't be able to do that if you're there. You're too…"

"Too what?"

"Never mind."

"Just say it."

She shrugs one delicate shoulder insolently. "Volatile."

"Volatile?" I laugh. "Honey, you have no idea how 'volatile' I am. And if you think I'm allowing my *wife* to go to a wedding unescorted that Troy Fucking Beckett happens to be attending, you've lost your pretty little mind."

"Can you stop calling me your wife? This is temporary. We knew that. We agreed on it."

"I didn't agree to anything, Sunshine."

"*God*, Colton." She folds her slim arms across her chest.

Her anger is so fucking cute I can hardly stand it. And I realize it fully in the moment: my Sunshine girl is my *wife*. Drunken escapade or not, this makes me stupidly happy.

I'm in love with my wife.

I mimic her, folding my arms and sulking. "*God*, Lila. You're so…" To play with her.

"So what?"

I wait until her eyes meet mine. "So beautiful it hurts."

But it bounces right off her forcefield, which seems to be extra thick this morning. "We should just appreciate it for what it was. We had fun, Colton. But that's all it was.

You can head back to your harem in New York and I'll—"

"I don't have a fucking harem. Those girls meant nothing to me."

"Well, *they* didn't get the memo. *I love you so much, Colton,*" she says in a breathy little voice like she's imitating them. *"I can't stop thinking about our night together, you beast.*"

I take a deep breath, trying to corral my patience. "Once again, I'll remind you that you and I had not yet met. What would you have preferred? That I remained a monk until the girl of my dreams—who I didn't know existed and I didn't believe *did* exist—sashayed into my life with her silver eyes glaring at me and her luscious pussy all wet and ready for me?" I glare right back at her, and my voice is low when I ask my next question. *"Are* you, baby girl? Are you ready for me now?"

"No. You escorted me to L.A. like you promised. Our pact is over now. You're off the hook."

Damn it. That fucking forcefield is impenetrable today. "Wrong. The pact just shifted up several gears, Sunshine. Because last night we took vows. To each other."

"Which I can't actually remember. It was the tequila talking. So you can get one of the limos you always have on call to take you to the airport as soon as we land and—"

"Jesus, Bailey. All this because of a couple of texts? I'm not the only one with a past, honey. We're about to confront yours head-on. And there's not a snowball's chance in hell I'm going miss a single second of that. I'm coming to the wedding with you whether you want me to or not."

"*No*, Colton. Please. Let's not make this harder than it has to be."

"You know what would make this harder than it has to be?"

"What?" she grumbles.

"Me crashing the fucking wedding like a goddamn caveman. Which is what I'll do if you don't take me with you. Do you think Jessie would enjoy watching a lunatic punching his way through the ushers on her wedding day, beating Troy Beckett to a pulp and then slinging his wife over his shoulder and carrying her away with him?"

More glaring. "You wouldn't dare."

"Oh yes I would."

She rolls her eyes, then she turns back to the view. "You're absolutely incorrigible, you know that?"

"*You* like me incorrigible."

"I'd like you a lot more if you didn't suddenly consider yourself the supreme controller of my entire life."

"I'm not controlling you, baby girl. I'm supporting you."

"Is *that* what you think this is?"

Her pout reminds me of that first day. Driving the open road, just me and her. But now the rest of the world is crashing into our perfect bubble. "Affirmative, Sunshine." In my best Terminator voice.

She huffs and turns away from me, but I see it: the barely-there hint of a smile. "Fine. But do *not* tell Jessie we got married. I want to be the one to do that."

"I can agree to that."

"*Finally*. He agrees to something. It's a miracle."

We're descending now. The sprawling green lawn and the wide-open ocean. The rows of white chairs and the arch, next to the beach, covered in roses. Tables have been set up. Waitstaff are milling around and a few people are already arriving.

We're in Malibu.

35

———

COLTON

Saturday
Malibu, California

THE HELICOPTER LANDS and a woman with blond hair sprints from the house and down the lawn to greet us. She could only be Jessie. She screams with excitement when Lila disembarks, jumping up and down and then bear-hugging her.

Then she holds Lila's shoulders and gives her a once-over. "Who is this glamorous New Yorker flying in on her private helicopter? Are you freaking kidding me with this shit?" She seems like she might burst with her enthusiasm.

And then Jessie's glance slides to me, becoming both intrigued and wary. "And who is this mysterious plus one? Wait a minute! I know you! You're Colton Maddox!"

It happens. I hold out a hand to shake hers. "It's a pleasure, Jessie. Hope you don't mind me crashing your wedding."

To Lila, she whisper-screams, "*Colton Maddox is your plus one! Holy shit!* How did that happen? You two *know* each other?"

"You could say that," I drawl, and Lila gives me a don't-you-dare-tell-her look.

"I've been waiting for *hours* for you to arrive," Jessie gushes. "I'm about to put my dress on and I *need* you."

"And now I'm here." Lila gives Jessie another hug. "I'm so excited for you." Lila places her hand on Jessie's stomach. She's barely showing. "Hey, little baby, I can't wait to meet you."

But if I'm not mistaken, Lila's expression has become distracted, like thoughts are going through her head she wishes weren't.

"Colton, I need to steal Lila from you for an hour, but they're setting up the bar over there and there are tables or there's a path down to the beach. Jacob and his brothers should be down there somewhere."

"I'll be fine. You two go ahead."

Lila's eyes meet mine, but there's nothing there I can take heart from. She's completely shut me out.

She and Jessie walk back up to the house, their arms around each other. I can hear Jessie questioning Lila about me and our road trip.

I watch them for a few seconds, feeling strangely

bereft. I'm trying to identify the feeling. *We haven't been apart for five whole days and I already miss her. My perfect little sweet, gorgeous addiction. I need my wife. She's mine.*

I need to get a grip.

Shaking my head because I've turned into a walking cliché, I do my best to cowboy the fuck up.

I'll see her in an hour.

It feels like an unbearably long time.

I start walking toward the bar when my phone vibrates in my pocket.

I pull it out, expecting it to be one of those bitches who made her mad at me, but it's a Zoom call.

From all three of my brothers.

Which almost makes me laugh. I answer the call. "Wow, a group chat. To what do I owe the astounding pleasure of having all three of my brothers interrogating me at the same time? Must be my lucky day."

"Where are you?" Alexander asks. I can see from the background he's by his rooftop pool.

"I'm sure you know from your tracking devices but I'll tell you anyway. I'm in Malibu."

"At the wedding?" Cash is clearly back in Hawaii. Palm trees frame the background and he's wearing a Hawaiian shirt.

"Not that it's any of your business, but yes. At the wedding."

"Dude, we're worried about you." Noah's in the Hamptons, out on his deck. The same deck where I first saw her. It's hard to believe that was only a week ago. So much has happened since then. "Tell us more about this girl you've run off with."

"She's the maid of honor." I offer the bare minimum. "She's helping the bride get ready."

"Are things getting serious between you two?" Cash sounds amused by this. Everything's amusing to him these days, which is a complete 180 from how uptight he used to be before he met Dusty. I finally get why.

Except that I'm even more uptight now. *Because what if she fucking leaves me?* "You could say that." Do I rip the band-aid off now? Or wait until I get back to New York? She made me promise not to tell Jessie, but she didn't say anything about not telling my brothers. Fuck it. "We got married in Vegas."

It's not often that all three of my brothers are speechless, especially at the same time. I almost savor the moment.

Alexander recovers first, shaking his head. "Very funny."

"We got married in that chapel right there on the strip. She's moving in with me when we get back to New York tomorrow."

Yes, I'm still ironing out a few of the details, but I'll get my way because it's the only end result I can live with.

Noah still thinks I'm joking. "Our lawyers didn't mention it, but I'm sure you did the only reasonable thing and drew up an air-tight pre-nup before vowing your life away?"

"Nope. No pre-nup. Just a pure love match that's going to last a lifetime."

Total silence.

"Still waiting for the punchline, Colton," Noah says.

"You want a punchline? Here's a punchline: I'm in love with her."

More silence.

Alex is still hoping I'm joking. "And you met her, what, a week ago?"

It's not *that* shocking is it? "What's the problem? Cash, Alex, you get it. We've had front row seats to your own total meltdowns and happily ever afters. Don't judge me. I found the girl of my dreams and now she's my wife."

Noah's incredulous, but Cash and Alex went down just as fast. "That's it, I'm coming out there. You've lost your mind."

"When you know, you know." I'm standing near a bench that looks over the ocean. I have a good view of the new arrivals as they get dropped off by the fountain beyond the tables.

Most of the guests have arrived and a few ushers are guiding people to their seats. Music is starting up.

And someone new has just arrived at the wedding.

I don't recognize his face because I've only heard his name in passing but I know exactly who he is.

He's a few inches shorter than me. He has brown hair.

I'm trying to gauge it and I guess he could possibly be described as handsome.

Troy Fucking Beckett.

The girl he's with is very L.A., with bleach blond hair, way too many fillers in her face and fake tits.

"I have to go," I tell my brothers.

They all look shell-shocked and concerned, but I'm too distracted to worry about it right now.

"Colton," Alexander says in his Big Brother voice, but my heartbeat drowns him out.

"We can talk about this tomorrow," I tell them. "I'll call you when we're on our way to New York."

"Colt—"

I end the call.

Because Troy Beckett's gaze isn't directed at his bimbo date.

He's riveted by the gorgeous little maid of honor in the tight, low-cut pink dress.

The one who's more beautiful than anything I have ever seen.

The one who's not wearing her wedding ring.

And that fucker is staring right at her.

36

"TELL ME *EVERYTHING*. Colton Freaking *Maddox*? How did you meet him?"

"How do you even know who he is?" I ask Jess.

"I follow him on Instagram."

"You *do*?"

"Lila, he's got, like, *millions* of followers. He's not on there that much, but he occasionally posts photos of himself, like on super yachts or at an event in some swanky night club in New York." I'm thankful she doesn't say it. *Surrounded by women.*

"I'll have to look him up." *Not.* Unless I'm overcome with sadomasochistic curiosity.

My stomach does that swooping thing again, which happens every time I'm reminded of Colton's playboy lifestyle, like I was so rudely at 3 a.m. this morning.

"I'll tell you everything, Jess—and I have a *lot* to tell

you. But it's going to have to wait. Right now we're focusing on you and your wedding." *Swoop.* A vague memory resurfaces, of Colton on one knee in the chapel in Vegas, sliding the Tiffany ring he chose for me—the biggest, shiniest one, that I also vaguely remember cost *two million dollars*. Surely I dreamt that. "This dress is so gorgeous."

Jessie's standing in front of a huge window with a view of the ocean down below. "It's more understated than my usual." The dress is a low-cut white silk sheath dress. My bridesmaid's gown has a similar cut but is pink and shorter.

"I love it. It's so flattering. And this *house*? Is this Jacob's?"

"Yes. Can you believe this?" Jessie has tears in her eyes. "My baby's room is going to have a view of the water." My stomach does yet another swoop.

I really need to google a few things.

Some of Jess's helpers and another bridesmaid arrive. The bridesmaid—I'm guessing because she's wearing the same dress as mine—is holding three bouquets. She has long honey-blond hair and green eyes. She's stunning.

"Lila, meet Lexi Black. Lexi and I met around a year and a half ago, just before you left for New York. She interviewed me about the short film I made—remember?—called *The City of Guardian Angels*. We've been hanging out ever since. Lexi's the artistic director and co-owner of Downtown."

Of course I've heard of Downtown. It's a trendy and wildly successful company that has its fingers in a lot of pies here in L.A. They have a movie studio, a lifestyle magazine, a publishing company and a bunch of other divisions. It's always being written up as one of the hip places to work in California.

"Lexi, this is my bestie, Lila Bailey. She ran off to New York for a while but I'm trying to convince her to move back home."

"So nice to meet you, Lila," Lexi says, hugging me. "I've heard so much about you."

Now that I think of it, Jess did mention Lexi to me during one or more of our conversations, and how she's married to some big shot who also happens to own the investment company Jacob works for. I was always so distracted and exhausted—or both—during our phone calls, I'd forgotten.

"Nice to meet you too, Lexi. Wow, artistic director of Downtown. That must be an amazing job."

She smiles. "Well, my husband is technically my boss. So I was basically allowed to create the job of my dreams. I got very lucky. But, yes, it is amazing. I love working there."

I like her immediately. She's humble and soft-spoken but you can tell she's not easily intimidated.

"You might have gotten hired because your husband is obsessed with you, Lexi," Jess says, "but you're also *very* good at your job. I've seen you in action first-hand and Downtown is lucky to have you."

Lexi laughs, smoothing one of Jess's errant curls. "Thank you, Jess. I like to hope so."

Jess's mom, Sandy, rushes into the room in a flowing yellow gown. She's basically my second mom and has been since Jess and I were tweens. Sandy's face lights up when she sees me and she gives me a huge hug. "Welcome home, honey. We missed you so much."

"I missed you too. And congrats, mother of the bride…and soon to be Grandma."

"Can you *believe* it?" Sandy obviously approves of Jacob. She's absolutely glowing with pride. "When are you going to find that special someone, honey?"

Jess answers for me before I get a chance to dodge the question. "Mom, her plus one is *Colton Maddox*."

"Who's Colton Maddox?" Sandy asks. At least *someone* on the planet hasn't heard of him.

"He's the youngest of the Maddox brothers," Jess explains, "the most eligible *billionaire* bachelors in New York."

"You're dating Colton?" Lexi hands me my bouquet of pink roses. "He knows my brother-in-law, Max. Max runs Black Investments, so he and Colton have a lot of contacts in common. Max is here at the wedding with his wife, Peach. We met Colton at an event here in L.A., just a few months ago."

"Oh." *No doubt with a different date. Or three of them.* Lexi's kind enough not to mention it.

And I'm relieved when Sandy changes the subject. "Let's go, girls. Jacob and his brothers are waiting. Rafe's ready for you downstairs, Jessie."

"Rafe?"

"Rafe is Lexi's husband," Jessie explains. "Since I didn't have anyone to give me away, he offered. It's so nice of him, Lex."

"He's honored to do it," Lexi says.

Of course I know the whole story of Jess's parents' bitter divorce, which happened a few years before we met. Jess hasn't talked to her father in a long time and I'm not surprised he's not invited.

Lexi hands Jess the biggest bouquet, of beautiful white roses.

"Let's do this," Jess says, like she's psyching herself up for her brand new life.

I kiss her cheek. "Congrats, sweetie. You deserve every good thing and the happiest happily ever after."

"You'll get yours next," she whispers back.

Swoop.

"There's Rafe," Sandy says breathlessly. The man she's staring at is waiting for us at the bottom of the staircase, dressed in a tux and scrolling on his phone. When he sees us, he slides his phone into his pocket and watches us walk down the grand staircase.

Rafe Black is a stunning-looking man. He's tall with

black hair and a dark, powerful vibe, like he's used to getting his way.

"You look beautiful, Jessie," Rafe says, but he's having trouble keeping his eyes off his wife. He can't quite hide how besotted he is.

Jessie introduces us and Rafe shakes my hand.

Then Jessie takes his arm and we get ready for the procession.

For a second I find myself wondering what it would feel like to be looked at the way Rafe Black gazes at his wife.

But I already know.

Because I see Colton in the second row and…he's looking at me the same way. Like he'd kill anyone who tries to come between us.

He's changed into a beautifully-cut suit. His blue shirt is open at the collar and shows off a hint of his powerful chest.

It's extremely connective to lock eyes with a man and know exactly what he *feels* like.

I still have bruises from the grip of his hands as he surged inside me.

I know what he tastes like when I swallow him in milky mouthfuls.

He looks so beautiful with his thick, breeze-blown hair and his fiery blue eyes.

I love him.

And I hate him.

Why does he have to go around breaking all those people's hearts and earning himself titles like the freaking King of Heartbreak?

He shouldn't be looking at me like he is right now. It's Saturday. Our time is up. Okay, the marriage has complicated things but I'm sure he can figure out how to solve the problem easily enough. Solving problems is what he does best.

It's probably jealousy holding him here. Some male conquest that means he can't walk away until he's proven a point.

I wish he'd spare me the agony.

I wish I'd realized that my period was actually due yesterday.

I wish he'd walk away before I'm too far gone to recover from him.

But it's too late.

Way, way, way too late.

37

It's a beautiful day in Malibu.

I've never seen Jessie so happy.

Jacob is waiting at the altar with his brothers. He has longish brown hair and he's wearing black-rimmed glasses. He's handsome in a slightly nerdy, wholesome way. He doesn't look nervous, and he doesn't look like he's second-guessing anything. He seems grounded and stable and like there's nowhere else he'd rather be. As he kisses my cheek, I can tell by the kindness in his brown eyes that Jessie *is* going to get her happily ever after.

I take my place beside Lexi and I can't stop crying as Jessie walks down the aisle.

Rafe lifts Jessie's veil and kisses her cheek. Jacob takes both her hands. Jacob and Jessie take their vows and exchange rings as they gaze into each other's eyes. It's the most romantic thing I've ever seen.

It doesn't matter that they've only known each other for a short time, or that it's a shotgun wedding and she's —almost—beginning to show. True love doesn't have a rulebook or a playbook. It looks a little different every time.

I think about how lucky her baby is, to have Jessie as a mom, and Jacob, with his kind eyes, as a dad. A dad who's not going to walk out on them with no forwarding address.

And I think about what my mom told me all those years ago.

Your father had trouble written all over him, but he was so beautiful I went with it anyway. I fell so hard for your father I didn't care that he would break my heart. I knew he wouldn't stick around, but I didn't regret a single minute of it. Because I'd never been so happy in all my life. And look at the gift he gave me, Lila Jade. He gave me you.

Lila Jade Danger Sunshine Bailey. I guess it has a certain ring to it.

Lila Jade Danger Sunshine Bailey Maddox, to be precise.

Maybe history is repeating itself. Maybe we do the things we do because we can't help ourselves.

Because I also knew Colton Maddox had trouble written all over him. And I also can't bring myself to regret a single minute of it.

Of course I'm aware that he's watching me. *My husband.* Grumpily. With a steely resolve I don't know exactly how to read.

It's not fair that he's the most beautiful man at this wedding, eclipsing Jacob and his handsome brothers like a god among men. Even Rafe Black isn't as…*Colton* as Colton Maddox.

"I now pronounce you man and wife," says the minister.

Jacob kisses Jessie and it's so sweet, I'm crying again.

A hazy memory resurfaces. Of *our* kiss. It was sweet too. *So* sweet, I felt it all the way down to my soul. And then it turned hot. *So* hot, Colton ended up carrying me back to our room where we couldn't get close enough fast enough and we consummated our marriage right there on that revolving bed in our swanky honeymoon suite in Vegas before we could even get our clothes all the way off.

Maybe I wasn't as drunk as I thought I was.

I wipe my tears as the music starts up. Lexi and I follow the newlyweds as part of their procession along the velvet carpet to the large white tent that's been set up with the tables under it. Candles have been lit and there are white roses everywhere.

People are congratulating the happy couple and the crowd starts moving into the tent. Some people are finding their place cards and taking their seats.

We all watch as Jessie and Jacob take to the dance floor for their first dance.

"Lexi, hi," a young woman says, and Lexi turns.

"Hi, Olivia." They hug and Lexi introduces us. "This is Lila Bailey, Jessie's maid of honor. Lila, this is Olivia

Jones. Olivia works at Black Investments, where Jacob works." I can't help but notice Olivia could easily be a supermodel. She's tall and waif-thin with long, lustrous dark hair.

"Nice to meet you, Olivia."

"You too, Lila. Lexi," Olivia's voice lowers. "I didn't know *Colton Maddox* was going to be here. Holy hell, I had the best night of my *life* with that guy after that party at Downtown a few months ago. But the bastard was gone by morning and never even called. I got his number through a contact, but he hasn't returned any of my texts."

My blood feels like it just turned to ice.

Lexi gets pulled onto the dance floor by Rafe before she can react to what Olivia just said.

I remember her name, of course. *Olivia. Kara. Bianca. Jemma.*

Olivia and I are both watching Colton try to make his way through the crowd. But Jessie intercepts him, laughing and pulling him onto the dance floor. "You *have* to dance with me," I hear her say.

Of course he does. Jacob is distracted now and she's the bride. She gets anything she wants.

"God, it's not fair, he's so fucking *hot*," Olivia says to me as we watch them dance. "That to-die-for asshole is loaded and *seriously* well-hung. He *told* me he wouldn't call me the next day, but of course I went with it anyway." She sounds almost unhinged about it. Almost like he broke her heart. "I would fucking *marry* him without hesitation if he asked me—but oh no, we all know he'll never commit. Which is a crying shame, if you ask me. I mean, just *look* at him."

I am looking at him.

"Oh my god, he's coming *over* here." Wild hope drips from Olivia's hushed murmur.

He doesn't even seem to see her. His gaze is fixed on me.

"Hi, Colton," says Olivia, watching Colton's arm loop itself around my waist. Possessively.

"Hey." He's somewhat dismissive, like he doesn't recognize her.

Is that possible? It was the *best* night of her life and he doesn't even *remember* her?

"Are you two together?" Olivia asks.

"We sure are," Colton confirms, pulling me toward the dance floor. "You have a nice night now. Come on, Bailey. Dance with me."

"Good luck, Lila," Olivia calls after us. "Don't fall for it!"

I wonder if he'll remember *me* three months from now. I picture us running into each other at some party in New York, a new girl on his arm and that same bored look on his face he just gave Olivia.

I pull away from him. "I can't do this." I start walking away. I have to, before he completely breaks me. I've been broken once, and it was my own fault. I'm not going to let that happen again.

"Lila—" Colton grabs my arm. I know how strong he is and I can tell he's taking care not to hurt me. I'm able to pull from his grip, and I stare up into stormy sapphire eyes.

"The problem is, Colton, I don't know if I can trust you. Trust is something I have trouble with anyway, and everyone keeps warning me that all you are is a mess of red flags. I don't want to dance with you. I don't want to talk to you. I don't even want to look at you right now. I want to go and enjoy my friend's wedding without it being all about you. So, please, leave me alone." I walk away, willing myself not to cry again. I can't handle his harem making its way into my bestie's romantic happily ever after. I need to get away from him.

But as I push through the crowd, I bump into someone.

Someone solid.

I'd completely forgotten he was coming. The one person I haven't been able to get out of my head for the last four years.

It's Troy Beckett.

38

"Hey, Lila."

"Troy." My voice sounds breathless. *He remembers me. He knows my name.* Once this realization would have sent butterflies through my entire bloodstream.

Now, it has…absolutely no effect.

He looks different. Older. Heavier. His bed-head of thick brown hair looks thinner. More groomed in a way that makes him look…tame. He doesn't look like a hotshot hockey player anymore. More like a middle management lawyer who doesn't win a lot of cases. I don't know why I say that, I have no idea if he wins cases or not.

The Troy in my memories was bigger and more imposing. He was almost god-like, built up by my dazed adoration. Now, he looks ordinary. Tired and unimpressive. His brown eyes are dull-looking, especially compared to the vivid blue ones I'm used to. And his suit is cheap-looking and doesn't quite fit.

"Wow, Lila," he says. "You look amazing." His gaze drops to my low-cut neckline.

Once this might have thrilled me. That he notices me. That he is, in fact, checking me out sort of…tactlessly.

"How have you been, Troy?"

"Oh, you know. Fine."

"You didn't end up going pro?"

"No." He runs a hand through his hair, regretfully. "Tried to, but couldn't quite get there." His face looks puffier than it used to, his body paunchier. I knew it so well, once. I kept a photo of him that had been taken for a magazine, shirtless and holding his hockey stick, in my wallet all through college. I gazed at it so much, it grew dog-eared.

God, what a waste.

"I'm a high school coach now," he says.

"I thought you were a lawyer."

"Yeah, well, that didn't quite work out. I got disbarred." He laughs. "One little mishap with some misappropriated funds and they never forgive you." Like it's a joke.

"Oh."

"How are things with you?" he asks me.

I have no desire to tell him anything about myself. My

hopes. My dreams. My regrets. "I'm a designer now," I hear myself say. It's actually true. It's no longer just something I say because it's a pipe dream. I've got over a thousand orders waiting to be filled that people actually want. *If I can do it without him, that is.*

"That's great." It barely registers. He's too busy staring at my tits. "You look really fucking hot, Lila. But then, you always did. Do you want to, like, go somewhere, just you and me? Let's take a walk and get to know each other better. I don't know why we didn't get together years ago."

Because you were too busy fucking every female with a heartbeat, maybe?

"Jessie said you're with Brittany now."

"Oh. Yeah." He says it sort of disinterestedly. "She's here somewhere. It's just a casual thing. Nothing serious. I'd ditch her for you any day of the week."

How romantic.

Troy reaches to touch a long strand of my hair, which he rubs between two of his meaty fingers.

I'm almost surprised by how repulsed I am by his touch, but before I can take a step back, a fist grabs his hand.

"Take your hands off my wife," comes the low warning, "or I will drop you like a fucking stone."

Troy pulls back, rubbing his hand with his other fist, like it hurts. "Dude, chill." Recognition dawns. "Hey, I know who you are. Harvard, right? Yeah, that's it. None other than the revered captain of the Crimson, Colton Maddox."

"Is there something you need?" Colton seethes darkly. The cold menace in his tone makes the tiny hairs on the back of my neck lift.

"Never quite made it to the NHL either, huh, Maddox? Sorry to hear about the knee." Jeeringly.

Was Troy always this obnoxious?

Yes, is the answer to that question.

My "crush" is officially and completely dead.

"Beckett," Colton says, his voice low. "I'm going to ask you nicely once and once only. *Fuck. Off.* Go back to whatever cubicle you crawled out of and do it now. If you don't leave this wedding immediately I will beat you to a bloody, unrecognizable pulp. And if you ever come near my wife again I'll fucking kill you with my bare hands."

"Wife?" Troy grins but takes a step back. "Where's the ring?"

Colton punches Troy in the face.

Oh my god!

Troy stumbles backward into a tall hedge.

A few people nearby look over at him, but the party has revved up several gears and most people are dancing or talking and haven't noticed. They might just think he's drunk a little too much.

Troy is holding his bloody nose. One of his false teeth has fallen out. When Colton takes another step toward him, Troy holds his palms up and starts walking away. "I'm going, I'm going."

"Hurry the fuck up."

As soon as Troy is out of Colton's easy reach, he calls out to me, "If you change your mind, Lila, you know where to find me."

I grip Colton's arm to stop him from going after Troy and it takes all my strength. "*Colton.* It's Jessie's *wedding.* Stop it right now."

"He fucking *touched* you." Like there's never been a worse crime.

"Barely. You didn't need to *punch* him."

"Of course I did. You're my *wife*." His eyes are blazing. "If he hurt you, I'll go after that fucker and kill him right now."

"He didn't hurt me. *Please,* Colton. Do *not* follow him. He's leaving."

"He fucking better be."

Troy pointed it out, that I'm not wearing my ring. But I notice then that Colton still is.

Of course I can't help comparing the two of them. Colton is dark and handsome and perfectly built. Glowing with male virility. Troy, as he slinks away, pulling his protesting date along with him, seems smaller than he used to be, in every possible way. Unformed, somehow. Like a guy who peaked a long time ago and who's now, slowly but surely, being consumed by his own shallowness.

Once, they might have been similar men. But now they inhabit different universes.

Jacob taps a spoon against his glass of champagne from the front of the tent. "Please take your seats everyone. Dinner is served. We've got a few speeches to make and then we'll get back to the dancing."

Colton's hand is on my back. Jessie's waving to me. My seat is next to hers at the wedding party table.

I don't know how to feel. I'd like nothing better than to escape and be alone for a while, to try to process this avalanche of emotion, but I can't let Jessie down. I'll just have to cowgirl up and act like I'm fine for an hour or two.

Colton escorts me to my seat and then finds his own, which is at a nearby table, between Rafe and a beautiful woman with red hair. She's obviously with the guy to her right, who looks so much like a slightly younger version of Rafe, with tattoos and a darker vibe, that he could only be Rafe's brother. He and the red-haired woman are obviously very much in love.

I guess this is a relief, maybe, that Colton isn't going to be flirted with again, but my emotions feel stone cold.

Troy is gone and the relief of being fully over him is indescribable. That chapter of my life is well and truly over and if I could rip it out of the book of my life and burn it, I would.

I somehow make it through the dinner and the speeches. I do my best to be fun for Jessie on her special night but I'm sipping 7-up instead of champagne because my stomach feels off—*and that other reason*—and all I can think about is how most of the women at this party are staring at him.

Olivia gazes at him from a far table with dreamy, unmasked lust. Like she'd allow him to use her all over again if she could only have one more night.

Meanwhile Jacob is giving a toast to his beautiful One and Only.

It sinks in, and I wish it wouldn't. But it's obvious what I have to do.

At this point, it's not going to be easy. But I refuse to put up with a relationship that isn't worthy of me. I spent years doing that and I can't do it anymore.

I hope he's better than Troy. *I know he's better than Troy. Of course he is. A trillion times better.* But the doubts and the warnings and the red flags are all I can see tonight.

I want my own fairy tale. And I won't share him.

I want something true and steady and *real*. Something that isn't going to topple over every time we run into one of his exes. Okay, yes, tonight's drama was more about running into one of *my* "exes" than his, but still. At least I only had one of them. Not so many we can't even go to a wedding on the opposite side of the country without running into at least one. Who even knows if there are others here.

There's only one solution that will ensure that my heart doesn't get smashed into smithereens like my mother's did. Some days I wonder if she died of a lifetime's worth of heart-brokenness. Maybe sometimes a person's body just gives up when they've had enough of it.

I love him.

But I love myself too.

I have to let him go.

39

As soon as the dancing starts up again and Jessie's back in Jacob's arms, I sneak away, making my way into the house and up the staircase to the guest room Jessie gave me. She begged me to move in for a while, for as long as I want to.

I swipe at my tears, hardly noticing the French-style windows that are open, offering a spectacular view of the ocean.

Damn him, that sadist.

It really did feel real.

Sloane wasn't kidding.

It's what he does. DO NOT GO THERE, GIRLFRIEND.

Why oh why didn't I listen to her?

Of course I wish I could believe there was more to this…*marriage* than there actually is. But I've also spent the last five days preparing myself for this exact moment.

This was *always* how it was supposed to play out. I knew that. I was *expecting* it.

He's free to go now and do what he does as a billionaire playboy from hell.

I'll figure out how to get the marriage annulled and I'll get my period any minute and I'll set up my business without him.

I find my phone and I google it through my tears. *Can you get pregnant if you miss two pills?*

Yes, indeed you can.

If you have missed two to seven pills anywhere in the pack, your protection against pregnancy may be affected. You should use back-up protection like condoms.

Coulda shoulda woulda.

If you've missed two pills or even one, make sure your partner pulls out until you've taken seven consecutive pills.

Bad advice and too late anyway. I was having too much fun to use any pesky back-up protection like condoms. I specifically told him we didn't need any. Pull *out?* Yeah right.

Instead of behaving like a normal, sensible person, I proceeded to throw all caution to the freaking wind and fuck him like a wild animal day and night for an entire week. In gondolas where any passing skier could have easily seen us. In private jets and luxury condos and in every goddamn penthouse suite across the continental United States.

An alert pings.

It's the one I set up in case I got another email from Eleanor Jaeger. I wipe frustrated tears.

Hi Lila,

I have met with the design team regarding your job offer. We've received several glowing recommendations since then and we've also had a thorough look through your website and social media platforms. We think you'll be a great fit for our team. I'm thrilled to be able to offer you the job of junior design associate here at RL. We'd like you to start as soon as possible.

In addition, Mr. Colton Maddox has been in touch and we're confident that we can also reach an agreement about a collaboration with you; this can be further discussed when you're back in New York. We'd like to meet with you both at your earliest convenience. Mr. Maddox mentioned Monday. How would 3:15 work?

I look forward to hearing from you soon. Congratulations, Lila. We're excited to have you on board!

Best regards,
Eleanor

Holy shit.

There's another alert too.

New orders: 1,695.

In addition to the other 1,283.

I sit down on the bed, covering my face with my hands and I cry like a baby. With happiness, because this is absolutely my dream job—and a collaboration is beyond any fantasy I've never dared to dream up. With nervousness and overwhelm but also excitement, because my business is suddenly exploding. With anger, because Colton Maddox has thoroughly infiltrated himself into every single corner of my life and now I don't know how to *un*-infiltrate him. With jealousy, because I absolutely *hated* the sight of that girl who he once had a fling with, staring at him with stars in her eyes, just like *I* do (when I'm not shooting daggers, that is). With fear, because *I'm late.* And I'm *married.* And this is all just a big mess that's way more than I can handle. *Without him.*

I miss him and I love him and I hate him so much.

I hear a loud bang outside the window.

"Fuck," says a deep, familiar voice.

None other than the devil himself is climbing through my open window, his jacket long gone, blood on his hand, his shirt ripped and his hair a mess.

He's the most gorgeous thing I've ever seen.

"What are you *doing* here?" I seethe, because I have a lot to figure out and I can't deal with more bombs going off in the middle of my life right now. Which he'll no doubt set off, like he always does.

Colton comes over to me in his disheveled suit porn and he falls to his knees in front of me, pushing my legs apart where I'm sitting on the bed, moving his big, warm body close to mine. He takes my face in his hands. "I love you, Sunshine. Please don't leave me. I love you so much. I'm sorry. Don't cry. I'm here now."

"I don't want you here!" Damn him! "You said you *couldn't* fall in love! So did Sloane. So did all the headlines about all those girls crying into their Cosmos. So did *Olivia*."

"None of that matters. I don't care about them. That was before. Before you. None of those people mean anything to me and they never did. I didn't love them or even like them. I can't remember their names or their faces. I know that might be hard for you to believe, but it's fucking true. I never called them back or wanted to see them again. I never *married* any of them or fucking fell in *love* with them, did I? No, Sunshine, I did not. But you know what? *Everything* changed the minute I saw you at that bar at Noah's with your silver eyes and your perfect little face. I fell *in love* with you. I think I loved you from that very first second, I just didn't know how to recognize it right away because I'd never felt anything like that before. Not even close. It was like getting struck by a Lila-Bailey-shaped million-watt lightning bolt and I was fucking *hooked*."

God, his eyes are blue. "How am I supposed to believe anything you say when you're flirting with every girl you see—*and who you've already slept with?* How, Colton?"

"I wasn't flirting. I told her to fuck off."

"You did not."

"I told her to have a nice night then I asked *you* to dance so I could get the fuck away from her. Same thing."

"In what, asshole-speak? I don't speak that language!"

He's looking up at me with so much…I don't know what it is. Passion. Tenderness. Devotion.

"Please, Colton," I whisper. *Please leave.* But I can't bring myself to say it.

"What do you want me to do, Lila? Grovel? Fine, I'll fucking grovel all you want. I'm fucking *sorry*, okay? I'm sorry I was a player before I met you. I'm sorry I had other unsatisfying relationships before I knew you existed. I'm sorry I was allergic to any kind of commitment at all because I never met anyone I remotely wanted to commit to. Until you. I'm sorry I didn't think I could ever fall in love because I was fucked up by my family tradition of fucking up relationships on an epic level and I felt like something in me was broken. I was *trying* to be an asshole because I thought it was baked into my DNA. But you proved me wrong about all of that, Sunshine girl. You blew it all out of the water with your lightning-bright eyes and your sweet, sassy mouth and the way you never take any shit from me. I suddenly wanted to be the best version of myself just because the *only* thing I want to do is be good enough for you. You're strong and you're smart and you're so insanely talented I just want to be close to you and bask in your glow. Do you know why I call you Sunshine, Lila? Do you?"

I shake my head.

"It's because you light up my life and you have from the very first second I saw you. And yes, I know that sounds cheesy as fuck but I don't fucking care because it's true. And you know what else?"

"What?" I whisper.

"I wasn't that drunk. I *wanted* to marry you. I'm sorry it was sudden and I shouldn't have done it like that, but all I could see was a chance to put a ring on your finger so I took it. But I want you to know that I'm going to give you the whole damn fairy tale, baby girl. I could read your mind today when Jessie took her vows. And *I* want that too. We'll have another wedding with all your friends and your perfect dress and everything you ever wanted. Then I'm going to take you on the most romantic honeymoon you've ever seen, to all the places you want to go. Just tell me what you want and I'll make it happen. I'm going to give you everything, Lila Bailey, because I can. *Now* I know why I've worked my guts out from day one. It's so I can make all your dreams come true. Please let me try."

I'm crying again because *oh my god.*

"Please believe me, sweetheart. Please don't doubt me anymore. I'll grovel and I'll beg and I'll buy you diamonds and sewing machines or whatever it fucking takes to convince you, every day for the rest of time until you believe me. I'm *all in*, Sunshine. I want you. I fucking *need* you. I *love* you, baby girl."

It's a lot. It's everything I ever hoped might be true. And so I do it: I make a choice. I decide to believe him.

"Lila?"

"Yeah?"

He hesitates. "You're not still in love with that douchebag, are you?" There's a note of vulnerability behind the question and it kind of makes me realize something. There are two hearts in this equation, not just one. "If you are, just tell me so I can kill the fucker."

"No. I'm not in love with him and I never, ever want to see him again. He's gross and awful and I wish I never met him."

"I'm glad you met him. Because it meant that all the stars aligned in a way that led you to me. Which isn't something I ever believed in before now. But when Lila Bailey walks into your life, you tend to start believing in magic."

I let my thumb brush along the stubble of his square jaw, letting his words rain onto my parched soul. And finally, start to seep in.

"That fucker was never good enough for you, sweetheart. I've been telling you that all along. He's a million miles from your league. I'm not in your league either, because your league is basically perfection, but at least

I'm a lot closer to it. Because I worship the ground you walk on, baby girl. And I'm going to prove that to you every single day starting now."

"Okay," I whisper.

"I know you've been holding back on me, and I don't blame you. I get it. I understand why. Your father left and it's hard to trust when something like that has defined your entire life. Then Sloane planted a whole lot of bull-shit in your head and most of it was probably true, but the thing that Sloane doesn't understand is that *you* are my absolute dream girl. And I didn't even know such a thing existed until you showed up. But then there you suddenly were and I just couldn't imagine letting you walk out of my life after you fucking *lit it up* like you did. That's why I wanted to drive you to California. I don't have any fucking meetings, baby. I never did. I just needed to spend all my time getting to know you and getting close to you because I was already addicted. And it just keeps getting worse. The more I have of my sweet, perfect Sunshine girl, the more I fucking need. And now I can't see straight I love you so much."

He's quiet for a second and I let my fingers smooth a strand of his thick hair. I say it quietly. "Don't break my heart, Maddox."

"Don't break mine, Bailey. You're holding it in your hands."

He's blurry now, but he still looks mind-numbingly beautiful. "Cole?"

"Yeah?"

"I don't think I was that drunk either."

A glimmer of hopefulness makes his eyes shine like blue embers. "We're still going to have the dream wedding. You'll move in with me and if you don't like the apartment I'll buy you something bigger. I'll buy you ten houses, wherever you want. Just say the word, Sunshine. I'll do anything. I just want you with me. Please, baby girl. Please believe me when I tell you that you're the one."

"Cole?"

"Yeah?"

"I forgot to take my pill two days in a row in Aspen."

He blinks up at me and I can see it takes him a second to compute what I'm explaining to him. As the information and all that it might imply sinks in and the only emotion I can see is pure, manly joy, it's then—right then —that I really allow myself to fall cataclysmically in love with Colton Maddox.

I remember what Jessie told me, about how Jacob's reaction when she told him she might be pregnant was happiness, and how it partly clinched her decision to marry him. I understand it now. Even if I'm not pregnant, the fact that Colton not only doesn't mind and isn't upset by that, but actually *wants* me to be…it's a very powerful thing. It's comfort and it's safety. Two things I was always starved for in my life, now being poured into it with the kind of force that feels remarkably like he just healed me.

"Do you mean to tell me that my wife might be having my *baby*?"

He's kissing me now and it feels so good to let go. To *allow* myself to love him. To fall, fall, fall.

Colton lays me back on the bed. He's peeling off my dress, sucking my nipples almost reverentially. "So it's settled then, Sunshine. No more arguing. My wife and my baby need the absolute best of everything. Lila Danger Sunshine Bailey Maddox, you need to be ready to be treated like the perfect angel you are. There is *nothing* you can't have."

"Cole?"

"Yeah?"

"I know you contacted Eleanor Jaeger again."

"Yeah, I did. Sorry about that, princess, but everyone needs to know how talented my wife is. We're going to turn your business into the next Big Thing."

"I got another sixteen hundred orders this morning."

"Yeah? Well, shit. We're going to have to hit the ground running tomorrow. The jet will be waiting for us at noon and I told Eleanor we'd meet with them on Monday."

"That's really taking another liberty, Maddox."

"You're my wife so I can take all the liberties I want if they mean your life is about to explode with all your dreams coming true. I'm about to take another major liberty right now, baby girl, so get ready for me. Obey your husband and lie back."

He's got my dress fully off now and before I can continue to protest, he licks his way down my body, kissing my pussy, eating me hungrily, lovingly. Feasting on my pleasure like he's so good at doing.

"Cole," I gasp.

"Yes, wifey?"

"Come here. I need you."

"I'm yours, baby girl." Colton lays himself over me, pushing his thick length all the way inside me, filling me completely with his hot, bursting beauty. "And you're mine."

"Cole?"

"Yeah?"

I hold his face and he's quiet for a moment, staring into my eyes as he possesses me fully and completely. I gasp the words and he says them at the same time.

I love you.

It feels so good to finally say it.

EPILOGUE

Five weeks later
Manhattan, New York

"Do you, Lila Jade Bailey Maddox, take Colton Benjamin Maddox to be your lawfully wedded husband—again?"

"I do."

"Do you, Colton Benjamin Maddox, take Lila Jade Bailey Maddox to be your lawfully wedded wife?"

"You bet your ass I do."

"Colton, you may kiss your wife."

Colton takes my face in his warm hands and he kisses me—and I mean *kisses* me. Right there in front of all our closest friends and family. "I love my wife," he murmurs, kissing me again.

In the end, we decided to have our second wedding right here at his—our—apartment. Colton told me he'd buy me a new house if I didn't like the one he has, but the minute I saw his apartment I fell in love with it. How could I not? It's the top two stories of an apartment building on Fifth Avenue. It has insane views of Central Park from its wall of windows. The outdoor patio has a pool, a jacuzzi, spacious living and dining areas and is over half the size of the apartment's lower floor.

The top floor is the master bedroom suite. It has the biggest bed I've ever seen. The wall facing the bed has a flat-screen TV that lowers to cover the entire wall with the press of a remote control button. There are couches and a coffee table in one corner that take full advantage of the view of the park and the Empire State Building. The whole room has the muted, soft tones of a very upmarket spa or oasis. The master bathroom is three times the size of my old apartment in Southampton and the view from the jetted tub is over Central Park. There's also a gym, two room-sized walk-in closets, a sauna and a home office.

The lower floor of the apartment has a huge open-plan living area and chef's kitchen, as well as three bedrooms, four bathrooms, a movie theater/den, a formal dining room, a private meeting room, and a bar/game room. Sliding steel and glass doors open fully to the outdoor living area, which doubles the size of the space.

Colton set up a meeting for me with an interior designer so I could make any changes I wanted. I told him this wasn't necessary but he insisted. He said he wants me to feel like it's mine as much as his. At the moment, the place looks like an extremely luxurious but also minimalistic bachelor pad. It's very New York but it also has a slightly Western flair. We're going to add a little more color and some art to the walls, but other than that, I love it just the way it is.

When I suggested I might need a table for my sewing machine and that I didn't mind where I put it, Colton told me he had another present for me. As a wedding gift, he bought the entire floor under our apartment. It's being renovated into a studio space, with mannequins and tables and *eighty* sewing machines, just like the one he bought me when we were in Aspen. New desktop computers have been updated with all the latest design software and synced to the new MacBooks. The studio has the same view of Central Park as the upstairs. There's even going to be a showroom with couches and a private fitting room where we can do fittings with clients.

Colton also put a new table with my new sewing machine in the home office on the top floor. I got so used to sewing all night in my old life, it's still sometimes a habit, and I often wake up with ideas I need to sketch.

But the few times I've done this, Colton always coaxes me back to bed, making love to me until I'm so sated I fall asleep again. There will be always be work to do, he says, and it can wait until morning.

My husband has cured my insomnia, with hot sex and comfort. And with the biggest gift of all: the absence of fear.

It's not just the money, although of course it's a relief to not have to worry about it. But even more than that, it's his devotion to making sure I'm both physically and emotionally swathed in his affection at all hours of the day and night. He hardly lets me out of his sight. If there's a reason we need to be apart, I have a security team and drivers. I told him this wasn't necessary but there was no talking him out of it.

You're my *wife,* is all he says about that.

He buys me the most outrageous gifts, every single day. My new closet is already full, not only with my own designs but with all the things he buys for me. I had to tell him to stop buying me jewelry because there's only so much a girl can wear. My favorites are the tennis bracelet and, of course, my diamond ring. For our second wedding he bought me a 24 karat pure gold band with *Lila Jade Danger Sunshine Bailey Maddox, love of my life* etched into the inside of it, which he slid onto my finger to join the diamond as we said our vows.

The vows we said in Vegas were written for us, chosen in a blur from the selection they offer at the Vegas strip chapel. This time, we wrote our own.

"Congratulations, love birds." Noah kisses my cheek

and gives Colton a man-hug. Noah is the brother I've become closest to. He's like a hot teddy bear, and is one of the nicest people I've ever met, in an unapologetically masculine kind of way which is hard to describe. He's funny and has a wry and quick sense of humor that's very often poking fun at Colton. This is something we both do, because we love him so much and we agree he deserves it. We've bonded over our playful banter. I absolutely adore him.

He's the only one of Colton's brothers who's still single and they make fun of him because he's a romantic and was supposed to be the one to fall in love first. We're all waiting for him to find his One and Only. There was a lot of discussion between his brothers when Noah disappeared for three days last weekend and no one knew where he was. He's being cagey about it so the whole family is speculating that he's finally found someone. We're all trying to get it out of him but so far he's admitted nothing.

"Where's your plus one?" Colton elbows him.

"None of your business," Noah smiles in a way that has me excited for him. He looks almost comically happy.

"That stupid grin on your face can only mean one thing," Colton tells him. "You got laid last weekend."

"Again, none of your business." Noah pops a bottle of champagne.

"Congratulations, gorgeous." Cash kisses my cheek, and Dusty hugs me.

Alexander and Ivy are next in line and they both give me a hug. Cash and Alexander are stunning-looking men. They're both easy to be around and it's been fun to get to know them. They're intense people and deeply intelligent. They're both so in love, it's entertaining to watch.

My arrival in New York as the new wife of their youngest brother was definitely a shock to begin with. They couldn't get over the change in Colton. I'm grateful that they've welcomed me into their family with open arms.

But it's Ivy and Dusty that I've become closest with. As an only child of a very busy single mother, it's been life-changing to suddenly have a *family*. Ivy and Dusty are both around my age and I absolutely *love* them. They already feel like my soul sisters and we spend as much time together as we can.

Dusty works at Invested Enterprises and—not surprisingly, since Cash thinks she walks on water—has a new executive role working alongside him. I loved hearing the story of how they met at a work conference in Hawaii, had a wild one night stand, then lost touch because they'd given each other fake nicknames. He searched for her for months until one day she showed up as the newest employee of IE. It's like fate brought them together and Cash is over the moon.

Alexander is equally besotted with Ivy. They met when Noah and Colton set him up with a fake date for a wedding, who happened to be Ivy. The two of them had never met before. He was supposed to be best man at the wedding and his evil ex was the wedding planner, so Alexander couldn't get out of it even though he tried. Ivy and Alexander ended up falling in love over that weekend and the rest is history. She's also pregnant. Ivy is a talented musician who has just recently hit the big time. She just released her latest album and it went straight to number two on the Billboard charts. Alexander is the most serious-minded, stoic CEO-type guy I've ever met, but the minute his gaze lands on Ivy, he completely melts. It's the sweetest thing.

Jessie and Jacob hug us next. Jessie squeals as she hugs me. She's really starting to show now and she's totally glowing with her pregnancy. Of course I had to have Jessie as my maid of honor and she's crying as much for me as I did for her. "I still can't believe you didn't *tell* me you were married to your plus one," she laughs. "And don't say 'what happens in Vegas stays in Vegas'. Because we both know that's not always true."

She's the only one I've told about the *other* thing that happened to us in Vegas. We're going to tell everyone else tonight.

Sloane is here too, with her new boyfriend Levi, who's possibly the nerdiest of the "nerd brigade", as she loves to call her work colleagues. She's a few inches taller than him, especially on the sky-high heels she loves to wear, but he follows her around like a lovesick puppy and I've never seen Sloane so happy.

The last five weeks have been an absolute whirlwind. Colton and I met with Eleanor Jaeger and her team the Monday after we got back to New York and I started working for them the following Monday.

Colton and I both negotiated the terms of my job and also the collaboration RL offered. I'm working one day a week in their design offices, two days a week in my own studio on our collab line—where two of their team members will join me—and one day a week on my own business.

My husband insisted I take Fridays off. He doesn't want me overworking, he said, especially in my condition.

We've hired a business manager to run my business, as well as sixty-four other new employees, including fifty dressmakers. With the new sewing machines and several other machines we purchased, the new team should be able to handle the production of all the new garments being made. Two experienced design coordinators will oversee the production to make sure it runs smoothly.

Twelve administrative staff will handle the orders, the billing, the marketing, the social media and so on. We thought about outsourcing some of the production work overseas, where labor costs can be a lot less expensive, but Colton's idea was that we could start by keeping everything in house as long as we can keep up with it, and that we'll see how it goes and revisit that option in six months. I agreed.

I work mainly on creating new designs, but at the end

of each day I get reports about every detail of the business, which is growing quickly. It really is a dream.

Colton and I met with his—our—lawyers and accountants to make sure the business plans and legal contracts are in place. He put a mind-boggling thirty million dollars into the company and legally owns five percent. Which means I own ninety-five percent. Of course we had a lot of discussion over this and I thought he should have a bigger share, but he said all the creative ideas are mine and, in the end, he got his way.

And it doesn't really matter. We're co-owners of everything now, including his six properties, which I didn't even know about until he suggested we go to Italy for our honeymoon, where he owns a hotel. Aside from the apartment in New York, he also owns a ranch in Austin, a villa on St. John—where he keeps his yacht— the hotel on the Amalfi coast, a house in Miami and a house in the Hamptons.

I couldn't believe that. I mean, I *could*, I was just… amazed that every single one of those places sound like dreams coming true.

My Instagram blew up and I now have over five million followers. Our new company made a profit of one million dollars in the past month, if you include all the orders we're in the process of filling.

What is this life?

Even more incredibly, *Vogue* did a feature article on me, wearing the wedding dress I designed and which I'm wearing tonight. It'll go to press next week—with *me* on its cover.

The media seems to have gone into a frenzy over the fact that I somehow managed to get Colton Maddox to marry me. *Many girls have tried and failed but according to one insider Maddox is "gaga" over his stunning new bride,* said one article Sloane insisted on showing me.

Of course my marriage has a lot to do with my newfound success, but the clothes themselves are also getting rave reviews. I'm getting a lot of press as "the" young new designer on the scene who "everyone in the know" wants to wear.

Sometimes I have to pinch myself.

As it turned out, the two pills I missed in Aspen were all it took. I bought a pregnancy test when we got back to New York and Colton and I watched together as those two blue lines didn't even hesitate. They glowed there together like they were *very* sure of themselves. To me it seemed sudden and not at all what I was expecting to be doing at this point in my life, but my husband was so overjoyed about it he immediately took me to bed and insisted on "breeding" me for an entire weekend. I told him I was already "bred" but that didn't seem to slow him down.

In my life, I've become so used to feeling alone and afraid and overwhelmed, the thought of having a baby at first seemed like a scary one. But I'm not alone now. I have my gorgeous, perfect, exasperating, fun, sexy, generous, loving rock of a husband. There's nothing Colton wouldn't do for me, which he proves to me every single day. I don't have to be scared anymore.

Colton's manly—and extreme—excitement over becoming a father has slowly allowed my new reality to sink in.

We're having a baby.

Will it be a little boy with dark hair and silver eyes like mine? Or a girl, with blue eyes like her daddy's?

For a while, I was viewing the whole scenario from the point of view of my past life, and so it took me some time to get used to the idea and to realize that this baby's life is going to be charmed and magical. *Not lonely or full of the fear of being abandoned or left behind.* The little family we're creating is so beautiful it makes me cry (I've been an emotional mess since I got pregnant).

Now, the love and protection I feel for this little thing growing inside me is *fierce*. Already, I love it with a passion I've never experienced before. It's a part of me. And it's a part of him, the beautiful love of my life. All the best of us combined and thriving with its little beating heart. The emotions are vast and life-changing.

Colton takes my hand. "Are you ready?" he asks, his voice deep and low. *I love his voice.* His thick hair. I love his face and his wide shoulders and the way he fills out his tux. Most of all, I love how strong and sure his grip is and the steadiness of his love. I love that he believes in me. I love that he's fixed me.

I nod, squeezing his hand. "I love you," I whisper.

He kisses me. "Love you more, Sunshine girl. You're my life." Then he taps a spoon against a glass of champagne sitting on a high table. Once he has their attention, he says, "I want to thank you all for coming and helping us celebrate our second wedding. We have some news to share with you all. Turns out I knocked up my wife in Vegas." All our friends and family exclaim and cheer.

"Is there something in the water around here?" Noah says, which leads to more cheering and attempting to coax information about whether he'll be adding to the gene pool any time soon.

The music starts up and Colton and I have our first dance, something we didn't get in Vegas. After the first dance, everyone joins in and we have the most beautiful night.

I didn't know a person could *be* this happy.

IT'S LATE NOW and all our wedding guests have gone home. Colton carries me to the elevator. We get to our bedroom suite and he sets me next to the bed and starts unzipping my dress.

He hands me an envelope. "One more wedding present."

"Another one? You need to stop giving me so many presents, Maddox." I say this at least once a day.

"Just open it, baby."

Inside the envelope is…a deed. *Venice Beach.* I gasp. "You bought my apartment?" My quirky little house in Venice, which is in desperate need of repairs and barely covers its own expenses.

"I bought the whole house. And the one next to it."

"You did?"

"It's all in your name. We're going to go there next weekend and meet with some renovations teams. You're going to turn it into exactly what you always wished it could be. Or you can leave it like it is, but I saw photos and I think it needs an upgrade. We need a house in L.A. so we can go back and visit when you feel like it. When you miss it."

"Cole." The deed is blurry through my tears. I don't even know why I'm crying again. It's just…it's the nicest thing anyone could have done for me.

"Hey." He wipes my tears with his thumbs and kisses my lips. The kiss is erotic in its lightness. "You're all right now, sweetheart. I'm here. I'm going to put you to bed and hold you close all night long until you don't feel scared anymore." Colton knows better than anyone that I still wake up sometimes and can't go back to sleep because the loneliness sometimes resurfaces. I never really even knew it was such a big part of my psyche until he filled it.

He helps me step out of my dress then he carefully hangs it over a chair. Then he takes off my bra and panties, like he's undressing a child. I could stand still and never do anything and Colton would do it for me. And we like to sleep naked.

Sometimes he's almost overly careful of me because he wants me and our baby safe.

But pregnancy has not only made me crazily emotional, it's also made me extremely…hot for my husband.

I know how to get what I want. I had a good teacher.

So I get onto the bed on all fours, crawling toward the pillows, looking behind me to see him watching me. "I need some more detention from Professor Berserker. It's my wedding night, after all. Come here, husband."

I don't need to ask twice. Colton's clothes drop to the floor and he's behind me, his strong, rough hands on my hips, his mouth already there, burrowing and feasting. I arch my back and let my knees slide wider, laying my head on a pillow, offering myself to him in every possible way. He's mine.

He makes me come with his mouth and then he lays his body over mine, his thick cock thrusting into me from behind as his hands guide my body into the position he demands. He's strong but tender, relentless but reading every moan and every gasp, giving me exactly what I need, as he drives into me, thick and deep.

Colton murmurs into my ear as the waves of pleasure start to overwhelm me. *"I love you, Sunshine girl. I love you so much. You're the most beautiful thing that's ever happened to me. I'm going to spend my whole life giving you pleasure and lots of babies and making sure you're safe and happy and all your dreams are coming true."*

And that's exactly what he does.

❦

Thank you so much for reading **Billionaire Devil**. If you enjoyed this book, please consider leaving a quick review or rating on Amazon.

Want to see what happens with Colton and Lila two years down the road? Get the free bonus epilogue: https:// BookHip.com/NLSAMRN

Below I've included the first chapter of **Billionaire Romantic,** the next book in the **New York Billionaires** series, starring Noah and Lucky.

I've also included a sneak peek of **XOXO I Love You,** a super-steamy obsessed hero billionaire romance, starring Rafe and Lexi.

xoxo,

Julie

Please come join my Facebook reader group, Julie

Capulet's Romantics, where I share cover reveals, insider info and we discuss all things romance!

Sign up for my newsletter to receive my free bonus content and get access to sneak peeks and exclusive giveaways!

Visit my website @ www.juliecapulet.com

Noah Maddox is a hot as hell billionaire who, as it turns out, is impossible to resist. He's also an absolute beast in bed...

Details I didn't know, of course, when my best friend sets me up on a blind date with Noah "Steel". It's obviously a fake last name. But then again, so is mine.

From the moment we meet, we're like magnets who can't resist each other's pull. The blind date lasts all night. Then the entire weekend. The best of my life, if I'm being honest.

But when Monday morning comes too soon and we both have to go back to work, I'm shocked to find out that my sexy blind date is actually Noah Maddox, the evil CFO of the company that's planning to take over my late father's struggling investment business. The takeover will cost me my job, every cent I have and, worst of all, my beloved apartment.

If only I hadn't spent the weekend in bed with the devil, cashing in my V-card and throwing all caution to the wind…because how does a girl say no to all those mind-blowing orgasms?

I thought he was perfect. Until I find out he's not the sweet-and-dirty-talking dream man I fell for at all, but a shark who's about to take everything I have.

It's entirely Noah Maddox's fault that my life is now in shambles. I don't care how drop-dead gorgeous he is, the man is obviously a nightmare.

So why is he obsessively trying to prove to me that he's the most devoted, head over heels billionaire in New York?

And how am I supposed to resist the hot romantic who has already stolen my heart?

Billionaire Romantic is a steamy billionaire romance starring a hopelessly romantic CFO and the sassy blind date he'll do absolutely anything to keep. Each book in the New York Billionaires series is a complete standalone with a sexy fairy tale HEA.

New York Billionaires

Chapter One

NOAH

As I weave my Ducati through the usual madness of New York City traffic on a Wednesday morning, I make a decision.

It's safe to say I'm different to my brothers in many ways. My brothers always describe me as the "nice" one out of the four of us. The "romantic" one. The one who's most likely to believe that something like true love actually exists, despite the train wreck of our parents' legacy. I'm the one who supposedly still has faith that good things can happen. According to my brothers, they're the cynics and I'm the optimist.

But the universe has a twisted sense of humor. Because over the past few months, all three of my cynical-to-their-bones brothers have fallen head over heels in love.

I'm happy for them. I'm over the moon that fate has somehow proved them wrong. That each one of them is capable of falling so hard and so fast that all three of them had rings on the poor girls' fingers before they even knew what hit them—and, in at least one case, or possibly more, they've already knocked up their wives-to-be because they're incapable of thinking about anything except getting that particular job done.

And I, the only one of us who isn't—at least wasn't—allergic to the words "relationship" and "commitment," am still thoroughly unattached, disillusioned as fuck and pissed off that my "optimism" has obviously jinxed me.

Here I was, thinking it was worth waiting for The One. I'm the only brother who hasn't relentlessly slept my way around the island of Manhattan because I idiotically convinced myself that I'd prefer to actually *feel* something for the person I'm having sex with.

No longer. That game plan has done nothing except provide me with endless disappointment.

The decision locks into place, right here on the corner of Fifth Avenue and East 34th Street.

I'm no longer going to wait for that one elusive, perfect woman who never shows up for me. My brothers can drool all over their one-and-onlies, freeing up the New York dating pool for yours truly.

Fuck it.

I'm going to go out and find myself some unsuspecting girl with fake tits and dollar signs in her eyes, like they all seem to do. I'm going to stop pretending that the woman of my dreams exists.

And I'm going to get fucking laid.

It's been way too long.

It's not that I *can't* get women to fall in love with me. I can, very easily. The only problem is, most of them are after me for my looks or, obviously, my money. My brothers and I happen to be some of the wealthiest and most successful investors and businessmen in New York

City. So was our father and so was our grandfather. It's well known that a shitload of zeroes are attached to my many bank accounts, which of course is a super-powered magnet for every woman with a heartbeat.

Being the fool that I am, I've mostly avoided meaningless sex because I was hoping I would find…well, *meaning*. Love. *True* love, even. The kind of love you'd kill or die for. The kind that completely blinds you to everyone and everything except the one true love of your life.

The kind of love that staunchly, relentlessly eludes me.

Unfortunately, my brothers know me too well. I *am* a fucking romantic. I *crave* it. I want to fall in love so badly I feel like I can't breathe some days. Like there's a huge hole in my heart and my life that only she—a phantom lover who probably doesn't even exist—can fill.

It's depressing. And infuriating.

Where the fuck is she?

I've clearly got it all wrong. The only people around here who are falling in love are the die-hard skeptics who don't even believe in it.

I pull my Ducati into my parking space in the private parking garage under our building so abruptly I can smell burnt rubber.

It's another point of difference between me and my brothers. All three of them prefer to be chauffeured around in their limos. I like the chaos of the traffic. The soundtrack of the city reminds me that there's a world outside our glass box that doesn't give a damn about our investment portfolios or our share values.

Not being a slave to city traffic also means that on mornings like today when I'm earlier than usual, I can stop in to get coffee at the coffee shop around the corner from our office that has proven to be by far the longest relationship of my life.

It's the first place I became a regular when I started working in the city, long before Cash poached me to be CFO of his company.

Our family company, Maddox Equities, which owns its own city block including the skyscraper that houses the company's headquarters, is directly across the street. I started working at Maddox Equities the day after I graduated from Harvard, as we all did. As we were all expected to do, whether we chose it or not.

Alexander, the oldest of the four of us, still runs the family business. It was always his destiny to be CEO.

Cash and our father butted horns too often to work together easily and Cash wanted out. Since there were more crazy family dynamics than even *I* knew what to do with, especially before our father died—and I'm considered the "diplomat" and the steadying force in our family—Colton and I jumped ship as soon as Cash offered it.

The skyscraper across the street from the main hub of my family's empire happened to be for sale. So we bought it and began building Invested Enterprises from the ground up. It's been incredibly hard work. We've worked our guts out and weathered more than a few storms, but it's all been worth it. Business is most definitely booming.

So the Daily Grind and I go way back.

I pull off my helmet and secure it to the bike, glancing at the watch Alexander insisted on gifting me last Christmas. A Rolex. It's not usually my style to wear half a million dollars on my wrist but even I have to admit it's a nice watch.

It's almost nine.

As I make my way out onto the street and around the corner, I vaguely notice as traffic stops and the rush of the crowd hurries across the crosswalk. But something's holding them up. A frail-looking elderly woman wearing a bright yellow headscarf is being very nearly trampled by corporate assholes. She's hunched over a cane, barely a third of the way across. The light's about to change.

Despite my mood, I can't help myself. I walk over to her. "Excuse me, do you need some help?"

Her eyes narrow as she stares up at me. "If you're thinking of mugging me, Buster, I don't carry cash and my diamonds are locked up in my son's safe in Hoboken."

I like her feistiness. "I promise I'm not going to mug you. I'm Noah. Let me help you across the street."

"Enid," she replies, sizing me up and apparently finding me trustworthy enough. When I offer her my arm, she takes it.

We start our slow, slow journey across the street. The traffic light turns green before we're even halfway and horns blare. Enid grips my arm tighter, using my support and her cane to take another step. "If I wasn't holding onto you, dear, I'd be giving those morons the finger."

This makes me smile. "Maybe let's not give any pre-caffeinated New Yorkers the finger until we get you safely across." A driver revs the engine angrily and screeches past us.

"Assholes. Everyone is always in such a rush these days," Enid sighs, continuing at her snail's pace.

"Big plans today, Enid?" I ask, in an attempt to distract her from the cab driver who's wound his window down specifically to yell obscenities at us.

"Oh, you know, the usual. Judge Judy and Jeopardy with my sister Mabel, then maybe I'll go shoplift some Tums later. Just kidding, they're locked up like Class A drugs these days. Mabel is ninety, a spinster and ornery as hell, but she insists I visit her every morning. And I have to be nice to her in case she dies first. She keeps threatening to leave her fortune to her hairless cat Nigel."

I didn't think I was capable of laughing this morning but Enid has proven me wrong. "Quite the agenda you've got there, Enid."

We finally reach the other side.

"Are you going to be okay getting to your sister's, Enid?"

"Oh yes, I'll be fine from here. I've walked to Mabel's

every day for fifty-seven years. I could do it blindfolded." Enid steadies herself. "I'm sure you have places you need to be, looking like you do."

"I'm happy to help if you need it."

She squints up at me. "Whoever gets to keep *you* is one lucky lady. If only I'd met you when I was a looker in my twenties."

"You're still a looker, Enid."

She cackles nostalgically. "And you're a good liar. And very charming. Not to mention tall, handsome and well-dressed. And *built*, good Lord. Tell your lucky lady she better appreciate the catch of New York City." She pats my arm and begins shuffling away. "Have a good day, Noah. And thank you."

"My pleasure." I watch for a moment as she makes her way down the street, concerned she's going to be knocked over by a guy who's reading on his phone and not looking where he's going. But Enid's ready for him. Before he can barge into her, she gives his leg a well-aimed thwack with her cane. He jumps back, letting out a little howl. Limping and glaring, he gives her a wide berth as he hurries away.

Enid's going to be just fine.

I make my way back across the street and hear someone yelling my name. Colton steps out of his limo. "Tell me you did *not* just help an old lady cross the street."

I don't bother confirming or denying.

"Dude, you're a walking cliché," Colton laughs.

"And you're an ego-inflated asshat, but we love you anyway." We make our way inside the Daily Grind.

"Hi, Noah." It's one of the baristas who knows me by name. Because I have to give a name for my order. I make a point of asking theirs because I come here a lot and it seems like the right thing to do. I happen to know her name is Elli with an i, because it's how she introduced herself. She blinks blue-tinted eyelashes at me.

"Hey, Elli with an i."

Her smile is doe-eyed. Colton elbows me but this girl is so not my type. She has piercings all over her face and a goth look that's never really floated my boat. "Can I get you your usual, Noah?"

"Make it three, please."

They always get my order first, no matter how long the line is.

Elli hands me my coffee, making a point of placing it in the cardboard three-cup-holder so I can see she's written her number on the side. "Thanks, Elli."

She bites her lip, blinking at me again. "Bye, Noah. See you again soon, hopefully."

We get out to the street and Colton is still laughing. "Jesus, she might as well have had 'Fuck me' tattooed across her forehead. You should call her. Getting up close and personal with a chick with *that* many piercings could be interesting."

"Give it a rest, Colton."

"Just go with it, bro." Colton keys us into our private

elevator. "You're too wholesome for your own good." Not entirely true. There's a side to me my brothers definitely know nothing about. "Unless the rumors are true," he smirks.

I don't bother taking his bait. "You're in a good mood," I observe.

"It's called getting laid, Noah. You should try it sometime." Ever since he met Lila, Colton has been insufferably *happy*. Cole was always the fun-loving Casanova of the pack of us, but now there's a new, fervent light in his eyes which, considering both his past and his usual devil-may-care attitude, is probably the best advertisement for true love I've ever seen.

"I'm not taking your place as the family fuck-boy, so you can drop it," I tell him. Then again, that's exactly what I just made a decision to start doing.

The elevator dings and the doors slide open. Directly opposite the doors is one of our main boardrooms, which Cash happens to be walking into. "Better than the Maddox Monk," Colton replies.

Which of course is all the invitation Cash needs to join the conversation. "How's the vow of celibacy going?"

"Fuck off," I tell him, handing him his coffee as I walk past him into the boardroom.

"Good morning to you too." Cash smiles at how easy it is to rile his usually Zen brother. He sets his coffee and some folders at the head of the table, pulling out a chair. "The mood hasn't improved, I see."

"My mood is none of your—or his—business. Let's just get on with the meeting you insisted we come to."

More grinning, but Cash tunes in to the fact that I'm really *not* in the mood for their rainbows and unicorns happiness right now—because they happen to be right. My epic dry spell is getting *way* out of hand.

Lexi

Somehow I got an interview at Downtown, the "It" company of the decade. Sure, I've heard the rumors about the CEO, Rafe Black. How elusive he is. How rich.

How *hot*.

None of it prepares me for what's about to happen. The white-hot lust at first sight. The attraction that sweeps me off my feet and tests the limits of what I can handle...

Rafe

Goddamn it all to hell. The second that goddess walks into my office, with her sultry green eyes and her body like something out of my wildest fantasies, I'm obsessed…

I'm whipped like nothing I've ever known. I've been a high-achieving Type-A control freak every second of my self-made billionaire life.

But *this*. This *girl*. She makes me want to f*ck everything up. Because she feels so unbelievably good that nothing else matters…and I'm already addicted.

LEXI

I step into the elevator. And I do my best to ignore how seriously unlikely it is that I'll actually *get* the job I'm about to interview for. I have zero experience, since I only graduated about a month ago. My English degree from Stanford will (hopefully) help, and I graduated (sort of) near the top of my class. But this is *Downtown*, the "It" magazine of the decade. It isn't just a magazine, but a *scene*, with its own fashion label, lifestyle website, pop culture news blog and even a film production company.

My roommate came across the ad for CEO's assistant

online only a few days ago. Given the glam factor, it almost seemed strange to stumble across it in a place like that. I would have expected Downtown to recruit from more exotic locations…like in Silicon Valley garages or on French Riviera yachts.

Anyway, I'd applied, and, by some miracle, I actually managed to get an interview. I knew every wannabe in California would be dying to get their résumés seen. Not because we have a lifelong dream to be a CEO's assistant, not at all. But because an underling job like this one might lead to other opportunities within the company— and it's a company every graduate on the planet would sell their teeth to work for. You knew that if you ended up working there, you'd not only rub shoulders with the rich and famous, but also maybe even *become* one of them. They were known for hiring young, hot, über-talented geniuses. Which kind of makes me wonder what *I'm* doing here, but I've decided to just go with it.

As much as I'd like to think I have half a chance, I also know it's definitely a long shot. The email informed me that I'd be meeting with an interview panel. I can picture it now: ten ultra-trendy, over-confident hipsters and one…me.

I take a deep breath.

At least I look the part. As I check out my look in the reflection of the mirrored elevator walls, I can't help but notice that my new makeover has definitely done wonders.

As soon as I arrived in L.A., my roommate Tess dragged me along on a two-day shopping spree and pampering frenzy. Tess runs a make-up and fashion blog that has around fifty thousand followers, so I figured I should probably take her advice. Now, I have a stylish new haircut. I've been massaged, waxed (and I mean *everything*), glossed and groomed to within an inch of my life.

New city, new priorities, according to Tess. *You're no longer a student, you're a hot young urban professional living the dream in the City of Angels.* I'd argued that I wasn't a professional until I actually *landed* a job, but she laughed that detail off as a technicality. *Looking like you do, it's only a matter of time. Employers love hot, and you, my sweet Lexi, are the total package.*

We're about to find out if she's right about any of the above.

I try to let Tess's enthusiasm rub off on me as I stare at my reflection. My long blond hair falls in sleek waves. Highlights of platinum catch the light. Those colorists really know their stuff. My eyelashes have been lengthened by some carefully-applied mascara, also by Tess. A light green silk wrap dress with a short, flouncy skirt hugs my curves and emphasizes the green of my eyes. I wondered if the dress was too fitted and the skirt too short for a job interview, but Tess ordered me to get real. *This is Downtown, honey. They work in bikinis half the time.* Which is true, apparently. She showed me an article about it. Their offices are cutting-edge, modern, ultra-hip and even have pools, swim-up cocktail bars, loungers and tread mill work desks.

To-die-for heeled Miu Miu sandals with feather detailing complete my outfit. The shoes cost a fortune even at seventy percent off, but Tess said I really need to up my fashion game if I want to be taken seriously. I begrudgingly admitted she's right. My wardrobe consists mostly of sweatshirts and jeans—the more comfortable the better, since I've spent the last four years studying 24/7, not to mention the years before that, which were much worse.

Tess also pointed out that my scary new credit card bill will spur my motivation to get earning as quickly as possible. I didn't bother telling her I have that motivation anyway, cringing every time I think of my gargantuan student loan.

Anyway, look out, Downtown, here I come.

The elevator pings and the doors slide open. I enter the lobby. It's all glass and chrome and is positively glimmering with bustle and excitement and glamor. A lone receptionist sits behind a tall desk with a massive print of the L.A. skyline mounted on the wall behind her. There's an etched glass wall next to it that gives a tantalizing glimpse behind the scenes: busy people and racks of designer clothing, desks and film promotion posters. Sliding doors are open, offering views of the pools and palm trees. Music is playing. Everything about it screams *YOU WANT TO WORK HERE.*

The receptionist watches me approach.

"Lexi Blondeau?"

"Yes, hi. I'm scheduled to meet with the interview panel at four thirty."

"Actually, Ms. Blondeau, something came up. You'll be meeting with Mr. Black himself."

Mr. Black.

According to Tess, Rafe Black is famous for his reclusiveness and also his ruthlessness when it comes to business. He's also rumored to be…ridiculously hot. Either way, I'm relieved. A one-on-one meeting sounds a lot less intimidating than a full-blown inquisition.

"He's expecting you," says the receptionist. "Go right on down this hallway. And take the elevator up to the 17th Floor."

The receptionist's phone rings and she points down the white marble hallway before she answers it. I want to ask her what number Mr. Black's office is, but she's already distracted. His door will probably have his name on it, I figure.

Fine, is what I'm thinking. *I can handle this. No problem.* Most likely, he'll be some aloof executive who will run through his list of questions, loftily mutter a we'll-call-you-if-we're-interested dismissal, then send me on my merry way. I already know it's a phone call that'll probably never come. I'll wait a few days before reality sets in, while I meanwhile scour the internet for something slightly more realistic.

I walk down the hallway, and press the button for the elevator. It might be a private elevator. It's not the same one that accesses the lobby of the building.

The elevator swooshes up in that ultra-slick, barely-noticeable way, which gives me vertigo. I reach the 17th floor in about three seconds flat. I teeter unsteadily into a hallway, which has floor to ceiling windows and a killer view of the hazy L.A. skyline, all the way out to the ocean. I take a few seconds to let my equilibrium settle more or less back into place.

So the 17th floor is the *top* floor. There are a couple of swanky leather chairs bathed in sunlight.

Everything is so *luxurious*.

I can't help thinking this would be a perfect place to sit and read a good book while appreciating the view. But of course I'm here for one reason only. To kowtow to the mysterious Rafe Black.

There's only one door. So Mr. Black is the *only* executive with an office on the 17th floor. Well, he *is* the CEO, after all. And the founder of Downtown. And now that I think about it, Tess might have mentioned that he owns at least part of the building. Or maybe the whole thing.

I knock on the door.

And I wait. I check my phone. 4:27.

It might be a full minute before the door opens.

He stands there, wide-legged, silhouetted by the sunlight streaming in from behind him. And—*whoa*—if I was expecting an ordinary, work-addled managerial type,

I was sorely mistaken. *Hot* doesn't even begin to cover it. In fact, it takes a few seconds for my eyes to adjust to… just *how* gorgeous Rafe Black actually is.

He's tall, and big. His dark hair is thick and more unruly than you might expect from a CEO. He's wearing an extremely well-cut suit but doesn't seem entirely at ease in it, as though it constricts a barely-controlled wildness that's a definite part of his vibe.

"Mr. Black?" My question comes out breathy and cautious.

His eyes are a deep shade of dark, smoldering blue and have a glint in them that's kind of…electrifying. He assesses me, more than a little cockily. But there's an edge to him, and I get the feeling I've somehow caught him off-guard. He's more tan and rugged-looking than any businessman has a right to be. It wouldn't shock me if he spent most of his time sailing the Southern seas or wrangling bucking broncos in the hot sun. I don't know why I say that. He's got this outdoorsy look, which sort of clashes with the ultra-modern lines of his office and his building. He's too masculine to be called beautiful but it's a word that comes to mind. And it's the kind of over-the-top male beauty that'll hit you…*right there.*

Yikes.

As he opens the door in an invitation for me to enter, his eyes trail intently across my face and my body.

Wow.

This is already…*intense.*

"Ms. Blondeau." His voice is deep, tinged with bass notes that sound almost like a purr. "Please, come in."

I hesitate. Some deep instinct flickers. For a second I wonder if he might be dangerous.

My hesitation seems to amuse him, and he barely cocks his head and scalds me again with those smoky eyes, like he's challenging me. *I dare you.*

The brief, deep-rooted warning is overridden by something else. A curiosity. A pull that feels more complicated than mere attraction.

What I'm thinking is…*I don't care if he's dangerous.*

I can't quite tear my gaze away from his brawny shoulders and his burly arms, where the muscles are defined even under the layers of his clothing as he clutches the edge of the door with gripping, brutal fingers. As alone as we are, I can't help feeling like I'm walking into Rafe Black's lair. *No one will hear you if you call for help.*

I step into his office, and feel a small rush of anxious excitement as he closes the door firmly behind me. *Is it hot in here?* The automatic lock clicks into place. I can feel my heartbeat in strange places.

"You're very punctual, Ms. Blondeau. I like that."

A good start, maybe. "Please. Call me Lexi."

"Lexi." My name, spoken in that molasses-rich voice, sounds strangely erotic. Almost indecent. I find myself wondering what it would sound like…in the dark…as a growl or even a plea as I take his…

What the hell?

I force myself to focus on the reason I'm here: To. Interview. For. A. Job.

This is not like me at all. I'm a clean-cut girl, punctual, reliable to a fault. Socially awkward. And embarrassingly inexperienced. I have never in my life felt such an instant and desperate pull of white-hot lust.

Damn you, Tess! Why did I let her talk me into wearing such a short, clingy dress? I feel like my clothes are entirely sheer, like Rafe Black is somehow penetrating them with his predatory appraisal as he watches me.

"You found me without too much trouble?"

He's making small talk, to put me at ease, maybe, but I get the feeling that Mr. Black is perceptive, freakishly so, and that he's somehow able to read me very easily. Too easily.

Small talk isn't something I'm good at, but it comes more easily this time, for some reason. "Yes, well, I was glad there was only one door."

He smiles, revealing perfect white teeth.

Holy hell. He really is…very attractive.

"I bought this building specifically for this office," he says. "I prefer total privacy. I like the feeling of being removed from the rest of the world. What do you like, Lexi?"

So he does own the building. "Uh…" *Is he teasing me?* "We had to take personality tests in one of my psychology classes and the results said I'm ninety-three percent intro-vert. So, yes, I can relate."

"We have something in common, then." His eyes do that sparking thing again and...*oh, no...I'm blushing.* "No one can access this floor at any time without my permission."

"Oh." I already know I'm locked in here with him. That no one can get in and that I can't get out unless he *lets* me out. I also know that if I don't *un*lock my eyes from Rafe Black's sinfully perfect mouth right now, I'm going to do something I'll probably regret.

I find myself desperately hoping my reactions to him aren't somehow...*detectable.* My nipples might barely be visible through the thin silk of my dress, which has a sort of light, built-in bra that might not be fully up to its job. My skin feels warm and flushed, and I'm getting all hot and...*oh god...*

Flustered, I distract myself by taking in the surround-ings. His office is huge. Three walls are windows and the fourth is black marble. There's the elevator and one other steel, space-age-looking door, with blinking electronic locks. A large desk sits in the middle of the room and there's a couch and several leather chairs. One of the glass panes has been folded open, and leads out to a huge patio area and a private pool. Tropical plants and palm trees decorate the space. Everything has clean lines and ultra-swish detailing. Clearly no expense has been spared. The design, at a guess, seems to suggest that Rafe Black is efficient, organized and…controlling. You get the feeling he does things his own way and will tolerate nothing less.

I walk over the window, looking out over the vast expanse of the city, which stretches out toward the distant strip of golden sand and the blue, blue ocean. "You have an amazing view." Okay, not the most ground-breaking observation, but I can congratulate myself on the blithe, offhand tone of my voice, even if it is slightly husked. At least I don't sound as shaken as I feel.

"Come, take a seat." He motions to one of the leather chairs.

I do, as he half-sits against his desk and folds his arms across his chest, causing his suit jacket to tighten against his arms. *Jesus, he's buff. He looks unbelievably…strong. If he wanted to, he could so easily overpower me.*

Lexi! I scold myself. *Get a grip right now, girl! He's interviewing you for a dream job, not "overpowering" you!*

I do my best to obey the little voice in my head because I'm still picturing him, *yes…holding me down… pinning me under all that big, hard weight…oh, hell.*

This is bad.

His mouth quirks in a languid half-smile, as though he's reading my thoughts.

Of course he can't. I just need to calm down, and now that I'm sitting, I do. I try to, at least.

But then he takes off his suit jacket and tosses it onto his chair. *Jesus H. Christ.* The man is *ridiculously* built. Tall and muscular, but gracefully so, like a sculpture of a perfect male form. A perfectly *ripped* male form, with toned, hard muscles, as though he's spent the last six months sweatily lifting hay bales in the Outback of Australia or something. As my eyes kind of rove and drink in the sight—don't judge, this guy is seriously freaking hot—I can't help but notice, as much as I try not to, that Rafe Black is impressively built in…well…in *every* conceivable category. There's a sort of…very large…*gigantic, in fact…swell…*

Help me.

"Let's get started," he says.

Yes. Please. I need any distraction I can get at this point.

He reaches for a silver bucket on a stand I hadn't noticed before, behind his desk. He pulls a bottle of champagne out of its bucket of ice. "This might seem a little strange, but this bottle was delivered only a few minutes before you arrived. It's from my brother, Max."

"Oh. Are you celebrating something?"

"Today's my birthday."

"Happy birthday."

"Thank you," he says. "Can I tempt you?"

I can't even begin to describe how tempted I am. I know I probably shouldn't accept his offer. A glass of champagne will only annihilate my self-control, which at this point I badly need. But I can hardly say no. It's his *birthday.* "Thank you."

He smiles, and his gaze lingers on my mouth, before

returning to my eyes. That brief, subtle glance has all the effect of a shot of pure, uncut aphrodisiac.

No one should be this good-looking. Or this much of a big, rugged, sexy tomcat. All I can think of is hot, sweaty, down-and-dirty sex—which I have absolutely zero experience with whatsoever—and it's freaking me out. I really have no idea what's come over me. "There's no reason we can't enjoy my brother's gift while we get down to business."

Rafe Black pours two glasses of champagne and hands one to me.

Then he sits in the chair that's next to mine. He looks even bigger this close. And even more manly and mouth-watering, if that's possible.

I could reach out and touch him…it would be that easy.

What would he do? Would he let me?

Somehow, I know he would.

His eyes blaze and I get that feeling again that he's able to read me—if not my thoughts, then…my vibes. With chemistry *this* off-charts, it wouldn't surprise me. I'm finding it a little hard to breathe with him this close to me.

"As you know," he says, "I'm looking for a new assistant. I've had the same assistant since I founded the company seven years ago. She's sort of a Moneypenny type. She's retiring."

"You must have been young when you founded Downtown, Mr. Black." I wonder if he's even thirty. He looks younger than that.

"Call me Rafe." His wicked mouth quirks. He's a rich, powerful mogul, obviously. And I'm an unemployed, entry-level nobody. I am, in more ways than one, at his mercy. His request for me to call him by his first name feels like…a small triumph. A connection. An invitation for familiarity that's ridiculously enticing.

"Rafe," I repeat. The name suits him. Strong, dark, commanding.

His eyes are intense, and I get the feeling that something about the way I've said his name has affected him. "I was twenty. Still at Stanford."

"I…also went to Stanford."

"I saw that on your résumé. It was one of the reasons I decided to interview you." I wonder what the other reasons are, but I hold my questions. Maybe it's best if he does the talking. My nerves have made me thirsty, and the champagne is the most delicious I've ever had. I sip again.

"Are you aware that Downtown is only one of the companies I own?" he says. "One of the smaller ones, in fact."

"I didn't know that."

"We run the magazine and all its off-shoots, as well as several hedge funds, an investment company and a real estate brokerage firm."

I'm beginning to grasp just how rich and powerful Rafe Black actually is.

"I have to be honest," I tell him. "I've never been an assistant before. I did an internship last summer for a literary agency. The job mainly involved reading manuscripts and writing up reports. But I'm a quick learner and a hard worker. And very eager to please."

His eyes spangle, and I realize what that must have sounded like. *What's wrong with me? Why the hell did I just say that?* I blush again.

"I'm very glad to hear that," is his soft reply. "I think your résumé and references speak for themselves." His long fingers curl around the stem of his champagne glass. He looks like he could easily snap it without any effort at all. His eyes burn as he takes another sip. "I'm impressed."

I think I might be combusting inside this potent cloud of alpha-male pheromones he's emitting. My senses are hyper-aware, and my body feels unsettlingly warm...*and soft...and—oh, hell, this is way too much...*

Rafe rubs his hand across his jaw. He's so freaking... *sexy*...it's overwhelming me. His cinnamon skin, the stubble of his beard. *I can just tell it'll be rough and might even hurt a little.* His mouth, his thick hair, his dark blue eyes rimmed with thick black lashes. The man is an absolute specimen of hot sin and alpha male energy. And let's be clear about one thing: I'm not usually the type of girl who goes around thinking about alpha male energy *or* hot sin. Until now, apparently. "I do require that whoever I hire must be available immediately."

"I'm available whenever you want me." *Oops.* I realize the double entendre only *after* I make the comment, of course. Clearly my brain has turned to mush. My cheeks burn. "I meant, of course, that I'm available whenever you decide you'd, um, like me to start, *if* you want to hire me, that is."

"It's a demanding job. Long hours. I need someone who can basically be at my beck and call, at any hour of the day or night. We have affiliates in New York, London, Paris, Sydney, and so on, so we're a 24-hour business. It can be hard on…significant others, if you were to be working a lot."

"I don't have a significant other. I have a roommate, but she's busy most of the time, building her business."

"Good," he says, and his smug charisma hits me in the low pit of my stomach. God, he's so freaking cocky. *And it's doing things to me I can't even begin to describe.* "There will be times when you'll be required to travel with me. Frequently, in fact. Do you like to travel?"

"I haven't really had much opportunity to travel." I don't tell him that I never had the money. Or, that as a graduation present to myself, I decided to get my passport issued. Or, that it had just been delivered in the mail. Last week, in fact. "But I've always wanted to."

"Perfect." Rafe tops up our glasses. Then he reaches for a pen and a small piece of paper. He scrawls some numbers onto the paper and hands it to me. "This is the starting salary. Negotiable, of course. I'll cover all business-related expenses. You'll have a driver, and an expense account, if you agree to take the position. In addition, my apartment is in this building, and I have an adjoining studio apartment available for your use, if you have need of it from time to time, which you will, when I require you to work late."

I glance at the number he's written and hold back a gasp, wondering if my eyes are deceiving me. It's more than triple what I might have expected to earn from an assistant's job. A salary this generous will allow me to pay off my student loan within two years, especially if I can cut down on other expenses. Which I'll clearly be able to do, with all that he's offering me.

"What do you say, Lexi?"

"I say…yes. This is absolutely my dream job. Thank you so much, Mr.—"

"Rafe."

His black-satin voice seems to penetrate the air as a physical force, touching me and ruffling me. *How does he* do *that?* "Rafe."

He smiles. "It's settled, then."

This is happening so fast. I can't believe I just got *hired*. By *Downtown*. More specifically, by its drop-dead gorgeous CEO.

Rafe places his glass on the table and leans in his chair. As he moves, I catch a light whiff of his scent. He smells of soap and mint and raw masculinity. And there's more to it. Something elusive and outrageously, crazily appealing. The manly spice unfurls something in me, intoxicating me along with the champagne. My nerves are gone now, replaced by…sweet, soft, brimming heat. I feel reckless and a little crazy, if you really want to know.

My eyes rove down his long, powerful body and—*holy hell.* It's obvious that he's getting as worked up as I am. *His…the front of his pants…is straining…unbelievably…almost like it might…bust out…*

I can't handle this.

What would it feel *like?*

Lexi. Stop. Right now. Seriously. "When…w-would you like me to start?"

"How about right now?"

Our gazes meet. I'm having trouble breathing in enough air. I want to breath *his* air, his breath. That scent of him, that one hit, was not enough.

He leans closer. His dark eyes are burning with some unfathomable emotion.

Then, his hand lifts, brushing against an end strand of my hair.

He's touching me.

His fingers twirl around a soft lock of my hair, forming a lightly ensnaring hold. Very gently, he pulls.

I follow his pull. My self-control has been obliterated. I want this job, but even more, I want *him.* Sensing my consent, he pulls me closer, and closer, until my mouth is close to his. My nipples peak into tight little buds of sensation. Concentrated lust seemed to center there, and radiates slowly through my body in shimmery, uninhibited waves.

His lower lip is close to my mouth, as plump as ripe fruit. I'm high from his effect, and so desperate for more of that scent and the *taste* of him, I can't control it. This lust. This craving. It's bigger than me.

"Lexi." The whispered word is so dark, so deep. "I wasn't expecting—" He stops, his breathing heavier, as though he's conflicted.

I have no idea what's happening to me, but whatever it is, it's profound. I'm falling. That's the only way to describe it. I can't stop it. And I don't want to.

When his mouth brushes against my lips in a feather-light kiss that promises so much more, I touch my tongue to the rounded curve of his lip. He groans, and his fingers graze my nipple through the soft fabric of my dress. He teases it between his thumb and fingers, kneading it into a ripe bud. Searing sensation surges through my body.

Oh my god. This is really happening.

I gasp as he pinches tighter, rolling my aching flesh more insistently, controlling me entirely with his touch.

"*Lexi*," he says again, against my mouth. He cups my breast in his warm palm, squeezing lightly. "*Fuck*."

I get what he means. The ferocious urges of my body are driving me, and I realize with a tiny shred of concern that's swept away by an ocean of surrender that I'll do anything he asks. Anything. His effect is flooding me with fire.

He pulls at the knot of my dress, untying it. The fabric falls open to reveal my breasts. They feel full and soft. The rosy hue of my swollen nipples looks almost—and this isn't something I'd usually stop to consider—*sultry* against the pale white of my skin. I feel more beautiful than I've ever felt in my life. Because of him and the way he's looking at me. Like he wants to eat me alive.

Rafe makes a soft, savage sound. He seems overcome. He's torn, I can see, by the thought of taking advantage of me, his new, young assistant, if he'll even hire me now. It's a strange and sudden turn of events, and completely unexpected. But I'm too far gone to allow his internal dilemma to steal from me this stunningly needy anticipation. I don't care. I want him.

"Lexi. Do you want this?" His voice is low and deep and so appealing it pushes me past some barrier of self-control. "Tell me to stop and I will."

No. Don't stop. No stopping …

Get the **free** prequel, **The Obsession Begins @ www.juliecapulet.com**

ALSO BY JULIE CAPULET

I Love You Series

The Obsession Begins (free)

XOXO I Love You

XOXX I Love You More

Love You the Most (free)

Sexy Standalones

Max

Cowboy

McCabe Brothers Series

Hopeless Romantic

My Hero

Arrogant Player

Music City Lovers Series

Nashville Days

Nashville Nights

Nashville Dreams

Nashville Lights

Hawthorne U Series

Lovestruck

Paradise Series

Devil's Angel

Wild Hearts

New York Billionaires Series

Billionaire Boss

Billionaire Grump

Billionaire Devil

Billionaire Romantic

Wilder Billionaires

Billionaire Falls First

Standalone Rom-com

Beautiful Savages

Julie Capulet is an Amazon top 20 bestselling author of steamy he-falls-first romance with heart, heat and fairy tale HEAs. She met her husband in a seaside bar on a tropical island and knew within five minutes she'd marry him. She's been writing romance ever since. When she's not writing, she's reading, traveling, on the beach or watching rom-coms.

www.juliecapulet.com